COLORBLIND

ALSO BY
PETER ROBERTSON

Permafrost
Mission

to Karen;

COLORBLIND

A MYSTERY

Peter Bru

PETER ROBERTSON

GIBSON
HOUSE
PRESS

GIBSON HOUSE PRESS
Flossmoor, Illinois 60422
GibsonHousePress.com

Printed in the United States of America
20 19 18 17 16   5 4 3 2 1

ISBN-13 978-0-9855158-6-7 (paper)

LCCN: 2015902212

COVER DESIGN: Christian Fuenfhausen

for my family

ONE

I STOOD IN THE RUIN of the front room. I was here in the pale blue house on Lizardi Avenue for the first and last time.

The house had long stood empty, tideswept and abandoned after the storm waters had destroyed and then departed. When I placed my hand on the top of the mantelpiece the wood was remarkably unspoiled, the varnished red-brown mahogany still hardy and resilient beneath a layer of dirt and dust.

Underneath the mantelpiece were exposed bricks that formed a small fireplace. Inside the hearth lay a few pieces of worn green glass attached to paper covered in a printed but illegible message.

The front room gave way to a larger living area, a dining room or possibly a bedroom at one time. A bathroom was off a hallway that led to a small galley kitchen in the back of the house. All the rooms were mostly empty but ruined and filthy, detached from their furnishings, never washed in a decade of sustained neglect.

In the hallway, strips of peeling wallpaper hung low, exposing the mottled plaster underneath. One ceiling section, wooden and tenaciously clinging to all its paint, exposed the rectangular outline of a trapdoor. Its metal handle, centered and rusty and several feet above my head, was beyond my reach.

In the kitchen a stark hole stood where the dishwasher had once belonged, while the old-style stove had been callously rejected and trashed. The plaster wall where the refrigerator had once stood was wet and crumbling to the floor, where pieces of inexpensive tile lay broken in pieces.

I went out to the overgrown back yard, where I inadvertently stumbled over a green wooden stool camouflaged in waist-high grass. It was upside down and miraculously intact.

Back inside the house, I stood on the stool and pulled hard on the trapdoor handle. After a struggle it slid slowly downwards and the steps stuck out like a metal tongue.

They were solid under my weight as I climbed.

The upstairs air was dry and segmented by shafts of sunlight.

The attic room ran the length of the house, with exposed wood beams triangulating to create a canted ceiling, low at the sides, yet high enough to let me stand up straight in the center. The space was still cool this early in the morning. The windows at each end of the attic stood half open to produce a gentle breeze.

In the center of the room, a sleeping bag folded in half had a guitar case spread across it.

Under the front window stood a wooden chair in shade, with cotton trousers folded neatly over a thin sweater. A pair of gym shoes with socks wedged inside was tucked under the chair. Beside the chair was a cheap plastic basin, with a dried-up toothbrush and tube of generic toothpaste tossed inside. A hard sliver of cracked soap lay on the floor.

On the wall by the back window a towel hung high from a nail. A decade of sun damage had leached most the color from the tattered fabric.

I held my breath and knelt down to open the guitar case. Inside was the instrument I had never expected to find. It was surely his guitar–the same instrument from the front cover of his only existing recording. There was almost no dust across the age-darkened honey maple wood, and the fretboard looked to be unbuckled and true. There were six steel strings, brittle and rusted out but still taut.

I lifted the guitar by the neck and held it. A compartment inside the case stored a black metal capo and a thin brown leather bracelet. Under the bracelet was a folded piece of notepaper. The capo was the exact same model as the one I owned.

I unfolded the paper. The lyrics of a song were inscribed neatly in permanent ink. A series of letter and number notations were written above the lines. I recognized minors and sevenths and sharps and flats, unevenly spaced but not random. This was a chord chart.

He'd titled it "Kind Words." The title was written above a simple dedication:

For my daughter, Catriona, whom I lost.

The paper had aged to a dark yellow.

On the back windowsill, an inch of melted white candle stood in the center of a small plate like a tiny monument. I reached out and touched the candlewick. It smudged black between my fingers.

If I waited long enough, would the room reveal something of its departed? Of its antiquity?

I refolded the paper as it had been. I took the bracelet. I placed them both in my pocket. I ran my hand across the strings, praying that the wood had stayed dry. I lifted the instrument up, tightened the highest string carefully, and plucked the harmonic at the twelfth fret. I played the open string. To my ears the two notes sounded alike.

It was a hopeful sign.

I drew my hand across all six strings. I kidded myself that this was one of his elusive tunings, and not a random sampling of time and damage and desertion. I held his old guitar in my hands and I shut my eyes.

Afterwards I put the instrument inside and closed the case.

I looked around one last time. There was nothing else in the attic— no miraculously preserved notebook containing his other songs, no other parcel of lost writings, no words of either enigma or explanation.

This place on Lizardi Avenue, in the crushed heart of New Orleans, was a southern place, where there was no escape from the heat. This was the extended midpoint of my journey in a town as far south as I would travel, and the longest I would stay in one place.

The aftermath of this journey would be a matter of loose ends. My month had begun in one of Chicago's southern suburbs on a cold spring morning, and would end on the waterfront in West Seattle on another chilly day.

The song I'd discovered would surely arrive at its intended destination. The bracelet I would also hand over, on a whim, and the guitar would be sent away, a play for time, for safekeeping, and for some gentle restoration. When it was all mended, I would decide what to do. I could wrap it up and ship it home, or I could offer to carry it there myself.

By then I would be more than ready to take another trip.

⚏

DURING THE COURSE of my journey I would drive over three and a half thousand miles, be proven wrong several times, and fail to answer most of the questions that I started with. All of which begs the multifaceted question: Why was I wrong so often? Why did I fail to learn anything?

Giving the matter some thought, the answer, I suspect, is that my failures illustrate a singular negative constant—the inability to recognize patterns. I couldn't see those that actually existed, usually because I manufactured and admired the more seductive and flamboyantly false ones of my own invention. I also erred in observing that randomness can easily mimic order and vice versa, when it chooses to, or when we stubbornly try to impose our own sense of an imperative upon it.

I'm well aware that this story is not starting at the very beginning. I should apologize for that. Unfortunately, I am still somewhere in the middle.

⚏

THE DOGGEDLY ENDURING city of New Orleans comprises a handful of long storied streets. These culturally iconic thoroughfares traverse and triumph over dirty water. They lead to areas of abject poverty and beaten down yet evocative locales that have stubborn and enduring sentimental value. Legendary streets like Chartres and Royal and Rampart are prime examples of this beguiling dual functionality. And all three of these legendary roads intersect Lizardi Avenue at some shameful juncture.

The distance between squalor and sentiment is a lot shorter than anything else in this languid place. This locale moves with southern slowness, either unwilling to break into an unseemly show of Yankee-like sweat, or risk cracking open the myth and exposing an underbelly ripe with despair.

The locals ascribe a pleasing symmetry to their town, referring to the city as a crescent. Tourists are baffled by the description. To most of us the town exists as an improbable sponge. Its low-lying land mass is intersected by brackish waters of varying sizes: lakes, rivers, canals, and drainage channels. All exhibit disparate levels of insistent menace.

Did I somehow fail to mention that the cursedly contrary place is also close to irresistible?

I did.

But I digress.

⁂

I CAREFULLY CARRIED his guitar case down the stairs. I stood on the kitchen's tile floor and looked back up. Then I pushed the trapdoor until it was tightly closed once again. I took the stool back outside and placed it as close as possible to the place where I had found it.

Back in the front room, I noticed the brown waterline stood a mottled and indistinct three feet above the warped wood floorboards. The smell inside the house was mostly mature mold by this late stage. A few remnants of abandoned furniture were now nothing more than kindling stacked against the far living room wall. Outside that pale blue house, the grass was thick and wild all the way to the cracked edge of the tree-twisted sidewalk.

Lizardi Avenue has no bohemian sections filled with boldly experimental charter schools and Creole/fusion restaurants. There are no above-ground cemeteries holding the remains of belatedly revered jazz pioneers rubbing marble bones with voodoo enchantresses. Their largely unremarkable lives have been histrionically embellished over the years, to vend tour tickets and plastic gimcrack talismans.

For one thing, Lizardi doesn't run the length of the city. It doesn't get the chance to reinvent itself every few blocks as the districts change. Lizardi cuts across the town. Its route is a shorter distance both geographically and socioeconomically. In the South it comes to an ignoble and anonymous end a mere matter of yards short of the levee that can only pretend to restrain the Mississippi River. Residents know the water lurks on the other side of the gently rising grass, behind a rusted steel wall and a no man's land of cracked mud and broken stone. All are parts of a verifiably abject folly.

Hurricane Katrina takes on different lives depending on which NOLA narrative you subscribe to. It was a blast from a bitter trumpeter god, a spiteful spy boy in a retributive second line blowing hard and righteously on an unrepentantly godless party town. Maybe it was the Army Corps of Engineers caught grafting and trimming, or a French Quarter/Garden District elite sociopolitical cabal armed with stress maps and well placed sticks of dynamite. Or was it simply one ING 4727 barge breaking loose and breaching the Industrial Canal walls before thrashing around in the Lower Ninth like a beached whale in an admittedly good-sized but hardly life-threatening late summer storm whipped up in the turbulent cauldron of the Gulf waters?

But whichever way, as Steve Earle would have it, there's "nothing holding back Pontchartrain."

There are a series of Katrina storylines that uneasily coexist by either relying on or beating against a number of hard, uncontestable facts. The storm was between Category 3 and Category 5 when it hit the city on August 29, 2005. There were a handful of major levee breaches over the next three days. Brackish water, measured to a depth of fifteen feet in some places, covered ninety percent of the city. The government response was disorganized at best. Most of the population followed the mayor's advice and evacuated. The people squatting on their roofs, or left in the Astrodome to fend for themselves, or videotaped floating face down, were mostly poor, were mostly black, were mostly hopelessly unprotected, and were mostly very callously disenfranchised.

It was a cataclysmic clusterfuck in every sense of the word and, a decade later, it is still both a raw wound and an endlessly protracted re-ascendance in progress.

Not far from Lizardi, the Mississippi River enters the Industrial Canal, which was breached during the storm and its protracted aftermath. The two sections of water meet close to the austere, derelict facade of Holy Cross School, which battles humidity and nature on a weed-choked section of Dauphine. Deeper inside the canal resides an unintended steampunk construct, The St. Claude Bridge, which carries four lanes of pothole-bruised traffic between the Bywater and the Lower Ninth districts.

Around three hundred feet in from the levee, the canal waters had punished the 700-block of Lizardi less than other parts of the Lower Ninth. While much of the parish was swept apocalyptically clean for a restricted rebirth in measured, kaleidoscopic movie-star-sponsored projects, portions of Lizardi were simply left in myriad states of wildly disparate distress. This one particular block was functioning as a virtual cross-section of the city's woes. It had a reserved resurrection at one extreme, an abject abandonment at the other, and so many illustrated stages easily observable in between.

I walked outside the blue house into the escalating warmth and leaned against my car. My one hand was damp inside the pocket of my trousers as I gently massaged the dried out leather of the bracelet back to life. I put the guitar inside the back of the car and cracked the two back windows open a bit more. There were now two guitars in cases in the Outback. I opened them both and pulled the matching black capos from each case. I held one in each hand for a second and quickly considered. Then I swapped them out, closing each case carefully before relocking the car.

A small act of deception. I wanted to have his for myself.

I unfolded the piece of paper and read it again.

It occurred to me that the names Katrina and Catriona were oddly similar.

I put the paper in my pocket and studied the post-storm tableau.

The first property on the 700-block was a double shotgun frame leaning hard on its neighbor like a loan shark on a delinquent account. The skeleton was both spindly and architecturally implausible. A wooden cart full of mature trash sat composting on broken axles and flat tires out front. The last remaining section of foundation was four sad concrete posts and a doorstep of pre-Katrina vintage, onto which the ramshackle latticing framework of treated timber was attached in a manner no self-respecting builder would wish to claim.

In an unlikely juxtaposition, next door stood a tiny single shotgun fully restored and all urban cute. The grass was neatly trimmed and the front door was new wood stained a lush blood red. An abandoned lot where the grass stood long and wild and gave no evidence of a building ever having stood there, stood next to it. Further down was another double shotgun fully upright. Pale yellow paint flaked off the front and Mardi Gras beads of indeterminate vintage hung gaudy and limp from the rickety wrought iron nailed loosely to the rotting veranda.

On the front steps, a pasty hipster-white trash hybrid male in a yellowing wifebeater sat listlessly, smoking weed and pointedly ignoring the large dog barking loudly somewhere inside.

From the side of the smaller and neater shotgun emerged a purebred hipster pushing an expensive black single-gear bicycle. He too sported a wifebeater and a shoulder bag and an instrument case, which I could only assume housed a tenor saxophone.

The two distinct evolutionary stages of hipsterdom glanced at each other with no visible display of emotion as the mobile one rode slowly away. The stationary guy continued to sit and sullenly smoke as the big dog kept right on barking.

I watched this silent exchange from my vantage point outside the pale blue house, which functioned as the final piece of this New Orleans tableau—the unintended memorial to Katrina's victims.

It was still standing, more or less. A ratty squat, slowly subsiding, it bore the diagonally crossed scrawls of dark graffiti that the authorities used as they searched through the waterlogged parishes. The markings were crude and overlapped the plywood boarding up the windows and the crumbling wood siding. They indicated the dates of the searches and how many still bodies were found inside the premises.

I studied the numbers. Four sets of diagonals meant four likely inspections. White paint. Orange paint. Brown paint. Black paint. Three sets had zeros in two places. The brown paint had the letters DEA in the left quadrant and nothing in the other three. I took the zeroes to be good signs. The brown was more worrisome. I opted for the optimistic view, choosing to believe that the blue house on Lizardi experienced no instance of hurricane-related death immediately following the flood, or later, even after three subsequent visits.

I was, I will readily admit, less than secure in my rosy conviction.

It was still early in the morning. A brace of thunderstorms had passed overnight, and deep puddles camouflaged the potholes that pockmarked the street.

With the two post-Katrina artifacts in my pocket, I walked the two blocks to the river, where I intended to make a right and track the worn stone footpath along the top of the levee. Then I would make my way to the gate for the pedestrian crossing at the St. Claude Bridge.

But here my simple plan floundered.

The beaten down grass on the embankment held a sea of people who all looked rushed even as they stood still. There were trucks parked and gliding cameras mounted along the section of the levee. Generators hummed and flimsy gantries of lights rose up to illuminate. In the calm vortex of all this studied kinetics sat two young actors on a bicycle made for two. One was tall and thin with a week's beard and lank hair falling adorably into his eyes. The other was a pretty Vietnamese girl, very much the shorter of the two. They were both dark haired, both astride the old-fashioned bicycle on the side of the path. The tandem-style red clunker had big thick rubber tires, dull silver mudguards, and a basket for groceries, and whatever else, leather strapped onto the front. From somewhere out of sight, a directorial command was issued, and suddenly there was action. The two actors rode the tandem very well, the boy in back doing most of the serious pedaling, and the girl in front doing most of the serious talking and giggling as mounted cameras pursued on each side of the bike.

At that point I gave up and turned around.

The day's heat was starting to accumulate as I wandered slowly back down Lizardi to where my car was parked. In retrospect I was much too close to the trash cart. I looked directly across the road at the ruins of a large structure. The faded lettering on the wall proclaimed the burned out remains of one Lost Tribe of Zion Full Apostolic Gospel Church. The tribe had been housed inside a big brown barn of a building. I couldn't help but notice that most of the weathered detritus in the cart on the other side of the street was the same shit-brown stained wood as the last remaining sticks of the ruins.

I wondered how long the church had been gone, and how long it would take to rebuild, and I suspected the answer to the first question was a good while, and the second to be pretty much anyone's guess.

But I did hope for the rapid resurrection of the Lost Tribe. And perhaps the spirit of stubborn resilience on display was an influence. After all, back at the café on Magazine where I'd had breakfast that morning, I'd witnessed a bus full of pasty church youth from a suburb of Milwaukee as they laid siege to a property. They scraped and primed and painted about as efficiently as I did, but what they lacked in skill they more than made up with daunting displays of turbocharged teenage zeal. As I ate my sweet potato pancakes and drank iced coffee in the brevity of the early morning shade, I watched them turn the shabby building into a vision of pastel pristineness.

⚜

THE EVENTS OF the day had distracted me. I changed my mind and headed back toward the levee, turning right to cut diagonally across the grass to the path on the top of the embankment. On the higher ground, where the river and the canal met, the air was agreeably cooler, and the film crowd had thankfully thinned out.

The bridge across the canal at St. Claude was being raised when I got there, and I was forced to wait as three small boats meandered through the narrow lock. When the bridge finally descended, two impatient teenage girls on bicycles rode partway across before the coiled gears of the mechanism were fully locked in place, and a series of honking horns only elicited a cascade of giggles as the bold twosome pedaled away.

Once on the other side of the canal, I turned left and climbed over a fence that followed the levee path for few feet before scaling a series of huge crumbling pipe and cement constructions, which I had to assume were no longer operational.

In a few feet I stopped. This was the place. It had to be. It looked exactly like the photographs taken by his fans, the ones who had made the pilgrimage to the place where he had died.

There was a barge far out on the river. It rested, still and low in the water, half filled with what looked like cubed and compacted old automobiles, incongruously glittering in the early morning sunshine. Part of the city skyline shone in the distance far behind it, curving bridges and tall anonymous buildings peeking out of a haze. As always, the city's topography defeated me, and I wasn't sure which direction I was actually facing. The New Orleans skyline is a remarkably generic one from a distance. But up close, the place becomes at once singularly unique.

Inside the blue house I had been obliged to wait. A place should be required to volunteer all of its dark history, to present an imaging of the events that had taken place there. But there had been nothing.

Now I stood here, at the side of the canal, and I waited once again.

It occurred to me that I could always jerry-rig the whole event; perhaps take the paper and the bracelet from my pocket and solemnly toss them in an elegiac act into the water, as I muttered a poignant phrase or two, before lapsing into an anticipatory silence.

And no doubt this would be a fittingly grandiloquent gesture of utter worthlessness. But I didn't elect to do that.

I lingered for a moment very close to the place where he had drowned.

There was the graffiti I had first seen in photographs on the website. Nothing more had been added since. The vase was dirty and empty and overturned on the grass under the painted letters. I stood it upright, although I'd brought no flowers to place inside it.

He had died in this water a short time after the storm had compromised the canal walls. An estimated eighteen hundred people died in the storm, and forty percent of the deaths were thought to be drownings.

The canal had a lot to answer for.

So I waited for the water to cough up its historical dead, and all their attendant secrets. Like the empty attic room in the house on Lizardi, it should be forced to proclaim its history as including so much pointless death. This one death had managed to somehow insinuate its way a decade forward, and then it all but demanded another senseless sacrifice, the one that had got me started on this journey.

So I waited once again, for the haunted past to be rendered. And once again, I waited in vain, as first the room, and then the waters, relinquished nothing.

There was one final place to visit before I would leave town.

The levee path followed Rampart as it ran close to the canal. At some point I turned right, climbed down over a pile of weeds, broken steps, and exposed metal and found a negotiable gap in a rusty fence. I soon reached the point where Dauphine dead-ends at two lines of abandoned train track. Two short legs were just visible under the front of a silver rusted-out Buick Regal. A brown dog was unleashed and barking and clearly impatient for the makeshift repair to be completed. I kept on walking for two more blocks before making a left onto Poland.

Boldly painted shotgun houses crowded the street. Each had almost no front yard. To compensate, owners placed berserk flower arrangements in window boxes that all but overwhelmed their narrow painted balconies.

On the corner of Chartres and Poland a wine bar stood well concealed. In the back of what had once been an old Creole mercantile building was a patio garden with black wrought iron tables and a handful of early lunchtime customers with wine and cheese plates and good beers in big bomber bottles. There were unlit strands of festival lights in the sunshine and the garden was warm. Almost all the outdoor space was masked in shade as the sun was still behind the shadow of the building.

He had played here once.

I pulled a cold bottle of Meadowlark IPA from the cooler in the front of the shop. The clerk was an older gentleman with a monster gut. He wore a tie-dye bandana and antique NOLA jazz heritage T-shirt. Without uttering a single word, he opened the bottle and handed me a tall glass. When I offered him my money, he shook his head.

"Startin' y'all up a tab," he muttered under his breath.

There was little point in arguing with him.

In the far corner of a small second-floor room, a young man sat bony and angular. He was hunched over a vintage blonde Telecaster processed through about a dozen effects pedals and a peeling tweed

Vibrolux. Beside him a young woman in a thin wheat-yellow summer dress and dark blonde dreadlocks sat very upright in a hardbacked chair. She moaned into a microphone. Her voice was far bigger than she was. The song rhythms were gently induced by varying delay patterns, and the droning melodies came from no more than two or three strings that were detuned, then plucked, then ground, then left alone to reverb gently. The young man spent much more time stabbing at the pedals with his two feet than playing the guitar with his hands. He constantly looked at the floor and frowned often, but still managed to raise his head on occasion and smile softly as the girl's voice drifted upward.

The twenty souls occupying perhaps a quarter of the room's seating capacity sat quietly. Some read. Some listened. A few checked their cell phones with the long-suffering air of attending to an odious yet necessary duty. Most were young but not all. They were all locals. Not visibly sweating, moving slowly, decked out in studied attire that tended towards too much, vintage hats tilted at a rakish angle, dashing and sloppily debonair if a little overplayed, especially in a locale so resoundingly, so swimmingly sultry.

I sat at a table near the back of the room in deep shade and watched as dust spiraled in a prism of sunlight from a bare window facing east. I pulled the paper from my pocket and placed it carefully on the table. I read the lyric again as I held the bracelet in my hands, gently working it between my fingers some more, softening the leather and removing the last remains of the patina of dust at the same time.

I took my phone out and figured my route north and west away from the city. Then I thought about the guitar I had found, and what I should do with it. I considered the guitar shop in Memphis where I had stopped on the way down. They would surely take it and would know what to do with it. I should probably text them.

When I did they texted right back and told me all they could do. Then they told me about a store in Boulder close to my house on 28th Street that could do the very same things.

It all seemed simple enough.

Dusty beer bottles were fastened in groups of four, conjoined at the necks, and fashioned into light fixtures attached to the bare brick walls. They made barely enough light to read from, and all I could think of was the diagonal death signs painted on the outer shells of the Katrina houses.

"Takin' ourselves a goodwill offering at this time."

I raised my head in some confusion. The girl held what I was fairly sure was a straw pork pie hat in one hand. It contained about ten dollar bills and was rimmed with antique sweat stains, which I was quite certain didn't belong to her, as she showed no other visible signs of wilting.

It was the singer. She gazed at me and raised her eyebrows. I noticed that one of her pupils was larger than the other. Just like David Bowie. I was surprised I had remembered this fact.

"How much are you asking?" I finally asked her.

She shrugged sweetly at me.

"Just what y'all think would be fair," she said.

I put a twenty in the hat and I could see from her expression that it was too much.

"Something you like that we could play for you this very fine morning?" She offered this gently.

Impulsively I evoked his name. I asked her if she knew any of his songs. She made herself look regretful. Then she shook her head. It had been a stupid question. His name clearly meant nothing to her, and she looked long and hard at me, as if I had played a trick on her.

But he had played here once.

"We could sing you some Neil Young."

It was a wonderful suggestion and I told her just that, all the while wondering what had made me appear like someone who would care for Neil Young. Was it an inspired guess? Or the law of averages, applied to an older gentleman trying to look casual in a room full of people trying even harder to look casual?

She returned to her chair and whispered to her partner who was tuning another electric guitar, this time a vintage Gibson SG, with an elaborate Bigsby tailpiece and a third Seymour Duncan humbucker pickup retrofitted onto a chipped body of cherry-stained wood. He nodded knowingly as she spoke.

After another minute of listless tuning and painstaking pedal selection they began to play the slowest version of "Heart of Gold" I had ever heard. The intro reverbed from an E minor seventh to a D major and then to an E minor, and the guitar chords swelled in a bludgeoning haze of chorus and barely restrained feedback; a sonic methodology I felt certain would have made Shakey quite proud. After four agonizingly lethargic repetitions the young lady seemingly coughed a few times at random into a battered harmonica as the guitarist morphed the chord progression into an E minor, C major, D major, and G major pattern.

I couldn't help looking down at the notepaper that was still lying on the table, at the letters and symbols above the words, at the chords he had chosen, at perhaps his last song.

"I want to live. I want to give." She began to howl the words across the room.

I swallowed most of the beer in my glass and closed my eyes. I contemplated today, and the last few days, and then the days ahead, in no conceivable order.

". . . and I'm getting old."

That nasty young girl surely threw these cruel words right at me.

Have I mentioned that all this happened somewhere in the middle?

TWO

I HAVE DRIVEN THIS FAR on little more than the slenderest of notions. First, for five hundred miles south, to the northern part of Mississippi, then for another five hundred, down here to New Orleans.

From here I will drive much more: another two thousand five hundred miles, diagonally north and west across the country, to arrive in West Seattle.

When I get there a woman in her mid-thirties will be given a thin leather bracelet because I want to give it to her, and a song, which I convince myself, was intended for her to have. Naturally she will not understand and naturally she will be quite confused at first.

The song is written on the piece of notepaper. It is dedicated to her by name. She will gingerly take it and hold it in front of her, and will begin to read it very carefully, and the start of a smile will take shape on her lips, and I will not fail to notice that her lips are a small part of a face that looks an awful lot like her late father's.

When she finishes reading she will ask me what the song sounds like, and even though I know in theory how to play all the chords written down, I will tell her that I don't exactly know. I will try to explain that, to my knowledge, the song was never recorded. There is no known melody line, no published sheet music to help, and her father's guitar playing is almost impossible to duplicate.

She will look sadly at me as I say this. But could I perhaps try? Could I guess? She asks me these things very nicely. So I close my eyes, summon up the opening chord progression and I give it a shot.

I've actually thought about the song a lot as I drove across the country. I've imagined her father singing it, and when I do this I have an imaginary melody running through my head that almost sounds like one of her father's.

So I sing her the song as I have fashioned it, as an unaccompanied homage. She smiles at me when I finish. In truth I've sung about as well as I can, but I will still feel slightly foolish.

I look into her face. It isn't clear if she likes it or not. But she is polite and she insists that she does.

I'm absurdly pleased.

And after I have sung we will talk some more, actually for a long while, and eventually it will begin to get much darker outside.

She will do most of the talking and she will spend a lot of time telling me stories from her past and about how happy she is, but I won't believe her either then or now because I think she's mostly lonely, even as I listen to her.

Because happy people don't spend much time telling you how happy they are.

Before we met I did consider placing the bracelet and the song on one of the low stone walls outside her house for her to discover. It was an admittedly idiotic gesture; equal parts *Brief Encounter* and *French Lieutenant's Woman* (incidentally one film I love and one I truly can't stand).

As I considered this option it did occur to me that, if she didn't retrieve them soon, the perpetual damp of the local terrain would quickly destroy the paper, and the leather almost as fast.

There again, I reasoned, I could simply knock on her door, silently hand her the two items, and stride boldly and enigmatically away.

But in the end I had been forced to do neither of these things, because Catriona was leaving her house on foot even as I approached. And that was the last thing I had expected.

‡‡

IT SEEMED BEST to follow her from a distance.

She walked quickly, and something in the purposefulness of her stride made me suspect that she made this journey most days. The bracelet was still in my pocket and I took it out without thinking.

I imagined it double-wrapped around her wrist; the leather dark, tightly braided, a little chunky and mannish perhaps. She was a slender, pale creature, and I imagined her wrist similarly.

Perhaps she will hold her hand away when she tries it on for the first time. Perhaps she will look at it, as she turns her arm back and forth playfully, a trifle whimsically.

There's a real danger of getting carried away with all this whimsy.

I did have enough time to admire her little house as I turned and gave chase. It was constructed of equal parts red-stained cedar wood and mossy weathered brick. Being two blocks above the main shoreline road, her view would surely encompass the car ferry, which runs on the hour and docks leisurely; an ancient outdoor swimming pool of quasi-Victorian construction and questionable practicality; a footpath; a small park; a beach of sorts; and, of course, the wide stretch of water that lies between West Seattle and Vashon Island.

I tried to calculate whether her house would provide the much desired view of the water from any of the small windows. I wasn't sure, but I strongly suspected that it wouldn't.

The wet stone wall runs the entire length of her garden, which is small and steep, a haphazard assortment of worn grey rocks bundled up in gnarly knots of brilliant flowers.

She soon arrived at the shore road.

On the far side a footpath dissected a recreational strip of lush lawn, where the grass fell at a sharp incline, fading from an improbable green to ever-damp mud, to dark brown sand strewn with flat round rocks and the strands of worn seaweed that constitute this particular section of West Seattle coastline.

Catriona patiently waited for the two moderately drunk men on road bikes to pass; they argued loudly and heatedly over the absence of professional basketball in their city. She crossed the street hurriedly, even though there was no other traffic in sight. The fish and chip shop was open. She entered.

For a minute or two I pretended to read the signs in the front window for missing purebred cats and desired nonsmoking vegan roommates, before I followed her inside. We sat down at adjoining tables. The place was almost empty, and I could hear an angry seagull trash talking the bleating horn of the Southworth-Fauntleroy ferry outside.

Inexplicably I found myself thinking about *Brief Encounter* again. Trevor Howard and an actress, whose name escaped me, in a drab café in at least one sensually tense scene. Had it been Deborah Kerr? I thought not. But I really couldn't remember. They had drunk a lot of tea. I was sure of that part at least. Did Deborah Kerr have a famous actress sister? I had a feeling that she did. But who was it? That I wasn't sure of.

After a while I stood up and walked to Catriona's table. This would be awkward.

"Pardon me," I said to her. "I think these belong to you."

I placed the items quickly on the table. Then I spoke quickly, breathlessly, before my nerves capitulated. As she listened she picked up the bracelet and held it in her hand. She didn't try it on, as I imagined she would. For a while she said nothing.

I finished. "I believe that your father would've wanted you to have them."

Then she began to speak. She still retained her Northern England accent. Her voice was slight and gentle.

"However did you find me?" It was a natural enough question.

I placed my finger on the inscription.

"It wasn't hard. It was your first name on the paper. That helped me. Catriona. It's an unusual name. And I guessed your age. And I guessed which part of England you were born in. There are websites about your father. They mention a child. They didn't mention your first name. They mention your adopted parents' last name so you see it wasn't hard."

She stared at the paper.

"But I don't understand why he wrote this for me. Such a long time ago. They gave me up. I was very small. I knew about him. My parents told me. So I did know who he was. Everything like that.

Did you know that he named me? Catriona was always my name. My parents had intended to call me something else. But they didn't, in the end. They liked it too much to change."

I told her I liked it too.

After she smiled she began to talk some more.

"You followed me here." It wasn't a question.

"I did." I told her I was sorry.

"Why are you doing this?" She wanted to know.

"A misplaced sense of order." I had nothing else to offer her.

"I like it here," she said.

I told her I did too.

"I come to this place a lot. Late in the day is the best time. It fills up dreadfully at night. I don't care for crowds. I used to be more comfortable with them."

"Why?" I asked her.

"Because I was a part of them." Her tone hinted that she might consider me dim.

"The vinegary smell of this place. When I first walk through the door. Doesn't it remind you?"

"Of what?"

"Of our home." I was clearly getting no brighter.

So she had noticed my accent. She was right of course. It did remind me of home.

"How long have you lived here?" I wanted to know.

"Four years this summer."

I asked where her home was and she mentioned the name of a seaside town in the Northeast of England. I knew roughly where it was. I confessed I had never been there and she didn't seem surprised.

As she talked Catriona played with her hair. She pulled it out from behind her ears then slid it back. Up close her hair was more dark red than brown and she wore it short, higher than her shoulders, lower than her ears. The constant pulling and sliding revealed a scattering of light freckles on her neck that resembled a constellation of stars that I couldn't identify.

I've noticed before that when the British first encounter other British people they tend to talk mostly about the brilliance of British things and the greatness of being British; it's a dreary form of conversational refuge that has sheltered me on more than one occasion.

Catriona and I were certainly no different in that regard.

So we plunged right in.

"There was a fish and chip shop at the end of the pier where we lived. Mum and Dad used to take me there. When I was very small. It was a special treat. Dad and I would each get fish and share the chips and Mum would sit and look out the window at the sea and keep us company. She hated the food. Said it made her stomach all queasy. If it was a warm night she had a small ice cream cone with a flake."

I told her I remembered flakes.

She told me when she was a teenager, she and her girlfriends would go to the shop after the Friday night disco dance in the church hall.

I told her I remembered Friday night disco dances.

"The dances were in the winter. It was something to do in the long hours of dark and cold. The haar used to come slating off the water and chill the town."

I nodded. Sea haars were also very familiar to me.

"We sat outside shivering in our coats all buttoned up. There were white plastic chairs and round tin tables left there from the summer, signs advertising Wall's ice cream that always got blown over. The wooden pier was green and wet. There were rusted metal bars at the far end to stop people from falling into the sea below."

"How old were you?"

"We were fourteen."

"Is the pier still there?"

"It's been a long time since I was there."

Was that an answer?

She pulled her hair free.

"The pier was boring in the middle of winter. The promenade lights were left on all day and night. The beach gates were locked but older children and town alkies climbed over and drank on the sand under the pier, between the seaweed and the rock pools and the wooden pillars and the support beams."

She pushed her hair behind her ears.

"In the winter the waves were stronger. They used to come up and over the bars at high tide. When I was little, I remember being too frightened to stand close."

Catriona suddenly smiled.

"Do you remember the seaside deck chairs? The wooden ones that folded up and down and had a sheet of colored cloth to sit on?"

I told her that I did.

She laughed. "My dad could never get the damn things to open or close. You could rent them at the chip shop. I don't remember how much they were. There were windbreakers too. You had to push the wooden poles into the sand. The big striped patterns matched the chairs. I remember them being such old things that belonged to the past. The sun and the wind and the rain and the salt in the air stripped most of the colors away. It's strange what you remember."

"Did you like the beach when you were little?' I asked her.

Then she changed the subject.

"What else did you find that belonged to my father?"

"I found his guitar." I hadn't intended to tell her. There was also the small matter of his capo, but that would stay secret.

"Where is it?" She sounded suddenly interested.

"It might need to be fixed."

"Don't we all?" she replied.

At an early point in the drive between New Orleans and Seattle my nervousness over his guitar had overcome me. In a suburb north of Dallas, I had found a UPS store, and there I sheepishly handed it over. The cost of packing and shipping was exorbitant, but the toothy young man in khakis and a brown polo shirt assured me that the instrument would make it to the repair shop in Boulder in its precisely current condition. This was both reassuring and opaque, because I had no idea how much damage the years of humidity and abandonment had done. I emailed the store and told them it was on its way. I texted Jesse and asked him to wander over to the shop in a few days and get a verbatim assessment of the patient's condition. He texted me back and told me to go fuck myself, which probably meant that he'd do it.

This would buy me a few days to decide what to do. At this point I wasn't sure where the guitar belonged. I also wondered if leaving the instrument in its original condition was preferable to fixing it. If it were mine, I'd want to play it at its best. But I could play. And it wasn't ever going to be mine.

"Am I getting it?" Did she sound eager?

"I really don't think so."

"Is it valuable?"

"I've no idea."

That wasn't strictly true. For a very select person it was likely worth a fortune. Even I would have been willing to pay a lot for it, and a sneaky alternative scenario flashed rapidly before my eyes. But I could let that thought go. It wasn't mine.

"What will you do with it?"

"I don't know yet."

"Is it broken?" I was being interrogated.

"I don't know. You sound like you want it."

"I don't want anything that belonged to him."

I was confused. "You took the song and the bracelet."

"You came a long way to give them to me. It seemed appropriate." Her smile wasn't especially warm.

The waitress chose that moment to approach us. We both ordered fish and chips.

"You were asking me about the beach," she reminded me.

"I was."

"I remember the bother of having to get there more than anything else. We got the chairs first and then we had to walk all the way back along the pier. We had to carry all the stuff, the chairs and the spades and pails and a basket with our lunch inside and the beach towels for after our cold dash into the water, which my dad insisted on. We had to climb down the wooden steps. They were steep and always sandy and wet and slippery. I wore plastic sandals. I hated them. They were red and they blistered my feet. We would try and find a nice spot to sit; in the shade, sheltered from the wind, and higher than the tide when it came in."

"Were there old Victorian bath houses?" I asked her.

She shook her head. "There were once. Knocked down before my time. My dad said they were still standing when he was a boy. They belonged to the posh families from the South who came north to our town on the coast train at the start of the summer, for the season. My father grew up there. My mother's family came later, when she was a teenager. She was about my age when she moved there."

I suddenly wanted to leave. I didn't dislike Catriona. I had driven a long way to give her something. Now I had done so. She wasn't especially grateful. But there was no good reason why she should be.

At this point in the conversation I calculated that his guitar would beat me back to Boulder.

And suddenly there was the mental picture of my house there— my little house and the big porch in the front. There was me with a guitar in my lap and a cup of coffee on a cold morning with a dusting of leaves that needed to be swept up and the Flatirons, warm fire red in the first sun. It was more than a little trite. It was dangerously close to approximating an ad for a John Denver retrospective, but I didn't care.

I wanted to go home then and there.

Catriona was in the process of talking. I struggled to concentrate.

"After the disco the shop was steamy and warm. We always bought the smallest bags. I forget how much they cost. None of us had much money. They were wrapped up in brown paper with a layer of real newspaper on the outside. The owners' son usually served. We used to smile for him. We thought he'd give us extra if we were nice to him. We were young and we thought we were so brilliant."

I asked her what the town was like.

"Like everywhere else. Provincial. It certainly wasn't a rich place, the town we lived in. My mum worked mornings in the post office. My dad was a salesman in a sports shop on the high street."

I wasn't sure what she meant by a sports shop. I asked.

"Sinclair Sports was on the church end of the main road between a kebab carryout and a dentist's. They sold football boots and football strips and football scarves and football hats and footballs and rosettes and posters and trophies and pennants and what-not. The sign outside said "Sinclair Sports" but it was all really just football stuff that they sold. My dad was the only full-time employee. He played for the town team. They were just amateurs. Dad was the goalie. He was actually good and he played into his forties but he wasn't ever good enough to play for a professional team. When he was a schoolboy he had trials for one of the big Yorkshire teams. They were just a second-division team. He said he was nervous and wasn't good enough. He let an easy shot slide through his hands and he didn't get signed. The first time I remember seeing him play he got nervous again and let in another sitter. Direct from a corner. The ball caught in the wind. The supporters booed. They were such little shits. It was awful. He pulled the ball from the net. His head was hanging so low. I just started to cry."

"So tell me all about the boys."

She laughed and took a deep breath. "We were a right bunch of mercenary little tarts. It was always the same. We eyed the boys at the dance. We looked and smiled then we looked away and tossed our hair and danced close and held them tight—but not too tight—when the slow songs played at the end of the night but we didn't let them kiss us. Not on the lips. Not then. When we left the church hall we talked loudly, about where we were going for chips. We were shameless. They followed us. They probably imagined that they were doing all the work, chatting us up outside the shop, talking their way inside our knickers with their stupid jokes. What a bunch of trendy wankers. Lambs to the slaughter in their silly cop show outfits. Perishing cold on the English Riviera in their baggy Florida pastels. The stupid show was no longer even on the telly."

I was growing to like Catriona less and less.

"It did get complicated. There were always the four of us. We went together. The very best of mates we were." She was joking. Then she paused and looked hard at me. Her hand held a strand of hair caught midway between her face and her ear.

"How do we choose our friends when we're that young?" She asked me.

"I'm not sure we do," I replied.

She shook her head in mock vexation. "There was me and Angie and Penny and Karen. I was the talkative one, Penny was quite plain, Angie was self-proclaimed gorgeous."

"What about Karen?"

"She wasn't pretty and she wasn't chatty and she wasn't ordinary."

"So what was she?" I was curious.

She sighed. "Karen Chisolm was irresistible to all men and boys. God knows why. She just was. A walking wet dream."

"You must have loved her."

She sighed dramatically. "Karen made it very difficult without trying to. We had these elaborate rules for the boys. There had to be four. One each. One we each liked. They had to like us. One each. They had to want to chat us up. And once we had lured them into thinking they were doing all the hard work, we had to want to get off with them."

I smiled at an expression I hadn't heard in a long while.

"How well did all this work out?" I wondered out loud.

She almost snorted at that. "Naturally the little pricks all fancied Karen even though Angie considered herself to be the prettiest. Angie was quite particular about the boys. If she didn't fancy any of them then the whole thing was off. This happened a lot. She would sometimes try to pinch another boy—mine or maybe Penny's. She had no luck poaching Karen's. She was very rude to boys she thought beneath her. She was mean to Penny."

"Why was that?" I asked, even if I knew the answer already.

"Because Angie thought that Penny was ugly and boring and Angie used to get annoyed because, in her queen bitch opinion, no boys ever wanted to chat Penny up. Penny used to get upset."

"Angie sounds charming," I remarked.

"Oh she was."

I hesitated to ask my next question. But I was curious. "What did you do with the boys?" I finally asked.

"We ate our chips and stood by the boys with their backs up against the wet metal bars and we necked with them until our mouths were sore. If the waves broke over the top of the pier we would get drenched. If the weather was great and the sea was calm, we would keep on kissing. If the boy was cute and kissed well, we both got soaked. If he was sloppy and smelled too much of cheap Boots aftershave we broke and ran for cover. I remember that Karen usually ran first. She and Angie didn't like getting wet all that much. Penny was usually the next to go."

"What about you?" I smiled at her.

"A right little trollop. Always the wettest and the last," she said mock ruefully. "I really liked kissing the boys."

I was forced to laugh.

"What about you?" She asked me suddenly.

I grinned at her. "A trollop. Just like you. I really liked kissing the girls."

⁂

SHONA NESBIT HAD red hair and ran fast enough to be allowed to compete in both the girls and boys relay teams in the school that I attended. She had long thin legs and wore navy blue knickers to gym class and had matching dimples behind her knees. She had an older sister with long dark hair who was even prettier than she was.

For almost two months we had been forced to learn the Dashing White Sergeant and other energetic Scottish reels in a compulsory class that met for half an hour after school and cut deeply into our afternoon football time.

There was going to be a dance at the end of the school year and we were required to be ready.

In between fits of nervous giggling we formed into circles of eight, frantically maneuvering so that all four girls and all four boys got to dance with their chosen partners. I recall the process being complicated and not always successful.

I had passed a note to Shona in class before the first practice. She already knew I fancied her, as did everyone else in Mrs. Harper's chemistry class. We called out the rhymes about the children who fancied each other; Andy and Christine, Kenny and Doreen, Tommy and Shona.

First comes love, then comes marriage.
Then comes baby in a baby carriage.

In the note I asked her if she would go to the dance with me. She asked me if I was sure, because she had heard that Marilyn Nicolson wanted to go with me. Marilyn had passed me a note telling me I was the best looking boy in the school. I was not the first to receive this accolade. Marilyn had passed many of these notes, and several of her previous choices had been questionable at best. I had passed Marilyn a note explaining that I didn't fancy her.

She had taken it well and quickly moved on to the next best looking boy in school.

We were fourteen years old.

After the jigs and the reels came a few choice pop nuggets from the mid-seventies (I do still recall all the boys slumped against the gym walls in a collective huff as the girls melodramatically swayed and swooned to the flaccid-as-shite sounds of the Bay City Rollers).

I tried to walk with my arm around Shona's bony shoulders all the way down the road from the school gate to the chip shop after the dance ended. When we got there I bought her a pie supper and chips and she kissed me fiercely with her mouth clamped tightly shut the whole time.

It was awkward as I walked her home. We were simply not used to each other's height, to walking as a unit, and Shona was just as tall as I was. Her arm was around my waist and our hips kept on bumping together. I remembered her pale-pink dress had been much too delicate for the weather.

We tried talking.

"I liked it when they played Bowie."

"Me too. My sister likes Roxy Music. She fancies Bryan Ferry."

"They played the Sweet."

"Aye, I ken. "Action." It was brilliant. I kent Marilyn widnae come. She kent she'd look right stupid after asking all thae laddies and gettin' her slaggy self kicked intae touch every time."

We both laughed and our arms tightened around each other.

We tried kissing again in the bus shelter at the corner of the road, with our mouths finally open, and our teeth scraping together. I could taste the brown sauce on the corner of her mouth. It started to rain after a while, and the raindrops drummed daintily on the corrugated iron roof.

We didn't have to talk then. It had been very pleasant.

The next day in school Shona told me that her father had been watching us from behind a twitching living room curtain, and that she had got a serious bollocking when she got in.

She giggled and told me she didnae care.

The next day after school she showed up at the playing fields and asked if she could play football with us. There were several voices raised in protest. No other girls were playing. Grudgingly she was allowed to join in. She played very well. A few boys were better than she was, but not many, and I wasn't one of them.

We played for an hour and afterwards we held hands as we walked home. My house was closer to the school than hers. So she essentially walked me home.

As we got to the front door my mother was standing at the front window with a smirk on her face.

"Should I thank her for bringing you home safe and sound?" She asked me sweetly.

"Very funny."

By Christmas of that same year Shona Nesbit and her family had moved to Forfar.

I didn't for a moment believe that it had anything to do with her father's noticing our kissing, but I now had to walk all the way home by myself.

⁂

"WHATEVER ARE YOU thinking about now?" Catriona looked mildly peeved. She listened politely as I labored to explain. When I was finished with my tale of chips and heartbreak she laughed at me.

I asked her how she came to be here in West Seattle.

"We lived in a big house in Madison Park for a few years when we first came here. I was married then. To Jeff. We were sent here for his job. Jeff worked in transportation. There's a hub here. We divorced quickly. He moved back. It wasn't especially sad or dramatic. We were young when we met. We were married for a short time. He's living near London. Madison Park is lovely. There's a public beach and the Japanese gardens close to our house. That house has an indoor wave pool and a sauna and was much too large. I moved here to something smaller. I live simply. I worked as a bookkeeper before I met Jeff, as I do now. I have a few clients. They need my help but they don't need a full-time employee or an actual accountant. I do their payroll and insurance. It works well. I have my little house."

"Do you like it here?" I asked her.

Her response was predictable. "It's brilliant."

The British use that word for anything that isn't actually horrific. I must have looked unconvinced.

"It feels right. The first part of my life ends. This is the second part. I had my long childhood, my short marriage, my fast divorce. Then I had myself two wanton years after I got divorced. Erotic times in exotic places. I went all around the coast of Florida. Gambled with a girlfriend in Biloxi."

"How did that go?"

"We lost enough that the management generously offered a proposal to work off our losses."

"What kind of proposal?"

The options were long-term cocktail waitressing or short-term prostitution."

"Which did you chose?"

Her answer was evasive. "I chose not to stay there for long."

I didn't get the chance for a follow-up question.

"Spent time with some hippies in Apalachicola. They sold their artisanal beads and leather shit along the coast near Panama City. Later in the season we worked our way south down the Gulf coast to Clearwater, where we took hung-over tourists from Germany and England out on expensive fishing charters. My job was to mix the Bloody Marys and explain why the fish weren't biting that day. The best part was renting a small beach house in Key West with the dosh from the charters. Single malts in the tourist bars on Duval. Posing as a colorful local, pretending to be reading Hemingway in public, rescuing a mean stray cat, swimming in the ocean before bed. A belated gap year times two on the hot sand, lathered in coconut suntan oil, smoking weed with boys who were way too young for me. It was..." She faltered.

"Brilliant?" I offered.

"Amazing." She corrected me.

"You're happy now?"

Her smile was determined. "I am. I'm mostly alone. I'm not so young. And I'm fine with that."

"Where will you go from here?" She asked suddenly.

"I think back home."

"Boulder?" I had already told her where I lived.

"Yes."

"Do you know any British people there?"

I thought for a second. "Not a single one."

"You sound pleased when you say that. Does it remind you of Scotland?"

I considered the question. "No. There's a lot of hills . . ."

"But not much else."

"No. I think I chose it for that reason. Fewer trees. Less water. More sun."

"When you speak you sound almost like an American."

"It's been a while. My mother thinks I sound like an American."

"Does she mind?"

"She thinks it's funny."

"You've lost your identity."

"That's a harsh way of putting it."

"There are two kinds of immigrants. The brave and the cowardly."

"I assume I'm the latter." I said.

"You're one of the brave."

"You surprise me."

"Did you know there are an awful lot of European transplants in this part of America?"

I did know this. I chose to play along.

"And you have a theory?" I gently inquired of her.

This was her theory: "We settle with the familiar. We want to feel safe and comfortable. If we can, we try to make it better. Perhaps it's warmer, the summers here always feel longer, even though I miss the late sun in the extended evening. The sea and the winter are gentler and prettier than they were. The plants in my garden are the same ones my mum used to try and grow at home, but they grow much easier and taller. The growing season stretches out. It's all just that much easier."

"So why is that brave?"

"It's not brave. It's cowardly."

"I don't understand."

"Immigrants mostly gravitate to the familiar. The Scots went to Appalachia because it looks like Scotland."

"They were misguided. They chose a place that was no better at supporting them than the place they came from."

"They felt at home."

"At home in more hardscrabble squalor."

"Portuguese fishermen found warm places to fish. Scandinavians headed up north into the cold."

"And the slimy English bagged all the best arable land as usual."

"How do you like my theory?"

"It's not complete shite."

"And you found yourself a place that doesn't remind you of home."

"I'm a modern day frontiersman."

"I'm trying to pay you a compliment. You are one of the hardy."

I wasn't sure what to say.

So I considered her theory more carefully.

Bullshit mostly. But not complete shite.

Then Catriona abruptly changed the subject.

"I was adopted when I was three."

But I already knew this.

‡‡

SHE GOT NO further. There was a tap on the window and we both looked up. She hesitated for a second, momentarily confused, then she smiled and waved. I looked questioningly.

The matter of her past was tabled for the moment.

The man at the window was a gangly construction of coarse wool and mismatched plaid. He smiled and waved, or rather he smiled and waved to Catriona. We both watched as he unloaded three wooden ladders and four metal buckets from the oldest extant piece-of-shit Datsun pickup truck in the world. With little fanfare he then commenced to wash the restaurant windows. It was a cloudy and overcast day, which I imagined was just right for window washing, the kind of day that the state of Washington generates habitually.

His face came in and out of focus through the glass as it became wet then dry. The woman he clearly knew gazed at her wrist, played with the band of leather that now circled it, and talked to an older man he'd never met, and that she had never met, until now.

Did he look a little nervous? Could he tell she was about to start talking about him?

"I don't know him." She was being too defensive.

"He's still waving," I countered cleverly.

She considered this. "We did meet once," she finally allowed.

"Well he keeps on looking and waving," I informed her. "So you must have made an impression."

Reluctantly she could recall her first encounter with this surely fine, certainly wooly, decidedly bohemian-looking gentleman. And then she proceeded to describe exactly that.

It had been a largely wordless event at a record shop on nearby California Avenue where they had bought the same recording. They laughed briefly and easily at the coincidence as they made their matching purchases, standing awkwardly afterwards, aware that a bonding moment was in danger of departing, both helpless to prolong it.

The record shop in question served a sensibly priced and sustaining breakfast all day, and offered Washington State organic red wines and craft beer from nearby Bend, Oregon, later in the afternoon. More traditionally, the store also carried a catholic selection of new and collectible vintage music on compact discs and vinyl.

As she spoke I pondered the alluring combination of beer and food and music and found it difficult to imagine ever having cause to leave such a wondrous establishment.

"I buy most of my music there," she said.

"I can't say I blame you," I replied with deep conviction.

"I try to avoid the food and the beer."

"That seems ill advised."

"They're both bad for you," she admonished me with a laugh.

"That's certainly true," I was forced to admit.

Having won the point, her conversation abruptly changed direction. "Did you know that Johnny Marr once played guitar for The Smiths?"

I surely did. And I told her so.

It transpired that The Smiths were Catriona's favorite band when she was younger and Johnny Marr was her favorite Smith.

"He lives near Portland. Or perhaps he did. I'm not quite sure. I saw him on television. He was valet parking his blue bicycle on a comedy show. Actually he wasn't parking it. He was trying to get it back. They couldn't find it. He was getting annoyed. I wasn't sure if it was him. They ran the credits. It really was him. It was funny."

I had no idea what she was talking about and told her so.

"The record we were both buying. It was Johnny Marr."

Now I understood.

Catriona and The Smiths apparently ran deep. She surrendered her virginity in her last year of grammar school to a pasty paramour who claimed to have played bass guitar in a postpunk garage band with Morrissey, before Moz turned all vegan and grumpy and famous, and met Mr. Marr.

"This was the first pouty, glam boy to lie to me and let me down. We all have a type. Effete romantics were mine. What do you like?"

"I like my women easily distracted."

"By you?"

I shook my head. "By other things."

"That's a shame."

"Quite."

Many of her pretty boys, she would add, would prove to be weak and undependable, but a sad few would become more violent; rendered boorishly contrary by the nature of their failings, and by their need to exploit the neediness they were convinced they saw in her.

"Do I seem needy?" She asked me suddenly.

She struck me as alone and self-centered, but I chose not to say this out loud. I told her she seemed smart and independent, and she seemed more than satisfied with my answer.

The window cleaner had gone by now. He had done a fine job and finished just in time for the start of the late afternoon rain.

Catriona said she began purchasing vinyl when her parents' old turntable became a somber inheritance.

She told me they died together.

I waited for more details.

"It was the first record I had bought since I was a girl. I listened to it in my living room. It sounded nothing like The Smiths. On the sleeve he had a raincoat and the same haircut. Why do rock stars always have rock-star haircuts? There was an old poster on my bedroom wall."

At that point in our conversation she took the bracelet off, placed it on the table, and then put it back on, all seemingly without thinking. She picked up the idiotic fish-shaped menu and stared at it blankly. There was no need to look at it as we had already ordered our food.

And then our food arrived. Catriona's came with a small pot of tea that she hadn't asked for, and one small cup and saucer. The waitress quickly left and returned with a second cup, also unbidden, and we had our afternoon tea.

Catriona looked down at her plate and smiled. "I always get the same thing. A small portion of the battered cod and too many chips. I never manage to finish. It's half price until five. I'm cheap."

"You do know I'm Scottish?" I told her. "We own the patent on cheap."

By now I'd lost track of time. The clock on the wall was also shaped like a fish and, as a result, it was difficult to read, but I thought it must be close to three thirty in the afternoon. We still had plenty of time to talk, and to eat, and to be gone, before the place got loud and busy.

We ate in silence. A Rolling Stones song played.

"Angie," she announced.

"You're too young."

"It was her favorite."

"Who?"

"Who do you think? Do you know the song?" She asked.

I told her I did.

"She always begged them to play it at the end of the dance. It's a slow song. She liked the words. Especially the parts when they sing about her being beautiful, how there's not a woman that comes close to her. Shouted out the words. She really was vain."

"What ever happened to her?"

She shook her head. "Don't know. I hope she has ten nasty kids, and an arse the size of a double-decker bus."

It was an uncharitable thought. I had to smile.

"Did you see him leave?"

Catriona had missed the departure of the window cleaner, his ladders, his buckets, his piece-of-shit truck. She looked momentarily sad.

I was certain she had enjoyed the brief attention.

⚓

THERE WAS A distant moan, the ferry heading out towards one of the small commuter islands. As it came into view I could see that the boat was mostly empty in the middle of a wet working day, except for a handful of shivering, underdressed teenagers standing on the upper deck gazing miserably into the distance, perhaps hoping for the sun, or else a glimpse of the mythical volcanic mountain that exists only in cruel and taunting local legends.

Our waitress returned with a fresh pot of tea. Her one bare shoulder was a seething tendril of inked foliage and nesting birds. She was a decade younger than Catriona, more than a generation removed from me—a young muscular woman with dark shiny hair in an angular cut that seemed designed to highlight that one lushly illustrated patch of skin. She frowned inexplicably as she filled our tiny cups quickly and silently, a welcome yet wholly unbidden act. I thanked her as Catriona asked for more milk, rather than using the tiny packets of flavored half-and-half sitting in the matching blue dish on the table.

With some dismay I looked down at the acreage of fish still hanging off the side of my plate. I had ordered the full portion, reasoning that Catriona's request for the smaller plate made perfect sense for her, but that I, who had to outweigh her by a metric ton or so, would clearly require far greater amounts of sustenance. I could plainly see now that her order would have done me perfectly well.

Maybe I could get a bag full of greasy leftovers to go, and feed the grateful gulls outside.

With a deep sigh and a sense of impending failure I picked up my knife and fork and got stuck in.

It was surprising to me how little she had spoken about him.

"My parents got me from an orphanage near Durham. It was a place for little girls. The town's not far from where they lived. It was pretty. Do you know it?" I assumed she meant Durham rather than the actual orphanage. I nodded.

"It's in the North, with a cathedral and a university." She hesitated.

"I've been there, or very close to there. Isn't Holy Island nearby?"

"Were you there?"

I nodded some more. "A long time ago. I was married. We drove across at low water and visited the ruins and stopped at a small hotel with a bar that was open on a Sunday. It was a windy spot. We had to rush back to beat the tide."

"People get stranded," she remarked.

"We cut it close."

"I tell people that I don't remember it. I do. There was an old greenhouse in the gardens. It wasn't used any more and most of the glass panes were broken. We couldn't play there. It wasn't safe. There was a sunroom with wicker chairs and glass tables with old dolls on them. These are images. I can't tell if they are real or if I made them up. Perhaps there was a huge hall with high windows and no curtains and wooden cots painted white in rows. I remember a shiny floor and ladies with mops and buckets of strong disinfectant. I must have crawled on the floor at some point. I was only three when I left. It's all gone now. The building is still there. The university uses it for student residences. They put their first-year girls in there."

‡‡

I TOLD HER I was sorry that her parents were dead.

She thanked me. "They died together."

She had told me this already. I said nothing.

"It was a car crash. Up north. They were in Scotland. Motoring in the Highlands. They loved it there. They had a little caravan that we always used for our holidays. They were traveling through the rain and mist and went off the road. My dad was driving. He always drove the caravan faster than Mum did. They were on a narrow road. There was one lane. The traffic behind them was impatient. They were honking their horns. If Mum had been driving she would have laughed at them. She would have gone slower. Dad would let them bully him into speeding up. He'd get all embarrassed and try to get to a lay-by and pull over to let them all pass. Mum used to get so mad at him for doing that. She always said the road was just as much theirs. When they went off the side and through a broken fence and down a hill there were thirty cars in a line behind them, the police report said, but only one man stopped and tried to help them. He phoned for the police and climbed down the hill in the rain and even tried to lift the caravan up. But it was too heavy and it had flattened their stupid little car."

There wasn't a lot I could say to that.

Then she hesitated. "You came here to tell me about my real father."

"You don't seem that interested."

There was another pause. "No," she said at last.

I said nothing. I wanted to correct her. As far as I was concerned, her real father had died with her real mother under a wet caravan at the bottom of a Scottish hill, two victims of lethally bad manners.

But I didn't.

"Is there anything you can tell me that will make me feel any different about him?"

"How do you feel about him?" I asked.

"I've listened to his songs."

"And?"

"They're nice."

"I think so too."

"You obviously like them more than I do," she said. I didn't reply.

She looked out the window. "Are you leaving?" she asked.

"Soon. I think. I want to drive some of the way tonight."

"So tell me something before you go."

And with that supremely indifferent request I would proceed to tell her almost everything I had learned in the past two weeks about her father.

⁂

LATER ON WE said our goodbyes. I got up to leave. The rain had begun to pour in earnest. I did notice that.

And I also observed that the old Datsun truck had returned and the window cleaner was lurking outside the shop looking decidedly sheepish. Wet sheepish, I should probably amend that to. Had he forgotten one of his ladders perhaps? But I thought not. No man waves that much to a woman. Not unless he has a cramp in his arm.

We brushed against each other as he entered and I exited. The urge to whisper "Good luck" was strong, but I was somehow able to resist. Had he changed his sweater? I turned around. It was certainly possible. Maybe he was wearing his lucky sweater.

I unapologetically turned and stared at them.

He stood at her table and they both smiled. He pulled off his soaked wool hat like a true gent and his hair, a wild fright of dripping curls, bounced into action. I had thought he seemed young but now, newly chapeau-less and freshly re-jerseyed, he looked older, closer to Catriona's age.

I wanted to stare more, but the dictates of decorum prevailed.

As I waited to cross the street I wondered if she would talk to him about the bracelet, and about the song, and about her father. She certainly did like to talk.

And while I really hoped that she would tell him, it was doubtful.

Catriona was mostly lonely.

Catriona mostly liked to talk about herself.

Catriona had lost her parents recently.

And nothing I had told her or given her had changed any of these things.

But I'm getting far ahead of myself.

Because all this would take place several days and several thousand miles northwest of New Orleans. Before I would get to New Orleans there would be a road trip due south, with a pit stop at the halfway mark, where I would briefly experience the refined gentility of life in Oxford, Mississippi.

And that road trip south would begin in the southern suburbs of Chicago.

Which is where the story really begins.

THREE

THIS WAS the beginning.

The lure of free Wi-Fi and a warm place to sit had led a young man in a cheery argyle sweater vest and pastel polo shirt upper-body ensemble and threadbare Madras cargo shorts, to an empty table in a crowded coffee shop twenty miles due south of Chicago. His outfit was certainly bold and eye-catching. His shorts were grimy. His laptop was an older model that stood open and running on the table. The black plastic was heavily stickered, scratched deeply in places, the screen patinaed with a thick filter of grease and dust. Old-school earmuff headphones were plugged into one side of the machine, while a generic red plastic flash drive was attached and blinking reassuringly as the images played out on the screen.

By chance I had occupied the next table, and was thus able to spy shamelessly.

He was watching something I was quite certain I hadn't seen before, period science fiction, from the indistinct past. My best guess was somewhere in the seventies. A pointy-chested woman with purple hair fashioned in a sharp, near eye-level fringe was poured into a slick plastic miniskirt.

The young man gazed fixedly at the screen as the woman placed a metallic helmet over her head and pushed an improbably huge button on a wall made entirely of glass. As she did, it slid noiselessly open to reveal a brightly lit hallway, complete with a moving floor of space-age deep-pile shag that whisked her away.

I watched as he picked up his coffee. He frowned and put it back down. His beverage had come in a cup with an orange and pink corporate logo on the side, whereas the rest of us were in lockstep with the host brand.

Yet he continued to sit there, utterly bold and shameless.

The cafe was busy in the middle of the morning. The Internet-accessible tables were lined along one wall facing the counter, and were clearly each intended for two people, two paying people. Yet there he was; a very singular and noticeable party of one who had purchased nothing here, with a soiled backpack squatting on another chair lined up directly in front of him.

I had already observed that several customers had glared his way ineffectually, even going so far as to stand over him, clutching their freshly purchased products like so many talismans of entitlement, but he stood—or rather sat—his ground. So they had eventually retreated, all fuming and foamy under a good head of self-righteousness.

I glanced at my phone. Good God. I had spent the past twenty minutes doing close to nothing but sipping my coffee and observing this young man on a chilly May morning.

When I had first arrived the lady behind the counter had asked, "What can I get you this morning, sweetie?"

That was certainly pleasant, if unexpected. I didn't get called sweetie too often. A decidedly more senior server than the usual sullen adolescent, she was close to my own age. I smiled, resolving to hit the tip jar hard, one kind word being all it apparently took to render me an emotional dishrag, ripe for a good wringing out.

I asked for a medium coffee.

"Which blend?"

I shrugged my response, then elected to try a little harder. I was a sweetie after all.

"It doesn't matter. Whatever's freshest," I replied with another smile. I can't, in all honesty, tell much of a difference between Midnight Dark French Roast and Shade Grown Organic Guatemalan, although I like to imagine I can at least distinguish brews of a more recent vintage from the stewed sludge distilled in the early morning in crappier establishments.

But I may well be kidding myself.

Her nametag said Gabby and she was relentlessly friendly as she attended to me and the rest of the walk-in trade.

Meanwhile, three pale youngsters in matching shirts, attitudes, and headsets jumped to the faceless bark of the drive-up intercom and took turns rolling their eyes at Gabby as they bustled past her. When I elected to scan my phone to pay, one of the youths suddenly lasered in on our transaction. Was he expecting the dithering old biddy to hopelessly bungle the operation? Dude, check out the hapless codger.

But, bless her heart, Gabby didn't. Scanned and done. Score one for the old farts. I was absurdly pleased for her, and would have favored the snotty adolescent with a knowing smirk, but he had turned away.

I smiled instead at Gabby and hastily revised my tip amount upward. We crusties have to stick together.

That was half an hour ago.

The young man got to his feet and walked slowly towards the two adjacent bathrooms located in the back of the store. He took his backpack with him but left the empty coffee cup and the computer on the table. The show was still running, and the woman with the asymmetrical purple hair was revealed as the pilot of what resembled a flying trimaran without a sail. Her co-pilot, I couldn't fail to notice, also wore a shiny helmet, which didn't quite cover his two enormous pointy sideburns.

The muted colors and the hairdos helped to more accurately carbon-date the production as definitely somewhere in the early part of the seventies. My best guess was television rather than film. An older actor now stood commandingly, in what I assumed was a bedroom on a larger space ship. His suit was too tight, the lapels would help him take off in a strong wind, and his face was more lined than you would probably expect today, with the ready and pervasive availability of cosmetic surgical work and the forgiving salve of soft-focus camera lenses. His teeth were also slightly crooked.

My phone buzzed and I looked down at the table. An incoming text awaited from Nye, the supercilious and the decidedly more active partner in our chosen commercial endeavors—the largely unrelated worlds of online art supplies and artisan brewing.

He posed three questions. They were as follows:

Where was I? Where did I keep the sugar? Had we passed?

I quickly composed the answers to questions one and three in my head. They would read as follows.

I was on my way home and indeed we had.

I hesitated over the second. His demand for sugar was trickier. I don't use sugar. Neither does Nye. What to make of this request? He was in my house. Was he perhaps entertaining? Did his guest possess a sweet tooth? Could Nye perhaps be baking? That last seemed singularly unlikely, but I was truthfully stumped.

I suddenly remembered some dried-out brown sugar from a bygone era in a white ceramic pot on a high shelf in the kitchen. Thus able to reply to his text in full, I dutifully did. Asked and answered. Take that Mr. Prior.

Nye was attending Hop Haven, a beer festival in Fort Collins, Colorado. I was visiting our art supply distribution center in the Chicago suburbs. Nye lives in Chicago and I live in Boulder. The explanation for the geographical mismatch is trivial and complicated and, quite frankly, not really worth getting into. Suffice it to say that the anomaly would soon be redressed. I was about to get on the road and drive back cross-country, an activity which I loudly profess to despise, but secretly rather enjoy. Nye was meanwhile hanging with other brewers and beer snobs, doubtless drinking too well and too copiously, and staying at my place for a few short days before returning to Chicago to resume his role as captain of industry—a role he performs well enough to allow me the longtime luxury of mostly malingering and sporadically meddling.

I had been with our crackerjack art supply team in the early morning for an inspection of the facilities by a local government agency. We had passed with flying colors and I was heading home after a session of sundry shoulder patting.

The highway was a handful of intersections away, and would take most of the thousand miles west through Illinois, Iowa, Nebraska, and the irritating three hours of faux Nebraska that is Northeastern Colorado. Iowa is green and rolling and mostly pretty, Nebraska is flat and brown and empty and endless, and the wait for the Rocky Mountains to finally make an appearance takes an agonizing forever, as the Colorado plains very gradually elevate, and only transform into the traditional images of majestic mountains close to Denver.

I had made the drive once in one very long day to prove to myself that I could, but it had been a wretched experience. Today I would go only as far as Lincoln, Nebraska, by the evening, find a hotel room and swim, eat a pizza with chicken and pesto and olives and feta and dried tomatoes in a hipster bar on O Street, and cover the rest of the trip the following day.

This was the extent of my plan.

I was made aware that I had been daydreaming for several minutes by the sound of loud knocking.

One of the younger coffee shop employees was pounding with some urgency on the door of the men's bathroom. There was clearly no answer. Another employee joined her and they looked at each other in some confusion. There followed a conversation loud enough for the whole store to eavesdrop. A customer was locked in the bathroom. He was not responding to their attempts at intervention. The store manager had the key and she had left to run some errands. She had been texted but had not yet responded.

I somehow knew without looking that the table beside me was going to still be vacant. The computer was still running the television show, as a singular and wholly unrealistic piece of space Styrofoam was blown into tiny fragments time and time again, each explosion accompanied by the close-up of an alternating space pilot's face, frozen in a stock reaction of either fear or triumph.

Both servers began to beat hard on the toilet door. One was shouting, her voice dreadful and shrill and no longer fully controlled. My Gabby stood firm behind the counter, all alone, attending to customers, with the brilliance of her smile still holding fast. A fourth employee pulled his headset from his ears and was using his cell phone to make an urgent call, standing at the front door, ignoring the drive-thru trade as it began to bristle and honk outside.

A situation was rapidly evolving and the public reaction varied. A number of the less curious or the morbidly uneasy had got up and left, those who stayed pulled out their cell phones and made ready to summon electronic help.

One of the two employees outside the restroom door was pawing at it thoughtfully, clearly considering a full-on assault on the locked wood. Would the door hold? Would her shoulder give out? And just how comprehensive was the company medical coverage going to be anyway?

What I chose to do next surprised me. I can offer no explanation.

Without thinking I leaned across the table and pulled the flash drive from the abandoned computer and stuck it quickly inside my trouser pocket. Next I got to my feet and walked quickly towards the front door, throwing my almost empty cup into the garbage and pushing past the employee now all but yelling into his phone.

I didn't look back.

Outside I could see that the drive-thru line was now a static eleven cars, rendering it no longer possible to drive either in or out of the café parking lot. At that precise moment a car horn broadcast that very fact.

I got as far as holding the front door open.

The car horn stopped. There was a moment of loud silence. And then came two sounds and a hesitation between: a splintering crash as lock and wood gave way, and an earsplitting and prolonged scream, a woman's scream, both sounds coming from deep inside the cafe.

I walked quickly across the parking lot to the street and got to my car. The urge to start the car and pull away fast was strong, but instead I sat for a minute with the doors locked and looked across the street.

Set back from the road was a narrow steel footbridge that spanned two parallel sets of train tracks. On one the Amtrak train ran twice a day between Chicago and New Orleans, and during the long hours in between, a series of protracted freight trains commandeered the rail. On the track, the commuter electric line connected the big city to a succession of Chicago metro south suburban towns. The electric trains ran at least once every hour, slightly more often during the peak commuting times in the early morning and evening. A stucco brown station building served double duty for the commuters going to and from work on the electric and those taking Amtrak for the longer haul going south to colleges downstate, all the way to Memphis, or to Jackson, Mississippi, or still further south, down into Louisiana, for whatever romantic or desperate reason.

I had taken that southbound train myself once. Close to two decades ago. I had gone to New Orleans.

A diesel engine jolted into life and I jumped. The graffiti-spattered line of freight cars jostled together in a loud staggered cacophony of cracks, an undulating sequence of rapid reports, and the freight train began to grind its serpentine way slowly southward.

I took it as a sign that I should leave too.

I started the engine and pulled away slowly. No one entered or left the coffee shop as I watched in the rearview mirror. My intention was to drive a little way north heading towards the next entrance onto the highway going west, making myself think only about the day's driving. Perhaps I would stop for some lunch later, in Iowa, and by the end of the day I would be in Lincoln, Nebraska.

There was a sign up ahead for I-80 West.

Think about the drive.

Don't think about the scream.

A billboard sign promised me an EZ car title loan. A handsome lawyer with a slick smile and his shirt sleeves rolled up for business would get me a big check pronto for my job-related accident.

I wasn't interested in either a loan or a big check.

Why had she screamed?

The young man had stood up. He had taken his backpack with him into the bathroom. He had carried it instead of putting it over his shoulder. He had picked up his coffee cup. It had presumably been empty. He had put it back down.

He had left his computer on the table. Most of the customers in the café had cell phones sitting on their tables. Did he have one? I thought not. The drive and the headphones had still been attached to the computer. The television show had still been running.

What was on the drive?

The scream kept replaying in my head as I drove away. It was distracting enough that I almost missed the unexpected left turn onto the highway heading west towards home.

FOUR

I DROVE FOR THE NEXT three hours without stopping. I endeavored not to think about anything but driving.

Internet service was being offered at each rest stop and it was a temptation, but rather than stop and satisfy my curiosity, I made myself keep on going, heading almost due west, crossing high over the Mississippi River at the Iowa border, and a few minutes later exiting into a pretty riverside town. Three short blocks later, I found the bar right where Google Maps had assured me it would be.

I had generously promised myself a beer with my lunch as some kind of fictitious reward. They made their own. I opted for a stout and ordered a late lunch of homemade shepherd's pie.

There were three other customers positioned equidistant from each other along the high-gloss length of the bar. I sat instead at the window and looked out onto the street across the empty red dirt parking lot that sloped all the way down to the river. High overhead, I could see the arches of the bridge I had just crossed. Three wooden park benches on a footpath followed the topography of the riverbank and were placed strategically amidst tall grass arrangements that the town had artfully placed along that stretch of water.

The flash drive I had taken from the coffee shop was still in my pocket. My laptop was on the table, fired up and ready. The Wi-Fi password was written on a blackboard behind the bar. I was hungry. My food hadn't arrived yet. As soon as I started on the beer, I badly wanted another, but I had a long way still to go before my day would come to an end.

A woman had screamed in a coffee shop in a small town over three hours ago. So what? It would hardly merit a breaking news segment in the online version of the New York Times, but it might have generated a mention somewhere, deep in the vast minutiae of cyberspace. My first and best guess was a hometown news Patch, where the good people regularly posted on matters of mostly local and lurid interest, with neighborhood crimes being a reliable opportunity for considerable electronic hand-wringing.

Within minutes I was proven right. A witness in the coffee shop had already breathlessly posted and, setting aside the copious exclamation marks, I learned that a young man had apparently knelt down on the clean bathroom floor, cut open his wrists, cleverly placed his hands under the cold water in the toilet bowl, and proceeded to bleed very tidily to death.

The last part was admittedly a matter of some speculation. The eager witness had noted that the body looked quite dead. The two servers who had finally managed to get the bathroom door open had seemingly commented on the deep red color of the water, which to them strongly hinted at a massive and life-extinguishing blood loss. The poster also mentioned that the hands had been milk white, and that there had been no blood dripping down onto the clean floor as the victim had been removed from the scene at a leisurely pace by the paramedics. This decided lack of blood and haste in the removal of the body indicated that the young man was already dead. The witness went on to list other random observations. A knife had been removed by the paramedics, who had also thought to pick up the dead man's backpack. The two police officers who had arrived shortly after the paramedics, had commandeered both items.

The witness strongly believed the death to be a suicide, and there seemed little sense in debating the point with her, unless breaking into a locked coffee shop restroom and escaping unseen afterward was an even remotely likely scenario for a murder. I had been to the coffee shop several times before. There was no window in the bathroom, and no other means to get in or out.

I finished reading through the rest of the Patch as my lunch arrived. The shepherd's pie came with cheddar cheese cooked into the mashed potatoes on top. It should have been delicious. It wasn't. I swallowed the first bite all but untasted. I was asked if I wanted another beer. I did, but I resolutely declined.

There were several related comments posted, which expressed a predictable smorgasbord of sorrow and outrage, mostly sorrow at not being there themselves, and outrage that the poster was not delivering a pre-cathartic deluge of repugnant revelations of a more graphic nature. A singular comment near the end essayed a kindlier tone, oddly sympathizing not with the dead young man, but with the "poor soul" who had posted the initial link.

"So very sorry you had to see that." The comment earnestly concluded, albeit unnecessarily, as it was quite obvious that the witness was close to wetting herself with ill-suppressed glee at her good timing, and at her being at the scene of something so hideously pleasurable as an unexpected and unexpectedly gory death scene.

The urge to get all self-righteous in the unseemly face of the macabre was a strong one. But I resisted. I was breathlessly reading this stuff after all. And I had pocketed the flash drive.

Speaking of which, in my reading of the Patch posting, I had looked for any reference to my theft and was relieved to see nothing mentioned.

The question was: Why had I taken it?

Was it an impulsive act or a twinkling of intuition?

Had I somehow sensed that a bad ending was imminent?

I plugged in the flash drive and I waited. There were only two files saved to the drive and I opened the first.

It was a short text file and it loaded quickly. The file was named kindsister. It was a biography of an English actress, and the style and content felt a whole lot like a Wikipedia entry. Her name was Margot Kind. There was a birthdate in early December of 1945. No date of death was recorded. Her parents had been schoolteachers and were both dead. A younger brother, Logan

Kind, was a singer and he was also deceased. There was a separate link to him. Margot Kind was a mother with a child of her own, a daughter, Tracy, born in 1975. Margot had been married once and was now divorced. She had attended university in Newcastle in the North of England and a drama school in London after going to a fancy boarding school for rich girls in the Borders of Scotland, where her mother had been the deputy headmistress. Her acting credits were listed chronologically, and I noticed in passing a theater production from the Fringe. That was near the end. The later listings were mostly plays. Earlier she had several television credits. None of the program names were familiar. The first ones had specific dates in 1972, 1973, and 1974. I guessed they were one-off guest spots on television shows. They were all from British shows. The longest citation was for a science fiction series called *Project Europa* that ran from 1976 to 1979. Margot played a character named Ceres. There was a picture posted of her in the part.

The purple-fringed hair and the tight metallic outfit were instantly familiar.

Her last role was in a revival of Noel Coward's *Private Lives*. It was in 2011. It was a small part. She would have been seventy-one years old at that time.

I closed the file and continued sitting.

‡

A BARGE APPEARED on the river moving inexorably upstream. A gull picked frantically at a piece of food in the far corner of the parking lot. The waitress smiled at me and asked again if I wanted anything else. I asked her for the check. She looked at my plate and asked if I needed a box. I declined her kind offer.

When the bill arrived, I noticed that my drink was half price.

I paid and left and walked across the red dirt lot to the river. The gull continued to eat, tearing into a big piece of Kentucky Fried Chicken with a carefree nonchalance.

It was warm at the riverbank. I sat down on the nearest bench. When I opened up the laptop I discovered that the Wi-Fi was still connected.

The traffic moved high over the bridge with a low persistent rumble.

The second file was much briefer. It was also a text file and was titled kindsongs. I read the handful of words. They appeared on the screen as follows:

Circumstance is The Town Where She Loved Me.
Like It Never Rained is Pittenweem Girl.
LOOK FOR MORE

What should I do now?

I picked the most singular of the typed phrases and googled Pittenweem Girl. I got several hits. Pittenweem was a small fishing village on the east coast of Scotland with a population of 1,600. I already knew that. Well, I knew where it was, at least.

Of more interest was the fact that "Pittenweem Girl" was a song by a folk singer named Logan Kind. I already knew who Logan was. He was the actress Margot Kind's younger brother.

YouTube provided a version that had several hundred hits and was accompanied by a repeating series of a half dozen still photographs. The singer was tall and thin and sported a white collarless shirt in most of the pictures. He held an acoustic guitar, an older Guild model. It was around his neck as he sat by a lake on a large flat rock and tried to summon a smile for the camera but mostly failed. In another picture he sung into a microphone on a small stage. In a third he leaned on a mossy wall with a handful of sheep behind him looking bored and soggy in the misty mountain rain.

The song itself was an amazingly fine one. He fingerpicked fluidly and beautifully. The recording was simply arranged: his vocals, a solo guitar, and a string quartet heavy on cello. His voice was breathless and soft and reverb-free. He enunciated each word perfectly. I listened all the way through in a trance.

On Amazon "Pittenweem Girl" was listed as one of nine tracks on the album *Crofter*, recorded by Logan Kind. I noticed that "The Town Where She Loved Me" was another cut, and that the photo of the lake and the rock and the singer was the cover of the album. There were only a handful of reviews but they were all positive, mostly very positive, and several were downright rapturous. On YouTube, the viewer comments were equally euphoric. I scrolled quickly down.

Somewhere in the middle of the reviews a gentleman named BiggieIke posted that, in his far-from-humble opinion, the song "Like It Never Rained" by the piece-of-worthless-shit Deltatones was pretty much the same song as "Pittenweem Girl," which was, IHHO, a true fucking masterpiece. WTF? was BiggieIke's succinct response to this dubious coincidence.

I found another review that took Biggie's side.

Then I found a Deltatones fan who responded to Biggie by calling him a large fucking douchebag.

I dutifully investigated further. The Deltatones had a much larger video budget. For "Like It Never Rained" they carefully lip-synced their song on the banks of a cypress river that looked misty and swamplike and amply southern Gothic, which the black-and-white cinematography garishly accentuated. There were four burly wispy-bearded plaid-wearing gentlemen on guitar, bass, drums, and banjo, with a nymphlike female accordion and fiddle player in tow. About four thousand had viewed the song so far and most of them seemed largely content.

I listened hard to the Deltatones then I went back to "Pittenweem Girl" and listened to that again. "Like It Never Rained" was louder and faster and the words were mostly different. But there was definitely something there. It was similar but not too similar, as if a pattern of minor chords had been transposed onto major ones. In addition, Kind's blistering flurry of sustaining hammer-ons had been replaced with rolling banjo notes. But in all honesty, without BiggieIke's suggestion, I wasn't sure I would have spotted the similarity. I did know that Logan Kind was a better musician than all the Deltatones combined. He was in truth as amazing a guitarist as I had ever heard. As I listened to the Deltatones I could begin to figure out the chords to the song. If I listened to "Pittenweem Girl" a million times I couldn't begin to know how to play it. For one reason, I couldn't fingerpick that quickly if I grew five more fingers on both hands and my life depended on it. And for another, Logan Kind wasn't tuning his guitar in any way I could recognize.

And back to Amazon. The Deltatones had only made three albums in fifteen years. None of their recorded songs were named "Circumstance." They were a bar band based in Oxford, Mississippi, and they were painfully anxious to be my friend on Facebook. I resisted their kind offer.

Instead I purchased *Crofter* as an MP3, and while I waited for my purchase to download, I reopened Margot Kind's short biography and clicked on a link to her dead brother.

⁂

HIS FULL NAME was Logan Alexander Kind and his biography was far shorter than his sister's. He was born in 1949 in the far North of England. He attended primary and secondary school and, according to his teachers, failed to fully realize his potential in both institutions, although his swimming coaches had nothing but lavish praise for him. His father sang in the choir and his mother played the organ in a local church. He had the one sister. He was a folksinger who had recorded just the once. His early career was mostly busking and begging on the streets of Glasgow, on Briar Road, outside the student bars and used record stores, near the university, at the start of the seventies, after briefly attending, but not actually graduating from, the city's biggest and most prestigious college. Kind played for years in small clubs all over the North of England and Scotland. In 1973 the album *Crofter* was released on a small record label. Logan gigged behind it for the next few years but declined interviews and most forms of publicity. This was all before the days of cell phones, and no one thought to record any of his performances.

After that Logan Kind pretty much disappeared for a while.

He worked as a gardener and gave swimming lessons and he lived mostly by himself, first in the North of England, and than later in a remote village in the Fens much further south, where he walked his dog along the flat mud paths that stretched between the marshes; tenuous links between expanses of land that were flat and treacherously porous. He was married for a short time when he lived in the north. He had a child who was subsequently given up for adoption. He enrolled in Open University classes in the south. He used the local library branch and never once had an overdue book.

And he never quite completely went away.

Logan Kind became a minor legend. *Crofter* was a record that other guitarists tended to discover on a regular basis, and other players would lovingly reference Logan as a seminal influence.

In 1998 he left Britain for a proposed tour of America that one of his earnest musician fans had talked him into doing; this was a tour that never actually took place. He lived anonymously for a year or so in Oxford, Mississippi. Then he moved to New Orleans in 2000 and lived there until 2006. He had been fifty-seven when he died, a suspected suicide, his skinny body pulled lifeless from the Mississippi waters. He was survived by the aforementioned actress sister, and by a former wife, whom he was married to for two years in the late seventies and who subsequently died. She was not named in the article. Neither was their offspring, yet strangely the last name of the family who adopted the child was provided.

I reviewed the facts as presented thus far. I thought about the principal participants and I created a rough chronology. There were considerable gaps.

A young man had killed himself today. A folksinger had apparently killed himself eight years ago. The folksinger's sister was an actress in a British television show the young man was watching right before he died. Ike on the Internet thought a band from Oxford, Mississippi, had ripped the folksinger off and the young man on the coffee shop bathroom floor had appeared to agree with Ike before he died. The folksinger had lived in Oxford. I had never been to Oxford. It was in the northern part of the state, an hour or so from Memphis where I had been. There was a big southern football college in Oxford. The writer William Faulkner had famously lived there. I had been too intimidated to ever try reading him.

I recalled that at the end of his life the author had worked on a screenplay for a Raymond Chandler novel that had been made into a Humphrey Bogart movie.

But I was seriously getting off track.

The folksinger had died in New Orleans. I had been to New Orleans several times, the first time after Michigan and Keith, before Boulder and Art, and was far from averse to returning there, and Oxford was conveniently located halfway to New Orleans.

It was a time to ponder the following sad truths.

Once again I had time on my hands. As usual I wasn't especially needed anywhere. Nye would have located all my sugar by now. I was driving in the wrong direction if I wanted to head south, but five minutes with Google Maps would quickly remedy that situation.

Which it did.

Oxford was over nine hours away. But Interstate 55 was about 150 miles away, and there was a hotel there where I dutifully made a reservation. I would get there early in the evening. I was going to Oxford in the morning. I thought longingly about my house in Boulder, but Nye was there keeping it safe, using my sugar, mysteriously baking or doing something else that didn't urgently require my presence.

I was going to search for traces of Logan Kind. And if I needed a reason, which I didn't, then it could be either that "Pittenweem Girl" was about as pretty a song as I had heard in a very long time, or that I felt slightly guilty and very weird about walking away from a death scene with the dead man's zip drive.

FIVE

THE DRIVE HAD BEEN A slow crawl through construction.

As promised, the hotel stood close to where the two highways met. The sign was unlit this early in the evening and rose high over the road, which was good because the entrance was well hidden. As a result, I took the turn too fast, then had to brake even faster as the road climbed and twisted up a steep slope through a bunch of tall pine trees to open into the parking area that ran all four sides, surrounding the brownish red-tiled two-level building.

"Continental breakfast served till ten in the morning. The gravy's homemade." Her name was Ruthie. Not Ruth. Ruthie. She handed me back my credit card. "Y'all like Mexican?" I was momentarily confused. Mexican what? Did she mean the cuisine or the people? Was the continental breakfast Mexican? Was there such a thing as Mexican gravy? There was a slew of options to choose from. I decided she must mean food.

"Yes Ma'am," I cautiously ventured.

"One cent margaritas with your dinner entrée over at Rosa's tonight."

"That sounds reasonable." I was a lot hungrier now than I had been at lunchtime.

"Only goes till six."

The clock behind the front desk read 5:47. We had both looked at it at the same time.

Ruthie was seemingly able to read my mind. "Rosa's is no more than ten minutes away."

"I might not make it."

She looked hard at me. "It ain't a real fancy place." Did she think I was planning on showering and changing into a tux?

Then Ruthie smiled a smile of quiet power, picked up the phone, and rapidly dialed a number from memory.

She barked into the receiver. "It's me. I'm sending y'all one over. He talks funny." She giggled then abruptly hung up. "They'll be sure and give you the special when you get there."

"Thank you."

"Hot tub and pool open till eleven tonight."

"That's good." And I meant it.

"The hot tub water is good and hot tonight. The manager likes to turn the temperature way down when he's on duty."

"Is he on duty now?" I asked with rising concern.

Ruthie smiled once. "Nossir," she said, "he's visiting his dirty self on a new young lady tonight." She certainly did like to giggle.

⁑

BY THE TIME I got to Rosa's it was a little after six, but the words "Ruthie sent me" had the desired effect, and a huge salt-circumferenced goldfish bowl of a drink came for the next best thing to nothing with my combination enchilada platter. I had to use both hands to get the glass up to my mouth, and when I did I realized I was poised to consume about a gallon of tequila lightly garnished with lime juice.

⁑

THE TEMPERATURE IN the hotel's indoor pool was only marginally cooler than the hot tub. Ruthie had not boasted idly. Both were piping hot and, for the first half hour, both were exclusively mine. The only question remaining was which location to broil in—the big pot or the smaller one? The small did have the option of bubbles. The big was theoretically just about large enough to swim in, but doing laps while marinating held little appeal. So I sat in the bubbling pot and stewed myself into a state of mild tranquility, helped by my monster bowl o' margarita.

"Can we share with you?"

It was a young girl's voice.

She was perhaps eight or nine—pretty running to puppy fattish, and squeezed into what I assumed was last year's swimsuit. Her mother—they were simply too alike for any other possibility—who was perhaps in her mid-forties, stood behind her. I smiled and nodded. They both smiled back and clambered in. I couldn't help but notice that the mother's green one-piece swimsuit was a loose fit. She was solidly built and stared off in a way that made me think she might normally wear glasses. Fighting my way out of my stupor, I smiled and nodded to them both once again.

As they started to submerge, the bubbles abruptly ended. The younger of the two was out of the tub in a trice, her little wet hand cranking the jet timer to the maximum setting. Then she got back under the water and settled herself down like an old pro. It's been my experience that the regulations restricting minors from hot tubs are rarely enforced.

The little girl sucked in her breath quickly. "It's hot," she announced loudly.

"You'll get used to it, honey." Her mother spoke softly. "You can go cool off in the big pool after."

There was little chance of that. She was mistaken, although it was certainly a logical enough suggestion under normal circumstances.

The younger one began to talk.

"We're going to Grandma's." I could only nod my head.

"It's a long way." I nodded some more.

"It's almost my birthday. I'm going to be nine." I smiled at that.

She smiled right back. "She'll take me shopping at the mall. She always does." I smiled some more.

"I need to get new folders for school. I'm almost finished third grade." I went back to nodding.

"Which kind should I get?"

This question would require a verbal response. I was in trouble and played for time. "What are the choices?" Good God, I sounded half asleep.

She thought hard for a moment. "Taylor Swift. Hello Kitty. Minecraft."

I was vaguely familiar with the first two.

It was time for more stalling. "Which do you like best?"

There was another pause. "I like Taylor Swift."

Then she changed tack abruptly. "Do you like to go shopping?" Without thinking I shook my head. That answer clearly surprised her. She looked disbelievingly at me.

"We're getting a pizza tonight," she said. I smiled encouragingly. "Do you like pizza?"

This was much safer territory. "I do."

"You could come and have some with my Mom and me. We always get a really big one. Would you like to have some pizza with us?"

"Honey . . . " At that her mother tried to cut her off.

I hadn't expected the question. I was slightly drunk, and very tired, and the water temperature wasn't helping.

"Good God," I found myself crying out. "No. I wouldn't."

She instantly looked kicked in. I had answered too quickly, in too hurtful a tone. Now I had to do something. Anything. Shit. I hastily backpedaled. "That's very kind of you. I've already had my dinner this evening but thank you so much for asking me." This was going tits up at a rapid rate. If it were humanly possible to sound any more like a pompous ass, I couldn't imagine how. There was a long moment of silence. I could think of nothing safe to say. The three of us sat in the tub as the bubbles continued to bubble.

Miserably I reviewed my remaining options. I could offer a retraction; inform them that I would indeed love to have pizza with them. Then I could find a convenience store, buy some ice cream, and offer dessert by way of recompense. Or I could stick my pompous ass head under the hot foaming water until they left or I passed out.

I was leaning hard towards the latter when they climbed out. It seemed an abrupt action. They said nothing. I noticed that mother and daughter tied the blue hotel towels tightly around their waists as they walked carefully across the wet floor and out into the cool of the hotel hallway.

A moment later the mother returned. She bent down and began to speak as I sat in the tub feeling stark naked and exposed and apprehensive. She wasn't smiling. This wasn't going to go swimmingly. She spoke in the slow measured way people do when they have carefully planned out what they intend to say, and the person they're saying it to isn't terribly bright.

"My daughter thinks I need a man in my life. She's a sweetie and she means well."

"I'm very sorry if I seemed rude. I wasn't expecting the question." I briefly considered the notion of admitting to general fatigue and partial inebriation.

"You were rude. She's only eight."

"She's very sweet."

"She's asked quite a few men to eat with us before."

I said nothing.

"Mostly they were good sports and said yes. A few were polite and said no but in a nice way."

"Then they clearly have much better manners than me."

This last lame-assed mea culpa elicited a withering response.

"That wouldn't be hard. Can I ask you a question?"

I was again silent. I waited on the rest of my impending bollocking with very little hope of salvation.

"Do you stay in places like this because you're cheap, or because it's all you can afford?"

"I'm cheap." I wondered where was this going.

She nodded. "That's what I thought. Some of us stay here because it's all we can afford. Sometimes it's more than we can afford. You're a snob and an asshole. You're probably hoping some skinny skank half your age will show up. You'd manage to eat with her I'm sure."

This conversation was moving along quite wretchedly. I prayed for an end. And mercifully it came. The woman stopped talking at that point, gave me a last look of abject pity, and walked away.

I waited for a truly shitty two minutes before I grabbed two of the blue towels, slunk out of the hot tub, and turned the bubble maker off. I sat at the side of the pool on a precarious white plastic chair beside a matching plastic table and pulled out my phone.

Then I looked up.

From where I sat the hotel foyer was partially visible through a wall of steamy glass. I could clearly see the mother and daughter. They both wore matching fluffy bathrobes as they sat side by side at a glass coffee table. On the table stood an open pizza box, a pile of napkins, a generic soda bottle half filled with alarmingly green liquid, and two red plastic cups. The mother was eating and laughing. The daughter was eating and talking and laughing. There was a television set mounted to a wall and turned on. They were both half-watching. Mostly hotels keep their televisions on the more rabid news programs, but this one was turned to a kid-friendly sitcom where long-in-the-tooth highschoolers in outlandish clothes spent their days engaged in wholesome hijinks in a bright locker-lined hallway.

The pair of them never looked once in my direction.

They both ate. It all looked so wonderful, and so blessedly simple. I could easily have shared a pizza with them. I could have offered to pay, and I could have steadfastly refused to take no for an answer. I could have spent some time in their company, watched some dumb television show, and tried not to be a snob and an asshole.

But I was, as identified, assuredly both these things: a snob, who eats a lot of his meals alone and pretends he likes it, and an asshole, who wastes inordinate amounts of time gazing wistfully at thin women who are considerably younger than him, and who never ever choose to gaze back.

⁂

THIS WAS GETTING me nowhere. I turned away from the window and fired up my phone.

I unwisely Googled the word "circumstance," which got me predictably everywhere and nowhere; the first few selections were word definitions, with a film on teen lesbians arbitrarily thrown in for light relief. I tried adding the word "song," and spent the next few screens wading through references to "Pomp and Circumstance," and more than a few strenuous YouTube school graduation ceremonies. I tried adding the title of Kind's song and got nothing.

"The Town Where She Loved Me" was, as I already knew, another track on the *Crofter* album and, editing it into a separate search, that was pretty much all she wrote. I liked the title. It reminded me of something, a poem maybe, or the name of a poetry collection. Adding the word "circumstance" to that song title produced nothing more.

Returning to the Amazon site, I scrolled more carefully through track listings for the three Deltatones albums and found nothing. I pulled up reviews of the *Crofter* album to see if anyone mentioned "The Town Where She Loved Me" by name. Lots of people did. Many people loved it. But no one cared to compare it to any other song, any other song titled "Circumstance" or titled "Pomp and Circumstance," or any other song by the apparently piece-of-shit Deltatones, or titled anything at all for that matter.

I opened Amazon music and located *Crofter*. The year of its original release was listed as 1973. A compact disc reissue had come twenty years later. The album length was short. I recalled that that was more normal in the old analog days; the nine tracks came in at a terse thirty-nine minutes. Perhaps the CD reissue had been extended with alternate takes and the usual bonus material of questionable value. I checked. It wasn't.

I opened the MP3. The first track was titled "Eddleston." I found my earbuds and began to listen. It began with guitar, either tuned high or capoed up. The fingerpicking was unbelievable—a lithe and dexterous blur. There was a droning, bagpiping sort of effect in the background as Logan Kind played. Were there two recorded guitar tracks? If there weren't, then the lower strings of his guitar were obviously detuned down to create that effect. For some reason, I was prepared to believe that the effect was created in one take on just the one instrument. I listened carefully. At first I was certain that indeed, a capo had been used to get his top strings higher, but the low bass strings refuted that notion. Had he used a partial capo perhaps?

As I indulged my half-baked guitar theories, it occurred to me that the realm of the Internet had to be a ready, if less than wholly reliable, depository of Kind esoterica, no doubt eagerly posited in frenzied postings by his loyal and persnickety fans. My tuning questions may well have a ready answer close at hand.

My body had dried and returned to a normal temperature by the time I entered the cyber confines of Croftertales.com, an unofficial website dedicated to Logan Kind and his solitary musical offering that contained a catholic selection of postings by the few, the fervent, and the frighteningly faithful.

On the site the few musicians who played on the album were listed and discussed, along with the producer and string arranger. The musicians' names were few and meant nothing to me. Most of the record was solo voice and acoustic guitar. Bass and drums were featured on a few tracks and credited to several session musicians. Logan Kind had not had a full-time band backing him for the recording of *Crofter*.

I learned much about Mr. Kind. He had once considered adopting the stage name William McGonagall to honor Scotland's arguably worst poet and most infamous self-proclaimed tragedian. Kind was reputedly chronically shy, and often turned his back on his audience when he played. He employed all manner of his own alternate guitar tunings as he played, and used some of the extended time facing away from the crowd to complete his tuning; thus his songs were performed live with long gaps between songs, as he spoke very little to the audience. Kind's songs were now very difficult to duplicate exactly, as no one could figure out precisely how to go about tuning a guitar to play them. No concert footage was thought to exist of a Logan Kind performance. At least, none had surfaced so far.

Some facts tended to appear almost randomly.

Kind had been deeply frustrated at how few copies of *Crofter* had sold.

He had loved his big sister deeply, and he was proud of her acting successes. He had hoped to someday create a soundtrack for one of her performances, but this had never transpired.

He had angered his parents by not completing his university studies.

He swam on his university team during his first year, but had dropped out of the team before dropping out of college altogether.

He had attended the local comprehensive high school before that. By contrast, his older sister had attended a posh public school nearby, but that was a girls-only institution where, I had already learned, her mother was the deputy head.

I paused for a moment to consider the irony that a college swimmer and one-time swimming teacher had managed to drown.

The recording of *Crofter* had allegedly been a troubled experience for all concerned. In the studio the producer had recommended a noted London studio arranger for the string parts on *Crofter*, but the usually timid Logan had apparently argued strenuously that a student he had known at the university could do a much better and cheaper job. Logan had managed to prevail, and Morris Dean had orchestrated the album, using himself, his younger sister, Margery, and two of her very young friends to play the two cellos, viola and violin parts.

If there was one thing that all the postings agreed on, it was that Morris Dean was a genius, and that *Crofter* was the finer album because of his participation. If Logan's career had all but nosedived, then Dean had gone on to become something of a star, or at least, an arranger very much in demand. His orchestrations became all but ubiquitous in British folk rock music for a remarkably long time. There followed an extensive listing of every recording Dean had been involved in. There were many I was familiar with, and several I had both bought and admired.

The record producer was Sebastian Winter and he too had gone on to make more recordings, exclusively folk music and mostly by Scottish artists. I scanned his discography. It was large, but clearly lacked the commercial firepower that littered Mr. Dean's more storied musical resume.

Winter was still alive and still working. I had already learned that Morris Dean had died fairly young, a victim of throat cancer related to heavy smoking. His death was lamented on the website for two reasons: he was both a marvelous arranger and musician, and was considered one of the few people who might have been able to shed some light on the secrets of Logan Kind's guitar tunings.

I learned what model of Guild guitar Logan played, and what year it was probably manufactured, although none of the faithful were exactly certain. He had played electric guitar on two of the tracks on *Crofter*. He had borrowed an Ibanez Les Paul copy made in the early seventies from Winter at the producer's urging, and had played it through a thirty-watt Marshall combo. Kind had reputedly hated the electric but had been talked into playing it by the producer for sound commercial reasons. I wasn't surprised that most of the Internet acolytes took the singer's side on this issue; yet their opinions came with very little assigned blame. The songs would no doubt have been better on acoustic, but no one seemed willing to assign too much blame to Mr. Winter. It had been a worthwhile endeavor—a brave but doomed attempt to garner *Crofter* a larger audience.

I played the aforementioned electric songs and listened hard. The years had been kind to the plugged Kind. In the wake of rootsy alt-country, and grunge, and whatever else Indie, Kind's raw and gnarly bursts of overdriven staccato noise sounded just fine. If anything, he perhaps tended to overplay, failing to note that less is often more, ignoring the endless sustaining capabilities of the amplified instrument.

Both the late Morris Dean and the living Sebastian Winter had their own websites, with links to various interviews, and both men had been asked, on occasion, to talk about Logan Kind. On this issue they presented something of a common front. Both men were sad that Kind hadn't become a bigger star. Winter was unable to shed much light on the commonly asked question: What was the deal with Logan's guitar tunings? Dean sadly was never asked that question during his abbreviated lifetime. Dean had been grateful to get his start on *Crofter*. Both men believed that *Crofter* was one of their best works. Winter proclaimed the electric tracks on the record to be his favorites and that, if Logan were around today, he would surely agree. Dean stated diplomatically that they had both been "interesting and worthwhile experiments." If Winter sounded a mite defensive on the matter it was hardly surprising, given the number of gently expressed opinions to the contrary.

As I read through the postings I began to note some curiosities. *Crofter* was an abject commercial failure, certainly on arrival, but one that had begun a modestly successful career for Sebastian Winter, and launched a stellar one for Morris Dean. Logan Kind had kept on playing live for a while after *Crofter*, but he hadn't chosen to record again.

Logan Kind sold few records as an active musician. But he continued to sell after he had stopped performing, and his popularity had grown still more after his death.

The music listings on Amazon include something called a best sellers rank and Logan Kind was currently in the 40,000 ballpark. While this number might not be enough to make Taylor Swift lose any sleep, it was more than respectable.

And then there was Croftertales.com.

I discovered that Logan Kind had a tribute website of his own, where his fans could avidly construct and tend and post to and wallow in an electronic monument to their boutique hero. Croftertales.com was both slick and professional looking and therefore indistinguishable from the Internet presence of any legitimate, mass-media–anointed star. It was where Logan endured as a cyber-entity; it was as real and as legitimate as any rock star's website. It functioned as a dumping ground for considerable smugness, as his artistic purity was celebrated, his initial commercial failure basked in and his reputation, undiluted by success.

The haughtiness was pervasive and weirdly justified since Logan had never gone disco. He'd never rushed out some unleavened sophomore effort, or cashed in on the bloat of a comeback trail. He didn't sell an FM chestnut to a car manufacturer, and there was thankfully no studio-enhanced duet disc with Willie Nelson.

His talent was undimmed by any kind of damning mass acceptance. And in their selfish little heart of hearts, the denizens of Croftertales.com wouldn't have it any other way.

Poor Mr. Winter took a measured amount of grief for lending Logan the Les Paul copy but I sensed an unstated note of relief in the Internet rumblings; even the voltaged Logan had aged pretty well, and most of his followers were happy to have their own broken and unheralded cult hero, in either the plugged or unplugged versions.

Reading on.

The serpentine tributaries of the Internet filled in a few more biographical blanks. The level of privacy afforded a reclusive soul in the present age is laughably slight.

Logan was known to have lived for a spell in Oxford, Mississippi, for about a year, for no apparent reason. He was twice spotted out and about, once in a second-hand bookshop on the square, and once eating at a meat and three Memphis diner, before he headed south to New Orleans. In Oxford he had rented a house on the rural edge of town, that had been photographed. It sat squatting in a weedy field on a side road that rose up and tumbled over a series of rolling hills heading out of town toward a reservoir.

In New Orleans he lived much longer. His first five years there were less secretive. After Hurricane Katrina, Logan resided more mysteriously for the remaining nine months of his life.

For one thing he played his guitar in public on occasion in New Orleans. He was photographed jamming on a summer night in a club on Poland Avenue in the Bywater district and was more than once observed playing his guitar on the streets of the French Quarter, metaphorical cap in hand for tourists to tip and the locals to presumably ignore.

According to the testimony from one giddy website poster, Kind was playing covers as a street musician in the Quarter. The woman in question asked him to perform one of his originals. He had politely declined. When she tried for a photograph he subsequently turned and fled. She had posted a picture of the location—the intersection of two streets. One of the streets was where Tennessee Williams had reputedly lived out the last years of his life, she proudly informed us. Finally, she had submitted a list of the songs she had heard him play. I had to admit he had chosen his covers well and the majority of online postings concurred.

Logan had been mostly observed playing before Katrina. His whereabouts known. The address of the apartment building where he lived was even provided.

What was stranger was that the posted dates of his street performances did include post-Katrina dates; one was only weeks after the storm, and a second, only weeks before his death.

Both were during the period when no one had a clue where he was living.

The faithful of Croftertales.com had come up with a plethora of theories.

I began to feel a little sorry for Mr. Kind, whose attempts at living the reclusive life would have been better served before the invention of the Internet.

There were some other sightings before the storm.

He had reportedly performed one of his own compositions at a young woman's funeral—a typical rollicking New Orleans street affair, with a second line brass band and a meandering cavalcade of friends, slight acquaintances, shameless interlopers, and one delighted tourist who recognized Kind. Logan had in fact played none other than "Pittenweem Girl" to a wet-eyed ensemble. Later, the girl's roommate and occasional lesbian lover had belted out

Led Zeppelin's "When the Levee Breaks" without benefit of a mike, augmented by a sprightly trombone accompaniment, all a mere matter of months before the levee did indeed break.

The Bywater club sighting was explored in greater detail in a link provided to the club's own website. Logan had been talked into getting on the cramped stage upstairs and jamming with a touring rock guitarist. My brief exposure to Kind's songs made me seriously doubt whether he had any real interest in jamming and perhaps I was right. According to a handful of unreliable witnesses, Logan had been drinking but wasn't by any means drunk, but he had, by his own standards, played badly. He had left the stage hurriedly with ill grace after only a couple of songs.

The guitar player, a genuine star and a longtime admirer of *Crofter*, was almost overcome with glee at getting Kind to play. In his modest view, Logan had pretty much blown him off the stage, but the shy Kind had clearly felt otherwise.

There was a link posted to a short newspaper piece. Logan Kind had died mysteriously in the Industrial Canal in May 2006. His death was ruled an accidental drowning, and the date of his death was recorded. His body had subsequently been cremated, his ashes scattered on the surface of the water that had swallowed his life a few days before.

But the exact date of his death couldn't be right.

Because that date was today—the same day the young man in the coffee shop had chosen to end his life, the same day I had illegally commandeered a flash drive and walked away from a crime scene in the making with a piece of evidence.

And on a decidedly lesser note, today was the same day I had first listened to Logan Kind, to his singular creation. *Crofter* was as remarkable a collection of songs as I had heard in long years of obsessive music-listening in teenage bedrooms and college dorms and coffee shops, in nice bars (including my own at Belvedere Brewing) and shitty bars, in nice cars and shitty cars, in stadium arenas on blissfully few occasions and small clubs on thankfully a whole lot more, and on badly scratched vinyl and shitty digital downloads, and every other format in between.

There was more to read about in Croftertales but I was too tired to continue.

Time to turn off my phone and instead consider the notion of serendipity.

SIX

"Ever been to a place called Colinton?"

"That's where the army barracks are?"

He nodded twice. "Stationed there during the war."

"Which war?"

He looked at me with pity. "My war. Most people got themselves a war. You got a war?"

"Not really." I looked hard at him. "You don't look old enough."

He looked sneaky. "Which war is it you puttin' me down for?"

"The Second." My hasty calculations made it unlikely that an American serviceman would be stationed outside Edinburgh for any other reason.

He nodded three times and looked pleased with both of us. "Yessir. That was mine. I'm eighty-eight years old."

"You look much younger."

"Black folks' skin keeps real smooth." He grinned at me challengingly.

"Is that actually true?"

"How the fuck should I know?" His laugh was like a gunshot. "We like to use us more lotion, that's for damn sure." Another burst of bullets.

He finished the bottle and put it down sucked out and empty.

"I know me a Scottish ghost story. Little Scottish guy once told it when I was there, in a bar in an alley in the center of the town. There's nothin' but bars there."

"Rose Street?"

"That one."

"Guy wasn't nothin' but a wee kind of laddie who told it to me. You'd call him that right? Swore it was nothin' but true. Kept it with me all these years. Scottish people, they ever known to lie?"

I smiled. "All the time."

He smiled back at me. "Then maybe it's just so much bullshit. It's about a green lady."

"A lot of them are. So why are you telling me this?"

"Thought you'd like to hear it. A thing from your home. A piece from the old country. You get yourself to missing it?"

"Sometimes I do."

"Best time I ever had was being there. Being a young man. In a place that was strange but not strange. Not many of us."

"Americans?"

"That. But more being myself a black man."

"I suppose not."

"Well? You want to hear it?"

He did have my interest now. "You go right ahead."

He looked at the empty bottle in front of him. There was a hesitation. "Cost you four beers."

"It must be a very long story."

He grinned. "Makes you think that? I drink me a Bud or two when I'm tellin' stories. Makes the words slide out. What is it you drinking yourself today?" He didn't wait for me to answer. "Bud's what they call the king of beers."

"So I've heard."

He pointed at my glass. "Less money than that dark shit water y'all are drinkin."

He did have a point, although he wasn't going to be the one actually paying.

"What do you do?" he suddenly asked.

I held up my glass of Copperhead Red. "I brew dark shit water like this." There was no response. "And I sell art supplies." Again a blank. "But mostly nothing."

At last he had the answer he was after. There was a knowing nod, and after that a prolonged pause. Defeat came after a while, and the bartender, who already had a Budweiser longneck in his fat hand, came our way with the proverbial shit-eating grin on his face. He set the bottle down on the stained coaster beside the old black man who was the only other customer in the bar, and the dark, shiny wooden Indian, who languished in the shaded corner of the bar on Marshall Avenue in Memphis, Tennessee.

He began his ghost story and my expectations were truncated. There are at least a dozen green lady tales set in at least a dozen Scottish castles. In the bulk of them she is glimpsed fleetingly in a high window late at night. She is usually gossamer young and pale and ethereal and profoundly mopey, because she has been deeply wronged, almost always by a handsome cad, and she has surrendered something of great value.

This then is the green lady story I heard in a Memphis bar that afternoon, which cost me four beers, and took close to an hour of my life, an hour I'll never get back, and which I'm truthfully okay with.

"The young lady in this story, her name was Jean. She was still just a teenager. They married them young and set them to workin' even younger in them times. She was real shy and in a little way she was real pretty and had herself this head of long dark hair. She worked as a maid in a high tall castle. This was hundreds of years back when. The castle was on an island in a small kind of sea. This was in the high country place in the north. Her family was mostly poor just like she was poor. They lived close to the castle by the edge of the water. What are these people you had then?"

"These people?" I was confused

"They were back in the day. Living the land. Not owning the place outright. Using slices of the dirt for their walls and roofs."

"We called them crofters."

The word clearly meant nothing. "Crofters?"

So I had to try again. "Like homesteaders."

He nodded an understanding at that.

So the story would continue.

"She didn't earn much of anything. Jean, she worked hard, and gave all the little she earned back to her crofter folks. Even though she was young she was already of a marrying age. So it was fixed that she would marry one of the older servants who was owed a favor. He was the master of the castle's personal manservant. A bad man by all accounts. He got her pregnant quick and she had his baby. He chose to drink mostly and he didn't care to love her much after the child. Then he lost his job for stealing the prize silver from his master. He took to his drinking more after that. Jean said nothing to him in blame. She wasn't ever mean and she didn't try to change him but in his nasty rage he fought hard with his young wife, and at the end of his last nerve he threw their newborn daughter into a burning fire where she sadly perished in the heat and flames. Poor Jean tried to pull the little body from the fire. She burned herself bad in her efforts, but she went on and lived subsequent to this. Afterwards the husband left her and he fled someplace away out of her mind. The young girl was recalled in her sadness, and she sat alone by the cold embers of the fire for days afterwards, holding tight the body of her dead baby girl. Her own badly burned body was hurting but she cared herself none for that, her bad life already over in the measure of her sad eyes."

"What happened to the husband?"

"They found his no account self and hung him from a tree for his nasty ways. Then they figured he deserved some more, so they burned his hung body till it was ashes and mixed them into the feed of the livestock they was planning to slaughter soon. Some who ate the meat said that it was bad and vile and tainted with his evil, that it tasted no damn good."

"What about Jean?"

"She lived on for a little time. Her face just a mess of ruined flesh, it was far too late to try to tend to. The little piece left of her sat days by that fireplace. She let no one burn the fire there. Said nothing else to anyone till she went and passed. Her pains must have been bad, but she lingered, until the grief took her away and she perished still young. People say they see her now, once a year, on the very same day that her little girl passed. She's all burned up and truly an ugly sight to behold. She wears a green dress and her hair is still dark and long and pretty but her face is plenty terrible and her hands are charred down to the blackness of the bones and nothin' much of anything else. The castle is just ruins now but visitors say they see her ghost in the same room where the old fireplace used to be. They say she sits and holds a loose baby shawl in her lap, nothing but empty now, the cloth lying across her burn-damaged fingers. Say that she says nothing, but cries herself some big sad tears that make their way down across the ruination of her face and onto the baby blanket."

He spoke slow and drank fast and he had all but finished his story after the first three beers, but a deal was a deal, and I paid for the fourth. By the end he was perhaps a little drunk, but I had drunk two, and I might have been in worse shape.

He told the story well enough. Maybe I did recognize some parts. We shook hands as I got up to leave. I had already tipped the bartender, but I left some more money lying on the bar, for the storyteller, or for the green lady.

⚜

OUTSIDE, ON THE street, the bright sun laughed away all but the hardiest of superstitions.

The bar had been chosen for a reason.

A few doors further down, The Memphis Music Exchange stood as a shrine to the elder gods of guitardom and I entered with all due reverence.

One store wall was made out of Telecasters: chipped varnish on aging butterscotch wood, one-pickup Esquire models from the fifties and onwards, the headstock growing smaller and larger, but the blunt economy of the bolt on guitar body staying remarkably unchanged.

Other walls featured various Fender and Gibson models. The prices were clearly posted and, to my untrained eye, seemed steep. Perhaps the suggested price was simply a courtesy, the taunting invitation to an opening salvo of bickering—a lofty plateau from which spirited negotiations could inevitably descend some, but I couldn't be sure.

In the back of the shop, hermetically sealed glass doors opened into the muted sanctuary of the acoustic instrument cloisters. Inside lay a bastion of unplugged peace, far removed from legions of pimply teenagers constructing their Metallica riffs from two- and three-finger power chords. There were couches and tall stools on plush rugs, guitar picks scattered on coffee tables and almost one hundred instruments hanging from the walls in the chilled air, both vintage and new instruments, the ubiquitous Martins and Gibsons, and newer brands I knew less well: Breedlove, Taylor, and Seagull.

A salesman walked past and saw me staring. Wordlessly he pulled down a new Gibson Hummingbird and handed it over with a knowing smile. Then he slid away, secure in the knowledge that the object of my affection had been correctly identified.

How wonderful.

All my adventures in shopping should progress thusly.

I sat down on the edge of the couch, selected a pretty abalone medium pick, and gingerly strummed the dozen guitar chords I had last played in my university days. To my rusty ear, the guitar was in tune and perfect, the neck butter velvet, far smoother and easier to play than I had expected, indeed far more forgiving than I remembered the cheap yet serviceable instrument I had once owned thirty years ago. I barred a B minor and smiled to myself. It had never been that painless.

"I'm going to hazard it's been a while." It wasn't exactly a question. The wordless guitar provider was now standing directly behind me.

"Is it that obvious?"

He stepped in front of me, looked down, and smiled with tenderness.

"A very long while," I finally allowed.

"It's a nice instrument." It was a statement of simple truth.

I nodded. "It should be for three thousand dollars." I was being crass.

He smiled apologetically. "The price is somewhat negotiable."

I gently held on to the guitar. "Can you perhaps answer me a question?"

He said nothing but waited expectantly.

"Do you honestly think someone who plays this badly should own this?"

His smile was still in place. "I don't get asked that too often. Let me put it this way. Most of our customers are older guys with newfound disposable income and suspect memories of their youth."

"That sounds a little pathetic."

"I guess. Not really. Now they have the money to buy the guitar they always wanted when they were kids. It's another form of midlife crisis. Like riding a Harley or a younger woman, but much cheaper and a lot less damaging. So. How long is very long?"

I did some hasty math. "It must be thirty years or more."

"Then welcome back. You actually sound better than you think."

I replied. "That's just bullshit diplomacy and the guitar talking."

He nodded slowly.

"Keep on playing," he said.

In the background a woman was singing in a place between folk and country. There was slide guitar and a distinctive guy's voice providing background vocals.

"Is that Emmylou?"

He shook his head. "Gretchen Peters."

"That's Rodney Crowell singing."

"Yup."

"But it's not Emmy?"

"Nope."

The salesman took a step away.

"We have fresh coffee," he said. Maybe I seemed like a drunk in need of repair.

"That would be nice." I held the guitar carefully. "Do you have any secondhand Guilds?" I asked him.

He looked pleasantly surprised by my question.

He returned first with the coffee, and I placed the Hummingbird down like a sleeping baby. The coffee was delicious as I sat and sipped and waited. The woman who was not Emmylou was still singing.

The exchange had two Guild acoustics in stock. One was a dark sunburst model, clearly close to brand new, retailing for just over a thousand. It was a nice enough guitar that sounded a lot like the Gibson but somehow thinner, while simultaneously feeling much bulkier to hold and to play. It had clearly been a novice's blunder to play the Hummingbird first; I had now set the bar much too high. I sighed silently. Was everything less than three grand going to sound like a piece of shit in my virginal un-callused fingers?

The second guitar was much older, well used, and Gary, for that was the salesman's name, began to talk it up as he placed the instrument in my hands.

"This is a D25M from the middle of the seventies with an all mahogany body. Only the fretboard here is rosewood. Someone has removed the original tuners and replaced them with Grovers. That's a pretty common thing to do. Not a big deal. It doesn't much affect the sound or the value of the instrument. They also put a strap pin at the top of the neck, which is also pretty standard. The rest of the guitar is original. Guild made their best guitars out of Westerly, Rhode Island, in an old furniture factory where they employed the old workers, till the company moved to California and changed owners a whole bunch of times until now. The back of the guitar is one solid piece of curved wood. Not all the D25 guitars were made that way. But this one was. There was a cutoff where the ones before a certain year were curved and the ones after weren't and I can't for the life of me remember when it was but this one was obviously before. The curved ones are more sought after. This is an entry-level guitar with none of the fancy binding and pearl inlays, but lots of people love them and love to play them."

He paused and took the instrument from me. He looked closely at the top of the guitar.

"There's a little finish cracking on the front." He pointed to various places. "That's to be expected. A little wear on the bottom of the neck, which again is normal given the age of the instrument. The frets are in good shape. Neck is straight. The guitar's been recently set up. Some of the original papers are in the case. The owner's manual is in there also. That's a nice thing to have. The original tuners are there too if you wanted to put them back on, but I wouldn't recommend doing that. We could do it for you if you really wanted. It comes with a nice Guild hard case." Here Gary hesitated. "I need to tell you this. Some stores wouldn't. The guitar is mid-seventies but the case definitely isn't. It's a decade newer, the kind Guild used in the '80s. You should be aware of that before you consider buying it. The two things don't belong together so the provenance isn't intact. The price would be a little higher if they belonged together."

He handed it back to me and I looked at the price tag.

Gary spoke again. "It's seven hundred and fifty plus tax. I can take off the fifty. A place like eBay might have it for less but this is a good guitar at a good price. The M models are actually pretty rare. Mostly Guild made their D25s with maple tops. The rest of the body was mahogany and the neck was mahogany and they came with a rosewood fretboard just like this one. The M stands for the mahogany top and it makes the guitar sound darker than most. What do you think of it?"

I carefully strummed G and C chords, then flatpicked the G chord slowly, adding the simplest of walking bass lines as I shifted between the two chords. The instrument was almost as easy to play as the Gibson, but the sound was a world, over two grand, and forty years apart.

"It sounds shady."

"These guitars aren't fancy. The midlifers want their mother-of-pearl inlays and onboard electronics, so they can sound slick at the open mic night."

"This doesn't have a pickup?"

Gary shook his head. "You could mic it up, which would sound fine, or else risk drilling holes in a forty-year-old piece of mahogany. If you want my opinion, clamping a Baggs active pickup across the sound hole would be the way to go here. We do sell them. So tell me, what makes you want a Guild?"

In silence I pulled out my phone and showed him the picture of Logan Kind on the cover of *Crofter*. He answered my next question before I could answer it.

"That's a D40. It's probably from a few years before this one. Not many. Nice." His answer matched the Internet consensus.

"Do you know this gentleman?" I asked Gary. He shook his head. I selected "Eddleston" and played it from the beginning. He listened. When Logan sang, I could see Gary lose some interest, but when the first instrumental break came he suddenly listened harder. He also began to look puzzled.

"How is he tuned?"

"The world is waiting for the answer."

Gary listened some more. He took the guitar from me and tinkered, unleashing a flurry of chords I'd never seen. He was clearly attempting to play along. He tried a few more chords without getting any closer. He looked slightly annoyed.

"Is the D40 a better guitar?" I asked when the song had finished.

He considered my question carefully. "Perhaps. It has more binding so it's a little fancier. The neck is really solid. It's a bigger body so it sounds loud, although all the mahogany body 25s are loud enough. The 40 had a maple top. I don't know. I like the 25 a lot."

"Is the D40 more expensive?"

"It is, but not overly so. New and used they generally go for over a grand. But old Guilds are mostly a great value, and they usually aren't too overpriced."

"And are they more appropriate for someone my level?"

He laughed. "I think maybe so."

I surprised neither of us with my next words. "I'll take it."

‡

GARY WANDERED AWAY with my credit card to write up the sale. I drank the last of my coffee and played my new guitar. When he returned he was carrying the black case. Gary had thrown in a dozen Fender medium pearloid picks in sea blue and a black Kyser capo. The strings, he told me, were light-gauge D'Addarios and were almost new. There was another fresh set inside the case. The case did look newer than the guitar, and the old tuners and paperwork were inside as he had promised. There was also a black leather padded strap with the Guild logo and a small Korg guitar tuner inside the compartment.

He left me again.

When he returned with the receipt, I handed him the guitar and he played a few simple chords gently. I said nothing but looked at him pointedly.

"What?" He could tell what I was going to say next.

"You can play a lot better than that," I told him.

So he did.

Maybe I should have been jealous, but instead, I could only marvel at how wonderful my guitar sounded.

Gary walked me to the front door of the store. He held a cell phone in his hand.

"What was that guy's name?" He typed rapidly as he spoke. I told him. He typed it in.

"He plays very well."

I could only agree.

"When was that song recorded?"

"The early seventies."

"Are there any overdubs?"

"I don't think so."

"Wow. Was that when the picture was taken?"

"I think so."

"That guitar would look a little different now."

"How?"

"Maple will darken with age," he said.

⁑

WE SHOOK HANDS on the sidewalk. The day's heat was fading.

"Are you staying in town?" He asked me.

"On my way south."

"Does your car have a/c?" He wanted to know.

I told him it did. I could guess why he asked.

"Good. So where do you go next?"

"Oxford, then New Orleans. I need to get something to eat first."

"Where were you planning on going?"

"For ribs."

"Where?"

"Over at Central?"

"Well," Gary laughed. "You don't need my help there."

⁑

AT THE END of that same day, with a fully loaded belly, I sat on a hard kitchen chair outside a hotel room in Batesville, Mississippi, halfway between Memphis and Oxford, and strummed along with the sound of transient traffic, as the sun dropped out of the sky.

⁑

THE HOTEL HAD been ridiculously cheap: one of those white-knuckle deals on the Internet, accessed half an hour away from your destination, where you only see a price. You enter your credit card information, hit a button, and offer a quick prayer before you get a text confirmation and the actual location of the hotel.

When I had arrived at the hotel the manager/owner smiled vaguely as I explained that I would prefer a room in the main complex, a pleasant and clearly empty building with an outdoor pool behind a metal fence that stood invitingly empty at the close of a hot afternoon. When I had finished talking, he nodded reassuringly before assigning me a place in the annex, some sort of quasi-military one-level barrack-style compound that stood at the other end of the communal parking lot, up against the highway, where two cars and a pickup truck stood alone and ostracized.

He kept right on smiling as I restated my request.

I was informed that the main section of the hotel was sadly unavailable.

It was a curious choice of words. Not full. Unavailable.

As I studied his guileless face I arrived at the conclusion that people who purchased their rooms cheaply were sequestered in the annex as a matter of course, whether the rest of the place was busy or otherwise.

"Can I have a towel?"

He looked mystified.

"Your room has towels."

"I'd like to swim."

His smile quickly diminished.

My request was considered carefully; he would dearly have loved to deny members of the thrifty caste use of the hotel pool, but somehow he couldn't quite figure out how to do this. In an act of curt dismissal, he handed me a wafer-thin tea towel.

My options for revenge were limited. I was irritated and overstuffed with beef. I instantly resolved to stay only one night. I would either find a place in Oxford tomorrow or keep on heading south at the end of the day. I realized that a crappy tip left in the room in the morning when I checked out would only impact his housekeeping staff. I could take a shit in the pool when I had finished my swim. It was certainly tempting but somewhat barbaric.

Right now I would have to settle for a small consolation: I would leave my guitar hanging out in the hotel room with the air conditioning unit cranked good and high for just as long as it took me to swim.

⚜

It's hard to walk along the side of a highway and not feel like a vagrant or a hitchhiker. Half a block down stood Lux Liquors, where I was able to purchase the last two big, cold pint bottles of Stone IPA from a freezer filled with cans of Colt 45 and Coors Light. I considered myself more than fortunate.

⚜

The room came equipped with a small fridge, where one of the bottles was carefully sequestered. I found my swim shorts and carried my other beer across the almost empty parking lot. The pool was old and set in peeling sky blue paint over cracked concrete, but surprisingly large, glittery and inviting. I knelt at the edge of the pool and scooped up a handful of water to sit on. With my toes submerged, I opened my beer and drank it from the bottle.

In the time it had taken me to shop and change my clothes, two other hotel guests were already installed poolside. The young girl swimming in the water was disconcertingly similar to the one in the previous hotel: same general age or slightly older, same baby fat-to-bones ratio, same constricting swimsuit. But this one was accompanied by her father, now languishing poolside with a cigarette in hand—a furiously inked presence, shirtless and boldly illustrated, concave-chested and dark trucker tan demarked. He was reading from a paperback. An empty plastic cup lay on the table in front of him, along with papers and pens and a large calculator.

He pointed to my beer bottle.

"The hell you drinkin' there?"

"Very good beer. Can I offer you some?"

Silently he held out his cup, and I poured him close to half the bottle. If I was expecting him to say when, I was going to be disappointed.

We clinked together chummily and proceeded to sip.

"Sure as shit didn't taste like no damn Bud." He observed this without rancor.

And he sure as shit had that right.

We went on sipping silently for a minute.

"Daddy, can we get some Subway?"

His daughter shook out her wet hair and plunked herself down in an empty chair beside us, wrinkling her nose in mock disapproval at the two late-afternoon drinkers. Out of the water I could see that this girl was older than I had first thought; my guess was twelve or so.

Her father gave a wry smile at her request.

"Y'all want something to eat?" he asked me as he got slowly to his feet.

If they had ordered blackened possum on a skewer I was going to share it with them. This was my second poolside dinner invitation in twenty-four hours, and I had blundered pretty ineptly through the first one. But this time I was determined to eat and shut the fuck up, and therefore rack up some much needed points for diplomacy. It wouldn't be that hard to do better this time.

Thankfully a black forest ham sandwich was offered in lieu of possum.

The father left soon after declining to let me contribute financially. His daughter pulled her calculator and her papers in front of her and got seriously busy ignoring me for the entire time it took her father to purchase and return with three footlong sandwiches and one large diet soda.

I did try once to be social.

"What are you working on?"

She didn't look up.

"Balancing equations."

"Is it hard?"

I was given a brief and pained look. "It's eighth-grade science."

"What grade are you in?"

There followed a massive eye roll. "Fifth." And then there followed a brief and taciturn stare.

I gave up and swam alone in the pool to work on my appetite.

When the father was safely back poolside, I headed to my room to retrieve my other bottle. Before we drank he coughed up a word that always sounds passably Gaelic, and is clearly meant as a toast that, to my knowledge, no true Celt has ever willfully uttered, but Mister Diplomat mumbled a polite response into his glass and we sipped together in pleasant solidarity.

"What are you reading?" I pointed at the paperback face down on the table.

"It's for her English class. *To Kill a Mockingbird*. Way too fucking smart for me."

"Are you enjoying it?"

"You know what? I am." He had sounded both surprised and pleased.

⚓

IT WAS NOW much later and the poolside lights were turned off. The traffic had all but ceased as I sat outside my room, facing the empty courtyard, with the room door closed but unlocked, a naked bulb lit above it, my guitar in my lap, and the noisy clicking of insects all around, the fingers on my fretting hand cramping. The guitar tuner had needed new batteries. The urge to blame Gary for this was a singularly petty one. My phone offered several tuner apps, and I chose the one with the most lavish reviews and ponied up the penny short of three-dollar charge. The guitar turned out to be pretty much still in tune—the warm afternoon drive and the chill of the air-conditioned room had done remarkably little damage.

On the Internet I found alternate versions of every song Logan Kind ever recorded. Some employed chords I knew and could passably play. So I gave it a try. I'd listened to *Crofter* more than a few more times by now. Again, much like the alleged cover by the Deltatones, the sound was superficially proximate, but also not really so at all. Digging deeper, other posted versions utilized all kinds of alternate tunings. I was pretty much clueless, but my tuner app offered some of these tunings so I got to work hitting the open strings, staring at the digital readout, twisting the tuners until a red and green line blurred agreeably together on the center of the phone screen.

This was deep in uncharted waters as I gingerly fingered the suggested chords. While this was definitely closer to the original Kind sound, it was still elusively absent the all-defining rightness. Once again so close, but still so far away.

It was time to take a break. This was more guitar-playing in a couple of hours than I had done in three decades. My baby-smooth, uncallused fingers throbbed.

⚟

MUSICAL THEORY HAD been a mystery at fourteen. My high school offered weekly music lessons to the first two dozen volunteers willing to skip a coma-inducing period of scripture studies every Thursday afternoon. The choices were piano, guitar, or bagpipes, although the third choice may well have been a joke.

My mother was persuaded to cough up for my first instrument. She found a cheap three-quarter-size steel-strung acoustic in a pawnshop, which I actually thought was cool at the time. My teacher was a small man with bad skin and a blonde Bowie cut. He traveled freelance between a handful of schools and shook his head in some disbelief when he tried to force the strings a fair distance down towards the undulant fretboard on my twenty pounds' worth of breath-thin varnish and slipshod wood veneer.

He didn't spare my feelings.

"It's a shite instrument, son." This came with a sad shake of the head. Part-time instructors, as opposed to the regular school staff, were apparently free to swear.

His honest appraisal wasn't too detrimental. We did other things. He showed me the chords for the Animals and the Moody Blues and two-fingered shortcuts to playing twelve-bar blues like Status Quo. Each lesson lasted a half hour. For the first twenty minutes he watched as I struggled. For the last ten, his natural empathy kicked in, as wordlessly he handed his huge blonde Epiphone hollow body over and his sore-fingered acolyte could actually get to play something.

My reasoning at the time was that guitar playing was a ridiculously cool endeavor, and I certainly wanted to be that cool. I knew boys my age who played well, but I suspected that they surreptitiously worked very hard at it, and I was loathe to visibly labor at something that clearly wasn't about to come easily, when there were other things that did.

The guitar joined a long list of activities to be performed with sporadic interest and a studied mediocrity, but never fully mastered. I did swap a denim jacket in my first year of university for a much better instrument, an Aria six-string. I could play it better than my twenty-quid special, which I left at home and would never see again.

⚟

SO NOW TO both learn and relearn. An A minor chord I could still remember. If I barred two frets up it was a B minor. Another fret up was C minor and the chord I was looking for, a C sharp minor, was right there on the fourth fret. I gave it a shot.

A limited success. Once again I was slightly surprised. I was far older, and my fingers were doubtless much stronger. The action on the Guild was low and forgiving. Yet barre chords were the bane of my teenage Axe-hero days, and now I could, with some effort, create them.

And as raggedy and hesitantly as I played outside my room in the compound, I already cherished the sound of the Guild. I looked at the dark aged wood and the cracks in the varnish as I kept on playing. I had read somewhere that wood instruments need to be played, that rich collectors often loan their priceless Stradivarius violins to lowly gigging musicians so that the instrument stays supple and fluid. Had this old Guild been played much of late? It was pleasant to think that it had.

In Memphis they told me it had been well cared for, the original paperwork and replaced parts had been retained, the frets worked on at some point, and Gary had professed the setup to have been of professional quality. In addition, a sturdy high-quality case had been found to house the instrument at some juncture.

How long had the guitar sat in the Memphis store?

I hoped not long.

Who had owned it before me?

Why had they sold it?

I should have asked these questions when I had the chance.

Because I needed more mysteries in my life.

I thought about Logan Kind, and the guitar he held on the cover of *Crofter*.

Gary had said it was a better instrument.

I was more than okay with that.

He was a better player.

That was only fair.

I played through the pain until it got seriously dark. Then I went to bed, a happy man, with four fingers in a state of near agony.

⚏

THE SLOW-GURGLING MASS was masquerading as sausage gravy, the lumps of pale fleshy dough posturing as biscuits. The fact that all the guests, even the social pariahs from the annex, were invited to partake should have alerted me to the grim nature of the proffered vittles.

Anyway, I took a pass, paid my bill for the one night, and drove into Oxford, Mississippi, in the white of the morning sunshine.

The main street that took me into the town was as blandly anonymous as any, with fast gas-fast food-fast drug stores alternating in a drab recurring pattern.

But closer to the town center, the roads narrowed and climbed, then descended. The gardens grew green and lush and were well tended. The porches were bright bursts of paint, yet partly obscured by vibrant explosions of spring flowers.

The town square was scrupulously in order and preposterously cute. Landscaped trees in a sea of dark burgundy tulips adorned the square. In the center, a white-columned building housed the county courthouse, and the four sides were given over to shops: a large bookstore with a separate entrance to a used books section, a starched old relic of a department store, at least one bar, and several restaurants.

I found a parking place under the shade of an oak tree and cracked all four windows open.

Directly across a narrow road from a clearly thriving Baptist church stood a storefront breakfast café and bakery filled with church comers and goers and legions of sorority girls in what looked weirdly like serious date dresses, full makeup and jewelry, and long big blonde highlighted hair that was pretty, if pretty dated. The ladies were turned out well enough to have attended the morning service, but I strongly suspected that they hadn't.

I ate a homemade bagel and drank good coffee at the counter. The servers were all toothy and smiling and patented Southern, which I found to be polite and languorous.

‡

ON MY PHONE, the online version of a major Chicago newspaper contained the details of the suburban coffee shop suicide, now two days past. Stephen Park had been just twenty-four years old and had lived with his father, Edgar, in a town twenty miles south from where he died. Park was attending the local community college and was near completing his associate's degree. He had dropped out of the larger state university in DeKalb after his first year. His mother said he was finally getting his life together. She lived on the north side of Chicago and worked at a theater box office. His father drove a remote parking bus at Midway airport. His parents were divorced and Stephen had been their sole offspring.

Stephen Park had listened to music all his life. He had taken part in theater productions in junior high school and worked on the sound crew in high school. He had been a Fine Arts major at DeKalb. He had apparently spent most of his time working at the college radio station producing and recording studio sessions, and researching on his own time. He had written a paper on modern Scottish poetry. His tastes were zealously narrowed to folk music from Scotland and Ireland. The Park family had roots in both. His father's family were Scots who had moved north from Kentucky a generation ago. His mother, whose maiden name was Donahue, had family originally from Cookstown in Northern Ireland. His mother said Stephen had wanted to go there, and was saving up for a trip.

She said she was shocked.

She said she had loved her son dearly.

She said he was always a happy boy.

There was no funeral information provided.

That Stephen Park seemed wholly unremarkable in every way made his death no less distressing.

I Googled his name and got exactly the same newspaper account I had just read. I typed his name again and added Logan's.

Pay dirt.

I had failed to dig deeply enough into the Croftertales website the first time. Stephen Park was in there several times, commenting, discussing, adding his views to a labyrinthine series of discussion group threads. It wasn't too surprising to learn that Park had loved *Crofter*, and that he had worshipped Logan Kind. In one long cyber-aside he offered his testimony about his first exposure to Kind. I soon learned that a woman named Margaret in DeKalb had introduced Park to Kind's music. Her last name was Munro. She was an artisan graduate student. There was a link to her earth-toned website, where she offered organic soaps and vegan edibles and wraps (it was unclear whether these last were edible or cleansing) and other earth-friendly, apparently endlessly sustainable skincare products, all with the lofty purpose of promoting a safe and reusable world and the more-intimate intent to foster a general epidermal improvement for all.

If I was secretly hoping that Park had a site of his own, where some deranged manifesto for Kind worshippers would be posted and readily available, and where a cult of folk-addicted suicidal mopes would be revealed, I clearly was going to be roundly disappointed.

On Margaret's granola-earnest home page there were raggedy soaps made from cardamom and pine and lavender and shea butter. But there was nothing that helped explain why Stephen Park was dead and why he had chosen to die on the anniversary of Logan Kind's death. There was also nothing to explain a young man's fascination with Kind, a model musical footnote. There was no mention of Park on Margaret's site, and no mention of Logan, for that matter. I Googled Margaret and got nothing more than a link back to her website, a handful of customer raves for her soap, and Stephen Park's lone mentioning of her.

Mentally scrolling back to my earlier searches, I tried "Circumstance" and Munro and Park together and separately and got nothing. I combined Park's name with the list of *Crofter* track names and got so many variations on a theme—extended comments in Croftertales where Stephen alluded to most of the songs in various stages of dewy-eyed deification.

Every permutation using "Circumstance" remained a veritable dead end thus far.

‡

OXFORD WAS THE land of the Deltatones. I circled back to them. Deltatones and Park was a possibility. It produced nothing. The flash drive text file had alluded to the similarities between their songs and Kind's. Had Stephen Park shared his opinion with the band on Deltatonic.com? It would seem not. I recalled that others had also noted the resemblance between the one Delatones song and one of Kind's. But "Circumstance" wasn't the name of the song. The band's website made no mention of this connection. But then again, why would it? It was hardly in the nature of being a compliment.

The band website did list sporadic concert dates. All were either in the past or a long way off. All were either in Tennessee, Arkansas, Louisiana or Mississippi. It seemed the band had a residency of sorts at one time in a bar called the Green Lady, which was in Memphis.

I thought about the old vet's ghost story, of wretched Jean and her murdered daughter, and her burned vigil by the dying embers of the fire. Scotland had a million green lady stories.

⚜

THERE WERE MORE pictures of the Deltatones. I looked once more at the compendium of raggedy beards and massed flannel. The young woman with the fiddle stood out as both refreshingly beardless and nowhere near as burly. Her name was Carly Williamson. I Googled her. She had her own website. She didn't make soap. She had appeared on every Deltatones recording. She lived locally. She was working on her first solo album. She had left the band. She had an old beagle named Wallace. There was a picture of her and Wallace outside what I assumed was her house. He looked very old and mostly brown and seemed friendly enough, but I barely noticed him because the house was far more interesting.

I went back to Croftertales and found the Wiki-like bio that formed the home page. There were precious few photographs accompanying the introductory text. I quickly found the one from Kind's approximate year spent in Oxford. It featured Logan posing with a younger Wallace the beagle outside a house with a neatly trimmed front yard and a green paint job, unmistakably the very same property where Carly Williamson and her pet were photographed.

Croftertales even went so far as to include the street address.

I opened Google Maps as I sucked down the last cold remains of my coffee.

"Y'all done here, Hon?"

I told the waitress that I surely was.

SEVEN

WHEN CARLY WILLIAMSON OPENED HER front door and took one brief look at me, she clearly found me less than mysterious.

"So let me guess," she began with a smirk. "You're going to be my seventh pilgrim so far this year."

"I beg your pardon?"

"I get them mostly in the spring and summer. You're kinda older than they usually are. Hope you don't mind me saying that, but you are. Shit. You are one aren't you?"

"Am I disturbing you? I should perhaps have called or something?"

"No. You're good. I was out shopping. I just got back. You timed it well."

"You mentioned a pilgrim?"

She laughed and pulled the door closed behind her. We stood on the porch of the house.

"Tell me if I get anything wrong."

"Okay."

"So you're a huge music fan and you want to know if this is Logan Kind's old house. They usually start with something like that, which is so much bullshit, because you already found the place on the Internet, so you already know that it's the right place."

It seemed prudent to say nothing and wait.

She continued. "So what is it that I can do for you? You'd like to take a picture for sure. Maybe I can give you a tour of the place? You're wondering if he left anything of value behind? Could there be a collection of his writings perchance? Or the secret cheat sheet with all his weird chord tunings? Or the master tapes he secretly recorded with Bob Dylan and the Rolling Stones. You're looking for some kind of seriously exclusive shit like that? Am I right?"

Once again silence seemed judicious.

Carly broke it. "Of course I could be all wrong and you're from the government out here taking the county census but I seriously doubt that." She pretended to think. "Maybe you're going to repossess my car."

I smiled. "Are you telling me you're behind in your payments ma'am?"

She held up her hands in mock protest. "Oh no. Not me, Mister Repo Man."

"Maybe I'm just the postman."

"The word you're looking for is mailman. Sweet Jesus fuck, you're actually English."

"I'm Scottish."

"Well. Pardon me." But she didn't sound all that apologetic.

My car was parked on a piece of dirt road that terminated outside her barn of a place. The yard was bare grass and sprawling, close enough to a half-acre, sloped down and away behind the wood frame construction to a slow flowing creek and a tangled copse of mangled brush and weeds on the far side. The creek was mostly narrow until a large stone dam effectively corked the water. There was a peeling wood bench and a low table at the edge of the water. An outbuilding door stood open with a late model Subaru Forester skulking inside. The house had a faded porch in front where we were standing, with a small dog bed and a single chair. I assumed the former belonged to Wallace, her dog, who had barked once to augment the doorbell.

Carly Williamson was still looking at me, her features wedged agreeably between pained resignation and mild amusement.

Her hair was much shorter than any of the web pictures of her I had found. She was also older than her website would have you believe—my guess was somewhere comfortably settled in her early forties.

"I'm getting to see more of you with each year. Gotta blame that on the Internet. Mostly I call them the pilgrims, or the Kind Kids, or the Kind Faithful. Like I say, they tend to be young. Just so many earnest kids who want to know about Logan."

"Did you know him well?" I asked her.

"He was here in town for about a year. I only lived three doors away but the houses are spread out. His house, this one, was a whole lot nicer than mine. Can I ask you a question?"

"It would be hard for me to refuse."

"Other than just being older, and I assume from that new-looking Subie out front that you have more money, are you still just the same as all the others? Are you heading on down to New Orleans? Are you following his trail?"

I neglected to favor her with my poker face. Instead I must have looked a little deflated. There was nothing to do but smile and nod.

Carly smiled back at me. "Don't feel bad. I'm making a little fun of you I know. Hey, at least you didn't have a guitar with you. Sometimes they want to sit on the porch and play me one of his songs. And I have to say they usually suck pretty bad when they do."

It was definitely not the time to mention the Guild in the car.

"I'm that obvious?"

"Yeah. Pretty much. Don't feel bad. He's a cult on the rise. It's kind of interesting to watch it happen. Anyway, I've just put all the groceries away. I like to talk and I like new people to talk to. So you go right ahead. Ask me some stuff. Do you want to sit down?"

She offered me the one outdoor chair, which I declined. So she took it instead and I sat down on her porch step.

"You live here now?"

She nodded. "The place belongs to an Ole Miss professor. She's on some kind of a permanent sabbatical someplace in Europe. When Logan moved on, I moved in. Been here ever since. I'd like to buy the place from her someday, if she's willing and we can agree on a fair price."

"Is that possible?"

"I guess. We'll have to see about that." She folded her arms challengingly.

There was a long silence.

She broke it first. "So ask me the one question that's burning you up inside. I'm bringing my dog out here if it's okay with you. He's old and slow, so you have a while to think about what you might want to ask. I always try to answer at least one question for the faithful."

"What should I ask?"

"Well. That's gonna be up to you, isn't it?"

"What's the usual one you get asked?"

"If I tell you, is that gonna be the one you want to use?"

I considered for a moment.

"Probably not," I finally allowed.

"Well since you did ask. The number-one all-time question is what was he really like?"

"Do you get asked about the Deltatones song?" I wanted to know.

"Oh. You mean the one about whether me and the Deltatones shamelessly ripped off Logan's "Pittenweem Girl" when we recorded "Like It Never Rained? That one?"

"That one."

She barked out a laugh.

"Nope. Never have heard that one."

Carly went to get her old dog and I was left on the step all alone.

She came back much sooner than I expected and had a question for me.

"So. Did we rip Logan off?"

I considered for a moment. "I don't think you did. But there's maybe something there. In the background."

Carly nodded slowly. "That's a good answer. We actually wrote that song before I got to know him and before I ever got to hear one of his songs. I used to see him around at first. We talked on the street sometimes then, about my dog and some other small stuff. We had Wallace in common. Logan liked to walk everywhere and my dog was still a puppy then. They both had way too much energy, so they took to hanging out together, most every day, as a matter of fact. I'd get calls from folk miles away, saying that a man and my dog were seen out walking a creek path or way out in the woods. Used to be they'd be gone off for half the day, and the poor pup was all tuckered out and happy as shit when he got back. I don't think I saw Wallace wide awake the whole time Logan was around. They'd go and swim too, out at Sardis Lake, which is a good ten miles from here. Logan didn't have himself a car to drive to anyplace."

"Did you like him?"

"Mostly. Can't say that I knew him all that well. He was just a quiet guy who loved walking and swimming and dogs. Eventually I got to hear his music, but that was after he left. It was just unbelievable to finally hear him play."

"Did he play for you?"

"Not once. I never once heard Logan play in person."

"Did he play in town?"

She shook her head. "No. I would have heard about it if he had. I remember the first kids who showed up at this house early one afternoon. It wasn't long after he left town that I moved in here. I was working in the house on a hot day. It had rained and then it stopped all of a sudden and they were at the door soaking wet and steaming in the heat. Did I know Logan Kind? They asked me that with their eager faces all shiny and bright. I told them that I surely did. What is he like? Of course they wanted to know that. One boy had his record under his arm. He showed it to me. Did I know about his songs?"

I had to ask. "And did you?"

She shook her head as she spoke. "Seeing that record was the first I knew anything about *Crofter*."

She continued. "They wanted to know where he had gone and I couldn't rightly answer that because I didn't know. Then things got a ways weirder and they started to ask all about my dog and whether my dog liked Logan. I had to tell them that Wallace probably liked Logan better than I did. They had some weed with them and they wanted to share with me. I politely told them no. Oh I like weed just fine, but they made me feel old and cranky. When they left, they waited outside the house for a good while and they took a bunch of pictures. Then they were gone. It wasn't too long before more showed up with the same doe-eyed look, same ditch weed, and mostly the same questions. I should put together a tour and sell tickets. Right after the first ones left I bought *Crofter* and got my first ever listen to his songs."

I asked her, "Tell me about 'Like It Never Rained.'"

"Like I said, that song was already written, before me or any of the Deltatones ever heard any of Logan's songs."

"So why does it sound . . . "

"Kinda like him?"

"In a weird way."

"Let me try to answer. Mostly we all wrote the songs together in the Deltatones. This song was like that. It was close to complete but we were still playing with it. Fine tuning it some. The chord chart was on my kitchen table. I was playing around with it. My old acoustic was there. A piece of cheap laminated shit in standard tuning. I was still in my early twenties and that was pretty much all I could afford to have. I was showering upstairs one day. Logan came in and got Wallace for their walk."

"Logan had a key?"

She shook her head. "Door was always open round here back then. I came downstairs later. Wallace and him were long gone. Guitar had been moved. I did notice that. I picked it up and played a chord. Holy shit, I thought. It was retuned completely. Sounded weirder than fuck when I open strummed it. I tried a few standard chords. They sounded interesting. Then I played 'Rain' . . . "

"And . . . "

"It was still mostly 'Rain' but . . . "

"But . . . "

"It was 'Rain' but it now had some kind of hidden counter-harmony that the song had never possessed before. I called Mark

James, who's the guitar player. He came on over later. We tuned his old Tele the exact same way as my piece of shit. Broke two of the high strings before we got it to work just right. We recorded some that same night with one electric guitar part in Logan's tuning and the other using standard tuning. It sounded out of this fucking world. Mark played the Logan-tuned chords. Later he got good and high like he always did with his dipshit girlfriend at the time, and the stupid-ass bitch must have got up during the night to stuff her face and then she went and retuned his guitar for him. No doubt she thought she was being all super cute and helpful. Logan came by my house the next evening. Maybe he knew I was out, or maybe not, but he retuned my guitar back to standard. I asked him about it a few days later and he just smiled at me. He asked me if I liked the other tuning. I told him I did. I asked him if he would play some, maybe teach me some of his tunings. I just got more smiles. I asked him about his playing. He just kept on smiling and shook his head. He asked me if our song sounded any good. I told him it did now and he grinned even bigger like he had a great big ol' secret. And we never said shit about it ever again. Mark tried to remember the tuning. He got close but he never got it totally right. The album version is the only one we played that way. When we performed live we played all the guitar parts in standard. It sounded okay. It was never a favorite. We didn't play it often and no one much cared. I didn't know anything about *Crofter* until these first kids showed up with it. I've listened to Logan's music a lot over the years since he left here. Each song has a different tuning. None of them are standard. The way he tuned my guitar I'm certain is the exact same way he tuned his for "Pittenweem Girl." I've met way better players than me who all agree with that. I think he must have figured that tuning that way was going to be the best way for our song. What's amazing is that he came to that conclusion without hearing our song."

She gave me a measured look. "I just bet you like his song way better."

I hesitated and considered a fast lie. "I do. I'm sorry."

Her laugh was bitter. "You don't have to be. Logan Kind was light years better than us. The Deltatones made a few bucks and sold a few albums, and we can fill a decent-sized bar within a hundred-mile radius of here, but that's about as far as we're ever going to get. Using his tuning was about the best thing we ever did by an ass-length country mile."

"You've left the band."

She smirked at that. "I have. They truly are good guys but I can do much better on my own. They're okay musicians but they lack drive. We made all of three okay albums in fifteen years. They're happy making enough for weed and getting to run up a bar tab at the end of the night. We traveled to all our gigs in a bus, and I swear they must've saved up their best farts all day for that fucking bus ride. I can pretty much fill the same places they're too lazy to play at most of the time, and I keep a lot more of the door doing it on my own. I'm playing out tonight. Larry's Firehouse is in town and I like it there. The cover is only fifteen. My cut is a third. It's a tiny place with a few tables but the tips are all mine. You can come see me if you want. Are you a big tipper?"

I grinned. "They call me Mister Moneybags."

She gave an unladylike snort at that.

"All right then Mister Moneybags. Now you get to tell me something you know about Logan."

I hesitated.

Then I told Carly Williamson all about Stephen Park and his last moments in a coffee shop south of Chicago.

When I had finished, Carly and I walked around the side of her house and down the steep hill to the creek water. We walked slowly, an unspoken pact, so that Wallace could walk with us. He allowed me to pat him on his flat old head.

"You're entitled to another story," she said simply.

"Tell me something you've not told any of the other pilgrims this year."

She thought for a moment. "So, this creek in back of the house, this pool, Logan dammed up the water himself. Went door to door for the rocks because there are none worth using on this property. Once he got it to be deep enough, he sat in the pool most days. In his raggedy-ass undershorts. He did it year-round. Wallace would go in too. The water isn't ever warm, even in the height of summer. Colder than owlshit in the winter months when Oxford can get all unexpectedly cold and northern on you when you aren't expecting. Logan used to claim he never missed a day. Sat in there for an hour at a time. I saw him on occasion. Eyes almost shut and smiling himself a proud fool's secret smile the whole time. Wallace won't venture in the water now. Too cold for him, and too hard for him to climb in and back out."

We stood in silence at the edge of the water.

Then Carly and I walked back to her front porch and talked for a while longer. Wallace came with us and we were formally introduced. He was an old and mostly deaf dog, so that when Carly talked to him she did it loudly and slowly, which made a strange kind of sense at the time. He circled his bed for an eternity before he finally dropped down with a bone-rattling thud.

Carly told me she worked during the day as a freelance translator. She spoke and read Russian well, and the university regularly sent textbooks and poetry collections her way. The textbooks were boring but paid much better. She enjoyed the poetry more. She enjoyed playing even more.

She asked a question then. "Why would you want to kill yourself? And why was it all because of Logan?"

"What makes you think Park wanted to?"

"Because he went ahead and did it."

"Maybe that just means he thought he had to do it."

"We don't know why."

"No," I answered her, "we don't."

"You said it was the anniversary of Logan's death."

"That gave him a special day to do it. It doesn't make Logan the sole explanation for why he did it."

"Do you know why?"

I told her again that I didn't.

"Do you want to know why?" she asked.

And I told her that I did.

Then I asked her about something else.

"Park mentioned another song of Logan's that he thought someone stole."

"Which one?"

"'The Town Where She Loved Me.'"

"That's a very pretty song."

"The song he mentioned is called 'Circumstance.'"

"Have you found that one yet?"

I told her I hadn't.

"You probably thought it was one of ours."

I smiled. "It did cross my mind."

"Well it isn't." Her tone was defensive.

"I know that."

"So whose is it?"

"That I don't know. Do you know what happened to Logan after he left here?" I asked her.

"He died in New Orleans months after the flood."

"He played his guitar in a club at least once. And on the streets too."

"I did hear tell of him doing that."

I asked her, "Does that surprise you?"

She told me that it did.

I asked her another question. "Do you know where he lived?"

"I heard that for a time he lived off Esplanade, near City Park. But he moved out after Katrina and I don't know where he went to then."

We shook hands when I left her.

Old Wallace slept right through the last of the pleasantries.

⁂

I HAD ASSUMED when Carly Williamson said she'd be at Larry's Firehouse it would be a bar. This was wrong. Larry had been a volunteer fireman and a compulsive drunk who had retired from the local force blessedly still alive and deeply grateful for that undeserved blessing. In recompense, he opened a coffeehouse without a liquor license. He promptly up and died of a stroke within a month of its opening. His two daughters now ran the place and tended to feature female performers, either singers or poets or artists or authors, often some singular hybrid combination of the four.

Carly played simple, angular pre-recorded guitar loops through an old Echoplex while she sat and sang and fiddled up a storm over the cascading pattern of chords. She sounded nothing like the Deltatones. The room was tiny and packed. I did some quick math. About a hundred of us at a five spot a head meant five hundred bucks for a little less than two hours of music in two sets separated by a large cup of black coffee that I had to assume was offered to her gratis. She sipped at bottled water between the songs and said little to her rapt audience. The tip jar was delicately alluded to once near the end of the first set and it got well fed during the break.

I drank my coffee and battled unsuccessfully through a mammoth helping of white chocolate bread pudding.

I listened to the recurring musical patterns. I decided I would text Nye about Carly and we would have her come and play at Belvedere if she was agreeable to the trip up north. Our room was bigger. She would have less of a loyal fan base to come out to see her in Chicago, but I thought she could easily fill our place in the big city.

The sonic undulations made me think of surface ripples decorating a body of motionless water.

‡

STEPHEN PARK HAD slipped his two hands and his two slashed wrists gently into the water and he was gone. Logan Kind had swum with Wallace in a reservoir in the northern part of Mississippi. He had been a swimmer in his high school and during college. He had worked once as a swimming teacher, choosing to live in the flattest part of England, a region as much water as solid land, and some of his few existing publicity photographs had him posed at the side of a loch. He had often lain still and satisfied and surely quite cold in the creek pond he had created behind his rented house in Oxford. And finally Logan had died, choking on the brackish liquid in the Industrial Canal. Shortly before his end, this same untrustworthy fluid had itself already swallowed up the city he called home.

Why was it always about water?

But there was more.

Long before all this, I had recreated Keith Pringle's end, at the edge of a vacation lake in the northern part of Michigan, and years after that I had struggled to avenge a number of tired souls who were taken and baptized, washed clean in the surging spring floodwaters of Colorado.

Still more water and death.

⁑

MY SENSE WAS that I could stay and learn a little more in Oxford, or I could follow the big river south, and perhaps learn all there was to know in New Orleans.

Carly Williamson was well surrounded by admirers, as I took my leave of her and Larry's.

Later that night I balanced on a very small bed in a very small guest room in a middle school teacher's house in Oxford. He was a reading specialist and his pay was frozen and his job was threatened and he wanted to retire with his full pension in three long years and then travel for an extended time, until he died discreetly on a remote beach. Hence his presence on an Internet bed-and-breakfast website for academics, and my last-minute booking, despite a serious lack of the desired educational credentials.

He told me his name was Jacobson and his long years spent teaching had left him unwilling to answer to his given name.

My bedroom was fully enclosed by books. There was a pile on the bedside table, more stacked on a wooden chair, and still more accessorizing the shedding wood on the windowsill. For the most part the covers featured all-knowing wizards hexing large unearthly creatures with befuddled expressions. Clearly these were adventures to divert jaded teens.

The selection on the top of the chair pile took place in an alternative version of London town, where only telepathic teenagers could identify and root out the perplexing infestation of ghosts that plagued an entertainingly idiosyncratic version of the storied city. I got to the end of the first short chapter before nodding off.

My last tangled thoughts were something about the elusive "Circumstance"—something ridiculously obvious, for less than a split second of lucidity, and then gone.

Oh well.

EIGHT

A PETULANT TEXT TO NYE had resulted in an address in New Orleans, on Elysian Fields, and a place for me to stay in the city for the next few days. Naturally Nye had this good friend, and this good friend naturally had this place, and this good friend was happy to have me as his tenant. My timing was perfect—there was a blank space on the calendar a safe distance from Mardi Gras and snuggled comfortably between the town's exhaustive pantheon of heritage festivals.

The key was to be found in the mailbox. Living room led into kitchen-dining room, into bedroom, into en suite bathroom, each one equally small, each identically square, each plaster-walled, most ceiling-fanned. Each room shot-gunned one behind the other. No air conditioning was offered. A fenced and deep-shaded courtyard in the back had a water fountain and a resident ginger cat claimed the sweet spots on the rotting wood furniture. The caretaker lived in a split-level frame house behind the shotgun, and the garden was shared.

The cat was hers alone, but paying guests in the front house were extended petting privileges.

I had followed the signs to Slidell, exited on Elysian Fields, and found the boulevard and the yellow stucco single-story dwelling. There was a place to park a block and a half away, outside a bike rental shop. This was a good sign.

I walked with my shoulder bag and my guitar case past a square city block-enclosed park with chained gates on all sides. Inside, dog owners and dogs and sprawling transients mysteriously coexisted, the mystery being their seemingly common purpose, and their collective method of ingress.

On one diagonal corner of the park stood Frenchmen Street and the restaurant Nye had told me to go to. Nye said to get there early. Nye said it would fill up fast. Nye said they would only take cash. Nye recommended the pork chop, but only if I was very hungry. Nye said there was an ATM upstairs. Nye warned me that the transaction fee would be large. Nye informed me that I had been warned. Nye asked me if I was okay.

I told him I was okay.

He was worried about me.

He had a lot of opinions.

I do have a biological parent living in a resort town in Spain with her new husband. Together their aging process seems largely stalled. Then there's Nigel Prior, a much more substantial parental figure who is younger than me in real years, an unequal partner in our two businesses, who does all the work I don't do so that I can succumb to myriad distractions.

Nye believes I'm alone far too much.

I've told him I'm okay with that, yet he's convinced that I'm lying.

I knew that everything Nye told me was true. I wasn't so certain if what I told Nye was true.

My solitary lifestyle masqueraded as a matter of personal choie.

‡‡

At the intersection of Elysian Fields and St. Claude I braked rapidly to avoid a wobbling cyclist crossing the street. She wore a pastel vintage dress that fell away from her shoulders under a gossamer lace wrap. Beneath a dirty blonde wig fashioned in a vague shoulder-length bob, the features were fleshy and raw and weather-scrubbed under pale makeup that left her features starkly exposed like cracked alabaster.

In high-heeled sandals, she rode her old red bike, a milk crate swollen with junk fastened awkwardly to the front. She stopped just as I did, glaring at me for something that clearly wasn't my fault. Then she lost her balance and tipped over. For an awful moment she was invisible to me, hidden underneath the front of my car. I waited anxiously for extended seconds. Then she slowly reappeared, scowling at me again, her mysterious crate of treasures now littering the side of the street.

She got down on her knees and began to pick up all her scattered shit as I sat and waited.

Should I get out and help her? Should I try to park? Should I just keep on waiting?

She was out of my sight once again. A horn sounded behind. Had she moved to safety? I could inch forward. Was she finished? Had she moved out of the way? Another horn bleated and I advanced. There was a crunching sound under the front of the car. I pulled over, got out, and looked tentatively down. What I had driven over was now just so much fine powder.

"I'm so sorry," I found myself mumbling to the still-kneeling figure.

"Just leave me alone, Mister Tourist." Her voice was low. I couldn't see her face, but I could hear her tears.

"Let me . . . " I trailed off and reached for my wallet. Inside were four twenties and seven tens. How much? I placed fifty dollars inside the empty crate.

" . . . For your broken things." My words came to a halt.

"For God's sake will you please just go away!" She cried this aloud as I backed away from her. Traffic was driving slowly around us. Someone in a passing car took the time to laugh.

I did exactly as I was told.

As I drove away she picked up a string of red beads and threw them at my car.

She missed by a mile.

Welcome to the Crescent City.

‡

I BOUGHT MY groceries later that night at a Whole Foods a mile away from the house. It was the act of an urban coward. I sat in the courtyard on a soggy cushion with a tall can of cold NOLA beer and fresh baked bread and asiago cheese and organic apples and listened to the chuckling of the water fountain and read Nye's texts again.

Paved stones were concealed under a sliding trap of old fallen leaves, and a tall oak tree had cajoled the fence over to one side of the yard, exposing the neighbor's back deck, a transitory project. It could have been under protracted construction, or else it was in the throes of demolition, the latter process either manufactured or organically driven.

Eventually the damp soaking through my trousers motivated me and I crawled off to bed. The overhead fan chilled the room and the noise kept me awake for a long time. In retaliation I listened to *Crofter*, with my phone docked and charging in a relic of a machine that played the downloaded songs through a single speaker mounted on one wall. The window of the house next door stood wide open and opaque a matter of feet from my own window.

I was almost asleep when a light came on next door. A dazzlingly lit kitchen was suddenly revealed and at the window a woman in her underwear and a red apron washed large green vegetables over a sink and stuffed them with chopped onions and celery and garlic. My bedroom glowed with enough refracted light that I was certain she could see in, even though her gaze passed straight through me as she lingered over the food.

She was talking to someone. Or else she was singing. She looked very satisfied, with her audience, or with the song, with the food, or maybe with herself. Her underwear was more utilitarian than playful, expansive cotton undergarments that looked comfortable and fitted.

I should turn away, but I hesitated.

What should have felt creepy and invasive felt inexplicably like witnessing a scene of happy domesticity, missing any kind of erotic charge.

But I told myself that this was still wrong as soft-core voyeurism and an invasion of privacy.

If Nye was worried about me being alone he should see me now. A solitary peeper cavalierly observing food being prepared by a full-figured woman in beige-toned Fruit of the Loom skivvies.

That the vision lacked sexual subtext was demonstrated by the gloomy fact that I soon fell into a guilt-free slumber unthwarted by the mild thrill of observing a woman missing most of her clothes. And then there was a good night's sleep. I had clearly arrived at the age where sleep trumps clandestine peeking at unexpected displays of female flesh.

⚜

THEY SERVED A breakfast of homemade boudin and cheese grits under fried eggs at a corner café on Chartres. It would be my first taste of boudin. The place was crowded, with aggravated locals conspiring to keep all the warm seats inside to themselves. But three open tables stood beckoning to the hardier breed of outdoor enthusiast. I seized one.

I had showered and attended to ablutions, troweled on several coats of dense sunscreen, perched a grubby University of Colorado baseball cap on my pale head, and dressed in old shorts, a T-shirt, and gym shoes. I looked suitably nondescript and a good deal less than prosperous. I had liberated a hard wood chair from the courtyard, my guitar was in its case with me, and I had over two dozen songs downloaded from the Internet and printed out, courtesy of the wireless printer that came with the house.

I had woken up in the morning with an idea.

Logan Kind had played on the streets of the French Quarter. The street corner he had chosen and the names of the songs he had performed were all posted online.

My plan was to go there and retrace his steps, play my guitar on the same corner, and duplicate his set list. Some of the songs were beyond me, some I didn't actually know, but a good few were both familiar and somewhat playable.

This would be an act of recreation and homage. This was my waking idea. It wasn't entirely sensible and it begged the question:

Did you need anything, beyond the basic desire, to sing poorly on the streets of New Orleans?

We would soon find out.

Several scenarios suggested themselves. There could well be some kind of unspoken system that allocated street performers their requisite piece of performing turf. In all likelihood I would be exposed as utterly feeble and devoid of talent. Both these possibilities would require beating a hasty retreat, pursued by either the authorities or a posse of discerning music lovers.

I was well aware that Logan Kind had been a good singer and a wonderful guitarist. I, on the other hand, was on track to be pitiful at both. I'd for sure make next to nothing in tips.

But my fledgling technique could certainly benefit from a day spent practicing. It was going to be a pretty enough day when the dark clouds departed. In fact, it was already beginning to warm agreeably. If it got too hot, there was always the option to up and quit.

When Kind had performed he had chosen a spot on the edge of the Quarter, at the corner of Dumaine and Burgundy. The location boasted the welcome shade of a grocery store awning, where a sit down and a po' boy lunch would be just the ticket.

It would be a blast to play on the street as Kind had done. I saw it as an act of deference and tribute. I could walk briskly there and back and exercise away the questionable nutritional merits of my fine morning repast. I could set my own hours, pause when I was sore or tuckered out. I would get some fresh air.

I could even break for alcohol and stroll a few blocks to Lafitte's to pound a voodoo daiquiri or two and still not sound any worse.

My whole plan was a masterpiece of unexplained spontaneity and inexplicable bravado.

What could possibly go wrong with such a plan?

I played "Perfect Day" capoed on the first fret to sing it in the same key as Lou Reed had sung it. I played it too slow. The chair was uncomfortable. My guitar case was wedged open expectantly and I placed a handful of dollar bills inside to encourage similar acts of generosity. Two college-age boys took the trouble to stop and tell me that I fucking sucked. A man on a bike threw close to a dollar in change without even slowing down. He was my one and only benefactor.

All this occurred during the first dreary dirge. After that, it rained explosively for almost half an hour as I squatted for shelter beneath the grocery store awning.

When the rain finally ended it was time to rock out.

I riffed on the E chord to open "When the Levee Breaks," alternating on the bass string between open and third and third and fifth frets. It sounded pretty decent. Then I realized that having the words printed out and in front of me and knowing how to sing them were two different things. So I played the chords and keened softly to myself. I arrived at the bridge of the song and noticed that my cheat sheet omitted that part. I slid to the ninth fret and hit the middle strings then slid down to the fourth and second. Then I did pretty much the same thing three more times. Not too bad. A partial save. At least no one was listening as I sat on the levee and moaned.

When I had finished moaning, someone from the grocery store came out and asked me how long I was going to be there. I had planned on asking to use their washroom at some point soon but instead I kept on playing in rising discomfort. My back was sore. My head sweated inside the baseball cap. The sun had moved upward and the awning was no longer capable of sheltering my pasty hide.

A couple of Scottish tourists came by and listened to me lay waste to an old Badfinger song. They were from Inverness and were far keener on talking about home than having me keep on playing. They were having a great holiday. Did I know there was a British pub over in Algiers that you went through a Tardis to get into? I told them I surely did. They insisted on handing me a ten-dollar bill. Maybe they hoped it would buy my silence. I told them it was too much, that I was doing this for fun, but they just looked sad and mystified and wouldn't think of taking their money back. So I gave up. Maybe they were right. With a surge of newfound capitalist zeal, I placed the larger bill in the open case to encourage others to up the ante accordingly.

Later on, as I gave the unsuspecting world one more mediocre version of "Hallelujah," a small boy approached the case, threw in a quarter, grabbed most of the bills, including the ten-spot, naturally, smiled sweetly at me, and ran like fuck.

My slim profit instantly became a net loss.

Undaunted, I played "Soul Love" by Bowie, and did just fine, until the key change. It was suddenly a stretch to sing, and it featured a chord or two beyond my ken.

It began to rain again as I finished my unintentionally elegiac rendition of a Steve Earle song about New Orleans. At that point I decided to continue on a thematic triad for the tourists, and promptly fired off the late Steve Goodman's biggest hit, then the Animals chestnut, which was the very first song I ever learned to play back on my piece-of-shit pawnshop special when I dodged scripture studies on Thursday afternoons.

Then the rain and my back both got worse.

I put the guitar in the case and carried it inside the grocery store. The restroom was available with any purchase. I chose a cold bottle of water, used the spotless facilities gratefully, and headed back outside to drink my pricey water.

My chair had been taken. The rain had stopped. I was soundly beaten and I knew it. After deducting the cost of the water I was behind by a few dollars and one chair. But my performance would still end on a high note.

"I know where you got them shoes." The old voice wheezed the words out at me.

"Corner of Burgundy and Dumaine." I knew that one.

"Shit." The word positively lingered.

I gave him a ten-spot anyway. The losses continued.

He pointed to my head.

"Go Buffs," he said.

With that last act of charity, I was now operating at a loss somewhere in the low double figures. A quick calculation: almost twenty in the hole, plus the chair, and let's not forget the loss of dignity. What price on that?

And, lest we forget, I fucking sucked.

⁑

BUT OUTSIDE LAFITTE'S a half hour later with my guitar case safely stowed under the table and a Turbodog half consumed, I was absurdly pleased with myself. I'd offered my tribute to Logan Kind on the very spot where he had performed, even playing a couple of songs he'd played. I'd performed a few New Orleans songs, a couple of old personal favorites, and I'd been paid and ripped off, been justly heckled, and had escaped arrest. I needed to replace one of the chairs in the courtyard of the house I was staying in, but, all in all, I was far from discouraged.

It was never intended as a career move.

All my realistic expectations had been met. My far more unrealistic one was the crazed fantasy where a nameless stranger approaches and, vividly recalling Logan Kind playing in the same place more than eight years ago, proceeds to answer every single stupid question I might have.

Of course that didn't happen.

Of course that was never going to happen.

⁑

"Y'ALL STILL ATTACKING innocent people with your big car Mister Tourist?" It was the fallen woman on the bike from the previous night, in the same anachronistic gauzy attire, on the same precarious mode of transport. But wait a minute. Was the crate on the front now just that bit more securely fastened?

"Just you, young lady." I offered up a riposte and raised my glass. "You threw your beads at my car." It was a lame response.

"You deserved much more. You do know that deliberate cruelty is unforgivable, don't you?" She toggled between laughing and pouting. "I'll be entertaining on the square this afternoon Mister Tourist. Y'all can come by and see me later, if you have a notion to, if you can spare the time." Her tone held nothing but a tease.

And with that, her bike picked up speed and she was gone.

I finished my beer.

⚊

I RETURNED TO Elysian Fields in the early afternoon with my guitar and used the house Wi-Fi to log back onto Croftertales.

There was much more to read on the site.

The biographical information about Kind became more extensive the closer his death loomed. But that made sense. *Crofter* was a stillborn release initially, and for a good many years after. The Internet wasn't around to jumpstart his legend until later, after he had left for the states. Even then there was next to nothing about Logan during his time in Oxford. He was believed to have lived alone, for close to a year, in the house that Carly Williamson had coveted and now occupied.

Carly had told me more than the web could offer. Why was that? My guess was that the death of Stephen Park had encouraged her to talk.

There was an extended posting from Margot Kind. When Logan had first arrived in New Orleans he had got in contact with his sister. She had been surprised to hear from him. It had clearly been a while.

Margot had known that Logan had fathered a child. She had known that his ex-wife had died in a hotel room in France of food poisoning or some other natural cause. The former Mrs. Kind had apparently suffered from poor health for a time and her death had been a piece of new information for Logan.

Margot's post proceeded to touch on several subjects. She was now the executor of Logan's estate, which, while not exactly a goldmine, was gradually becoming more lucrative. There was talk of a Logan Kind film, independently produced, commensurately budgeted. Margot was planning to write about Logan herself, thanks to a small publishing house and a modest advance. Each passing year brought more sales, and more interest in her late brother. It was easy to identify her pride in Logan and his music. At the conclusion of her post she personally thanked all the good people at Croftertales for keeping her brother and his legacy alive.

The next posts covered Logan's final months on earth, and in New Orleans. They were immediately post Katrina, and by then Kind no longer lived in an apartment on Esplanade and no longer lived close to the house where the artist Degas had visited for five months in 1872. Logan's third floor apartment had survived the storm, but he had moved out abruptly, abandoning his few pieces of furniture and his security deposit, and leaving no forwarding address. There was a series of photographs of the outside of the apartment.

But even as he all but disappeared, he was seen twice more on the street, still playing his guitar.

The last recorded sighting was from a man named Alex who lived in Portland, Oregon. He had been in New Orleans with a convention of librarians, actually the first brave delegation to visit the city after the storm. He had performed an afternoon's volunteer work in the Treme and was walking through the deserted quarter in the early evening. Alex loved *Crofter*. He loved Logan Kind. He almost couldn't believe it when he spotted Logan playing. He stopped and listened. He didn't have his camera with him and the battery on his cell phone was dead. He was alone. Logan would be dead in two weeks.

Logan had played as Alex had watched. But he hadn't played covers that day. And he hadn't played old songs from *Crofter*. Alex was convinced these were new, unrecorded songs. He stood stunned and helpless as Logan played one more Alex didn't recognize. When Logan started to leave, Alex tried to talk to him but Logan put away his guitar and kept on leaving. He asked Logan the names of the songs. He asked Logan where he was staying. He asked Logan how he was keeping.

But he got nothing. Logan left.

It would be fair to say that Alex's post caused a veritable flood of cyber conversation on Crofterales. There were skeptics who questioned Alex's story and outright cynics who believed they could spot a Kind hoax when they saw one. And there were the faithful who clamored for more details, actual song titles and descriptions.

After the bombshell from Alex, the rest of the posts were mostly posthumous.

Several were strictly of a historical nature.

The location on the Industrial Canal where Logan had died had become a pilgrimage destination. There were photographs of a raised metal structure resembling a balcony, intersecting a piece of rusted out fence and suspended twenty feet above the ground by a pair of concrete supports easily ten feet square and beginning to crack and crumble. The balcony structure became a steep ramp that dropped down into a shallow bank. On one of the supports the letters KIND RIP were clearly visible in a mélange of black and red graffiti. One photograph showed fresh flowers protruding from a cheap vase located just below the letters.

For as long as I stared at the photographs of the death scene, the nature of the structure remained a complete mystery. Was it some outdated fragment of industrial construction or an abstract waterfront sculpture? I would have willingly believed either explanation.

Other images displayed the nearby St. Claude Avenue Bridge and the loose stone path that ran along the top of the levee and came to an end at the side of the road.

The next posts clearly owed a debt to Wikipedia.

The bridge connected the Bywater district to the Lower Ninth Ward. When Katrina washed over the Lower Ninth, people climbed up into the structure for safety as the levees burst along the canal. After the flood the bridge was the only passable, if restricted, route upriver from the flooded areas to the rest of the city for several months. At one time in its history, the bridge, built in 1919, carried trains as well as cars. It still functioned as both a bridge and canal lock.

I studied the death site images more carefully.

Close to the shore, tall poles stood like cranes. Further out in the water, thirty-foot-tall edifices in asymmetric rectangle configurations extended skyward, with a handful of support beams still extant. Again, whether I saw modern art or chunks of industrial refuse was still open to interpretation.

Out beyond the raised balcony and the ramp and the rectangles stood the two canal jetties, lofty scaffolded wood-lined walls of surviving functionality. These jetties housed the narrow water passage for shipping of assorted size and function. Traffic waited or painstakingly progressed, depending on the status of the bridge.

The pictures taken from Logan's death scene had been uploaded in the last year or so, and they were some of the very last things that had been posted on the site.

The flowers still looked fresh in the photographs.

Croftertales finally ended with much assorted minutiae. In the last postings were the hopeful and the sentimental and the paranoid and the crazy. Logan was still alive and would show up one day. His death was a stunt. After all, he was a very good swimmer. There was no suicide note found. He was even singing new songs.

Other singers were discussed, specifically ones who sounded like Logan, or ones who had chosen to cover his songs. Comparisons were made, and to a fault Logan's work was considered to be superior. Logan had been killed for any number of convoluted reasons. Someone actually asked us to consider the Deltatones as possible murder suspects. For at least one person, their act of possible piracy was merely a precursor to far worse villainy.

It all sounded increasingly unlikely.

As I closed my computer it occurred to me that the mysterious "Circumstance" that Stephen Park had mentioned had not been mentioned once by anyone on Croftertales, including Park himself.

I found "The Town Where She Loved Me" on my phone. It was the song Park had cited as another example of plagiarism.

I sat on the bed and listened.

What was it I had been thinking about two nights ago as I fell asleep?

NINE

THE NEXT MORNING IT WAS time to walk.

Esplanade and Elysian Fields met close to the French Market, where I had my chicory-infused coffee with the rest of the tourists. We were easily identifiable, with our squeaky new exercise shoes lightly sprinkled with powdered sugar.

As I walked the length of Esplanade, I found Degas' house, one of a number of similarly painted colonials. I stood expectantly outside, awaiting some form of high-toned cultural visitation that utterly eluded me. A little further along Esplanade, the apartment building where Logan had lived had since gone condo. It was much prettier than I had expected.

Esplanade Avenue dead ended at the edge of City Park two miles from the market.

I arrived at the section of levee at Bayou St. John. It was well manicured and ornamental, more like a section of grassy public park and less like a working barricade.

Inside the park I strolled through the rose gardens, past a bizarre model train map of the city with peculiar details and little regard for universal scale. At the sculpture gardens, I took a picture of three posed figures on benches. Two faced the water and the other faced towards me. Out in the water, a gangly blue structure rose up and stretched enigmatically upwards towards nothing.

At the furthest point in my walk I stopped in an ocean of blossoming flowers clambering all over remnants of brick and stone walls laid across fresh-cut lawns. It was an onslaught of miscellaneous oranges and browns and yellows. I tried to imagine what they truly might look like.

But I could only hazard a guess because I don't see these colors well at all.

For almost forty years I have encountered several variations of what I refer to as my colorblind dreams: a gradated selection of nighttime visions that tend to accurately barometer my stress levels.

These images vary according to my degrees of anxiety, from mildly perplexing to flat-out scary. The mildest and most conventional version closely follows the actual scenario that took place when I was fourteen and at secondary school. It coincidentally occurred during the very same year as my guitar lessons.

We were summoned to the nurse's office in alphabetical order. This would happen twice in that same year. The first occasion was, for most of us boys, the more traumatic of the two. It included the firm and clinical grabbing of the tender teenage testicles with an icy hand, the assorted shifting and separating of the yeasty male appendages, and the mystifying final inquiry delivered in a tired and listless tone:

"Have you experienced any discharge?"

It wasn't a word that offered much in the way of clarity. That her hand was where it was indicated, that she wasn't talking about my nose or eyes. I further assumed she wasn't alluding to the act of taking a slash. Did she mean a wet dream? I didn't think she did. I felt certain she was after something more infectious, more pain-related, more running, more oozing, for want of many better words.

So I followed my first instinct, whispered in the negative, and was briskly tucked back into my waiting underpants and sent back to Latin class.

Naturally in the playground debriefing later that same day these events assumed comic distortion. The nurse's eastern European accent became much more Germanic and guttural. Her top lip sprouted dense tufts of hair, garnished with the occasional wart. Several of her patients claimed unexpected stiffies, and one even boasted the much needed administration of a swift wank post examination. All trauma was soon forgotten, and we and our manhandled willies would live and flourish.

The second and more harrowing visit that year, for me at least, was for an eye exam.

A series of charts featured random letters in descending size. I told the optician which letters I could read, prepared to lapse into silence when the letters became far too small to decipher. She didn't say much. A few students had already returned to class and reported their progress. Some had given up the fight early, barely three charts in, and letters home advising the hasty purchase of spectacles were en route.

I was still in the game, five charts in, doing fairly well, thank you.

Then the exam changed. Impenetrable patterns of color were silently placed before me.

"Can you see the number?"

There was little point in lying. "No," I said.

"I see." There was a pause, and another assault of color was produced. "What about this one?"

"No. Should there be a number?"

She nodded sadly. "I'm afraid there should. Can't you see it?" Her tone was almost plaintive.

I shook my head. "I can't see it."

"I see." There was another sad pause.

Then she tried again.

"What number do you see now?"

"I can't see a number now."

"I see."

Our conversation followed this sorry pattern for a few more minutes. Then she explained that the numbers on the chart were formed in a pattern that most people could identify. Because I was colorblind, the number in the pattern was invisible to me. My worst scores seemed to be in the spectrum of yellow to orange to brown.

She told me I was colorblind.

Naturally I had a question for her. "Why am I colorblind?"

"Well," she said. "It's a question of genetics. You get your colorblindness from your mother's side, from her genes. It's not so very uncommon in men."

"What does it mean?"

"Well," she said. "I'm afraid you can't join the army or be a pilot."

"I see." I could play this game too.

I was curious. "What number can't I see?"

She pointed to the chart. "The number in this pattern is twenty-eight."

I stared hard at the Technicolor snowstorm on the paper, and as hard as I tried to make myself see that number, it was no use. It wasn't there.

She took the paper away after a minute.

"Let me give you the second part of the test."

A second series of patterns was produced. I looked and saw a number clearly visible amid a blizzard of colored dots. I smiled knowingly at the nurse. This was going much better.

"I can see thirty-four."

She shook her head. "I'm very sorry. There's no pattern there."

This was even more irritating. "I can see one," I told her. "It's thirty-four."

"I'm afraid that's because you're colorblind. There's actually no pattern there."

"But I can see it."

"I'm afraid there isn't one."

I was given a note to take home to my mother. In the note I was declared colorblind and, as the nurse had already explained, several career options were henceforth declared off limits to me.

For reasons that I've never fully identified, that second battery of tests has always been troubling to me. The best way I can articulate it is to just say that telling someone that something they can plainly see isn't really there is somehow an unsettling concept, especially for a fourteen-year-old.

I remember getting annoyed with the nurse then. The number was clearly there. I could see it as clear as day. Her response was patient and infuriating. As my temper began to unfurl, I was suddenly seized with a small moment of triumph: I could see the fucking pattern, and she couldn't, so tell me who was the colorblind one now?

But it was a short-lived moment of triumph.

So the incident stayed with me, and that second test fashioned a transformative preview for a recurring sequence of dreams. In a mild incarnation, I dream often about colors forming a pattern that I can clearly read, sometimes a word I can read and understand, but more often a picture of someone I can recognize in my dream state, rendered tantalizingly unknown to me the very second before I wake up.

This is a dream I have at least once a week.

It's never a good start to the day.

In this version, no one needs to tell me that no tangible pattern exists. It's a given at this stage. My dream is constructed on the prior knowledge of my condition, but I'm still annoyed because I can see the image nested inside the pattern.

The process initially feels like a success, until I am made aware that my dream will soon end, and the image will no longer make much sense to me. At that moment I become aware that this is a dream I've had time and time again. So I try to save the information for my waking self, but to no avail. I wake up each time with the word or picture always gone, but always teasingly close to being identifiable.

In a darker and rarer manifestation, I struggle to see a safe place to land a plane, peering out of a cockpit into a kaleidoscope of colors, my hands gripping the controls as the ground suddenly materializes much too quickly in front of me.

I always wake with a start before the crash occurs.

In the worst variation, I hopelessly peer into a deep jungle of brown and yellow and orange looking for an army of well-camouflaged killers that I know are out there, the fiends naturally decked out in a uniform I can't quite see. In this version there is a constant level of frustration, as I know that my colorblindness is what places me in peril. I know my assassins are visible and therefore avoidable, but sadly not by me.

Again I wake, at the exact moment before I spot them, seconds before they kill me.

This dream is doubly unsettling because it cunningly utilizes a secondary source of fear.

When I was very young, I may have watched a film on television. It was in black and white. It was a jungle scene, where a man waits to die. I don't remember why, but his killers are in the trees bearing down on him. He can't run away for some reason. He might be wounded or he might have used all his bullets. I suspect he wasn't a particularly good man, some sort of immoral white hunter, and his death may well be a richly deserved one. I don't remember exactly what pursues him. But he waits and his death is inevitable and the film ends there. If I remember correctly the last shot is of something moving in the trees above him, as he sits and waits for his turn to die.

And here's the problem with this memory: I have no earthly idea if this is another dream or a real film I saw. I don't recall the title, or the name of the actor, or much else beyond these scant images that probably amount to five minutes of screen time, if indeed they really were images on a screen.

So in this composite of a dream I sit in a jungle waiting to die and the thing that is going to kill me is up in the trees, and I am colorblind, so naturally I can't see it.

I don't have this dream often, which is a good thing, because I really dislike it.

Being colorblind since I was very young has required that I often circumnavigate some variation of the following tiresome piece of conversation:

"So you're colorblind," someone will say.

I unfailingly answer this in the affirmative.

Then they point up to the sky or down to the grass.

"What color is that?" They ask me challengingly.

I answer blue or green for two reasons. One, I happen to know that the sky is blue and the grass is green. And two, I can see that they are blue and green. I can see blue. I can also see green. I can even see red and yellow and brown and orange. But I suspect that when these four colors bring all their various hues together and stir up the pot, the end result appears a lot more muddled in my eyes than most. But this is purely speculation on my part as I've only seen through my defective eyes. What I see might be very close to what everyone else sees, or it may be very different.

My point is that there exist two kinds of patterns.

There are patterns that are there that you can't see, and there are patterns that you see that aren't there.

I defy you to tell me which of these two experiences is the more real.

TEN

W HEN I RETURNED TO THE house, the courtyard in back was occupied and I met the caretaker and her friend for the first time. They were sitting by the fountain drinking white wine and sharing an auto trading magazine. She asked me if I needed anything. I could think of nothing and said as much. She told me what day to put out the trash. She told me that glass bottles were not recyclable in New Orleans. She apologized for the shower pressure. The house, she hastened to explain, was a hundred fifty years old and could be cranky. Was I using the Wi-Fi? Had I found a parking place close by?

I explained about the missing chair and they both found this amusing. She told me she needed to find a new car. She couldn't decide between a Camry and an Accord.

I wasn't much help in that area.

The caretaker and her friend both seemed friendly, and I was encouraged to hang out and share the courtyard. But I declined and left them to their wine and car shopping.

The inside of the house was warm and airless in the late afternoon. I opened all the windows and turned on the ceiling fans. The front door opened onto a small concrete porch framed by a black railing. Four steps descended directly onto the pavement. There was an ornate metal gate behind the front door that opened and locked using the same key as the front door.

I got my guitar, locked the gate behind me, and sat down on the steps to play.

Elysian Fields was a busy boulevard with a grassy avenue running down the middle of the road. Several people walked by and we nodded to each other without saying much. A couple and their dog jogged determinedly past without looking in my direction. The sun descended slowly but the temperature stayed where it was. My fingers began to hurt. I tried playing my songs in different keys. My singing voice was lower than I thought it would be, or I was older than I thought I wanted to be. I sang much more comfortably in the lower keys, and I was grateful to have the capo to get there. I remembered my elegiacal recital of the previous morning and endeavored to play and sing faster.

I went back inside the house and got a cold Hopitoulas from the fridge and my laptop. I hunted for more songs I could play: old ones from my long time past, strummy melancholic numbers for the most part. I found an early Moody Blues song that I once knew how to play. I went back outside and played it, but it was a terrible song, or else I was terrible playing it. I sung "Maggie May" and "Reason to Believe." One made me happy and the other made me sad. Which is weird because, when you get right down to it, they're both essentially sad songs.

> If I listened long enough to you
> I'd find a way to believe that it's all true
> Knowing that you lied straight-faced, while I cried
> Still I'd look to find a reason to believe

"That's a sad song you've got there, Mister Tourist. How come you didn't see me this afternoon?"

I looked up. "I'm very sorry about that."

The woman on the bike smiled at me. She wore the same dress. She looked languid in it.

"You don't have to be. This is where you're living?"

I nodded. She looked up at the front of the house.

Her verdict took a while to arrive. "It's nice and pretty," she finally allowed.

"How did you find me?"

She laughed a little. "I didn't. This is the way I go to get back home. I like this street. All the way down to St. Claude then I make a right." She hesitated for no apparent reason. "Up one old narrow street then down another."

"Is it very far to go?"

She seemed to consider this longer than was necessary. "Not really."

"Are you fully recovered?"

She looked confused.

"From the crash."

She smiled a little. "I'm just fine now." Another inexplicable pause. "I'm very adaptable to circumstances."

"I'm sorry again."

"It wasn't really your fault."

"Did you replace your things?"

"No. There was no point. It was only things. You called them broken. I really should give you some of your money back."

"I'd rather you didn't."

She stood with her legs on either side of her bicycle and gazed at me. Inside her crate were an assortment of colored beads, a shiny white dress, white high-heeled shoes, and a very blonde wig. She was wearing the same clothes she had worn the previous night. Her dress was oddly old-fashioned and looked well worn, like a mandatory uniform. I thought she looked a little sullied.

"Would you like a drink?"

"That depends. What are you offering?"

"I only have beer to drink."

"Then a beer to drink will be just fine." She held out her hand. "I'm Mel. It's nice to finally meet you properly."

I told her my name was Tom and we shook hands.

Mel propped her bicycle slowly against a trash container and I found her a kitchen chair from the house and brought it outside. We sat in silence for a while. Then she spoke.

"You're new to this place."

I nodded.

"So why are you new to this place?"

This seemed like a good time to tell Mel all about Logan Kind. So I did.

"He lived here before Katrina?"

"Yes. And a little bit after that."

I told her where he lived and where he played.

"I don't think I ever saw him."

"Were you here before Katrina?" I asked her then.

She answered me slowly. "I've been here a good long time."

"Would you have stopped and listened to him?"

She considered my question carefully. "I might have. If I thought he was interesting. I like show tunes and songs you can dance to. Would he have played anything like that?"

I thought it was doubtful and I told her so.

Mel looked at me thoughtfully.

"So you're following his path. You're playing on the street where he played."

I nodded again.

"And why would you want to be doing this?" Her tone was playful.

"The long answer or the short answer?"

"Oh, the short answer, please."

"I'm looking for him?" I said it as if it was a question.

"But you said he's dead."

"I know."

"So why would you want to be doing that?"

"It's just something that I do. I've done this before."

"What do you mean?"

"I hunt for the dead."

"I see. And how does it end for you?"

Mel had asked a very good question. I thought for a moment.

"It's happened twice before. There were dead people both times. They were killed both times. I found out who killed them, and I found out why they died."

It was about as eloquent as I could manage.

"What about this time?"

"This time there's two people dead and there's a connection between them. I don't think anyone got killed this time. But I don't really know why they died yet."

"And you want to know why?"

"I do want to know why."

"Is it your job?"

"It's not exactly a job."

There was a long pause. Then I spoke.

"One of the dead people was Logan Kind and he played on the street where I was playing this morning. He played there over eight years ago. He was a folksinger and a guitar player and he made one truly great recording and it was a long time ago. He drowned a few months after Katrina. The other was Stephen Park. He was a fan of Logan's. He killed himself in a café a few days ago. I was in the café when he did it. It was the anniversary of Logan's death when he died. It was sad. They both were sad. Stephen Park was young and he died and I do know partly why. He died because it was the same day that Logan died, and he chose to die that day, just like Logan probably chose to die that day too. But do you see that that doesn't really explain why either of them died. Not properly. Not enough."

Mel was kind enough to nod at that point.

Then she spoke. "He played on the corner of Burgundy and Dumaine?"

I nodded my head.

She shook hers. "That's not much of a place to be making a living. There's nowhere near enough eager young tourists out walking around with their lovely money in these parts."

"I don't think he was playing for the money."

"So why was he playing?"

"I don't really know," I was forced to admit.

We lapsed into silence. I had told Mel as much as I could, but it wasn't quite everything.

I could have told her that in my adventures in Michigan and Boulder I had followed firm convictions, that I was certain that Keith Pringle had been murdered, that I was equally positive that someone was killing homeless people in the town where I lived, in the creek waters close to where I rode my bike most days.

I could have told her this, as I could also have justly claimed to have been right on both those occasions, but telling her this would probably have led to the revelation that I was now operating with no such strong conviction. I was far less certain of anything I was currently doing.

And that revelation would have brought me to a sobering notion: that I was wasting time; that all this was for want of anything better to do; that I was simply bored. These were grim possibilities for two reasons. The first was that I was probably wasting my time. The second was that I was probably not going to find much of anything.

"Where is it you work?" I asked her then.

"You can usually find me by the Square."

I had a follow-up question ready. "And what is it you do?"

There was a hesitation before she answered. "I create enchantment. Why don't you stop by tomorrow and see for yourself?" At that she stood up and handed me the glass. It was still half full. "Too much strong beer for me. I do thank you for this, Tom."

I watched her as she rode her bike along the length of Elysian Fields as the sun dropped out of the sky.

⚜

THERE ARE FADED showbiz personalities, B-level stars for the most part, whose final act devolves into a nostalgia-drenched retelling of their lives and times. They stand on a stage and chatter on about their career, usually gossiping, always shamelessly namedropping more famous people, creating an aura of easily broken confidentiality, as their audience is suckered into the sham intimacy of the show.

The town where Nye and I have our art supply distribution center has one such famous son, a singer and comedian who almost made it to the very top in Hollywood. He worked as a support act to the truly legendary, he guest-hosted talk shows when the star was unavailable or drunk, he wrote autobiographical memoirs that elevated self-effacement into a fine act. They even named a street after him because he never forgot to be kind to the place that he came from. He came home often and he performed benefits. The town had changed its color and fallen on hard times in the years since he'd left, but he was still loved and he was still remembered.

Nye and I attended one such benefit. His act was the slickest hokum and his extensive list of Tinseltown buddies was too many degrees of separation away from the rap stars and ballers his younger audience could relate to. But it was a warm day and he stood sweating in a loud jacket for the longest time. His wife was a frosted blonde in a tight tailored suit and high heels, who looked tired. He called out the name of the town every two sentences and they cheered him each time he did. He named the park and the main street where the department store used to be. He told us it was where he worked his first part-time job every Saturday. The building was long demolished. A storefront church, a gold-into-cash store, and a hair stylist now shared the property. The park stood next door to an elementary school that never used it; there were too many broken bottles and discarded needles in the long grass for the little kids to play there safely.

I thought of this kind of self-referencing monologue the next afternoon, as Mel stood on her crate on the Square and simply talked. Around her performed the usual trashy theatrical detritus: tiresome robot figures caught inexplicably motionless for a stretch of time considered admirable only by the most hapless of tourists. There were Dr. John lookalikes hawking preposterous and outlandish fortunes to grimy college kids from Wisconsin. They had heaved up their cherry red hurricanes on a side street off Bourbon half an hour previously, and were thus weakened and susceptible to the smoky liquor fumes and the whispered opaque platitudes.

Mel's performance was slight but novel in its giddy economy. There were two acts and two personas. She was indomitably sassy and southern and flirty for the first, as she gathered a handful of young men drunk and bored and more than willing to be teased and flattered; her eyes unerringly sought out the best looking of the young boys as she lasered her innuendo-soaked words in his direction.

The opening recital was diluted Tennessee Williams filtered through a modernistic gauze. Mel was channeling Blanche DuBois, if the over-delicate and doomed Blanc to recite her life and times standing on a milk crate several times a day. I had seen the movie with Brando and Vivien Leigh, and the costume now made more sense. Mel and the boys in the audience fell into a joshing pattern of give and take. They would listen and grow listless and make as if to leave, and Mel would implore and pout and cajole and they would reluctantly return; they were utterly adolescent in their predictability.

It would have been nice to say that, through it all, Mel never once had to depend on the comfort of strangers.

At the end of the first act, the audience would place money in the crate and she would kiss them on their cheeks and place a string of beads over their heads. Older tourists and women were largely ignored. The chosen boys were close to half her age in my estimation. When they walked away she too departed, carrying the contents of her crate, her bicycle left chained to the gates of the park for the briefest of intermissions.

Act Two featured a tighter white dress cut at a weird angle so that the skirt appeared to be blowing in the air on one side. The bodice was flat on the front, the shoes were high white pumps and Mel's legs were smooth and bare.

It was instantly recognizable as the iconic image of Marilyn Monroe standing, if memory serves, over an open ventilation grate somewhere in New York City. I have to confess to not being a fan. Was the image a press stunt or a scene from a film? Who else was present? Was it an actor or a husband? And if it was the husband, was it Arthur Miller or Joe DiMaggio? Was she still young, or was she older?

I couldn't say for sure. I saw her escape cartoon gangsters with Tony Curtis and Jack Lemmon and only once again, in the twilight of her short career, alongside the creaking shells of the once fine actor Montgomery Clift and the usually hamlike Clark Gable.

Mel stood on the crate in her heels and bubbled vapidly and breathed in and out suggestively, and a fresh crop of boys hollered and catcalled. She made a little more money in the second act.

I left the show at the end of the second part. Mel saw me leave. I waved once and she tossed a kiss back with all the requisite Hollywood Va Va Voom! she could muster, which, in her Norma Jean guise, was not inconsiderable.

The Square was hot and hectic. A high school marching band played "Smoke on the Water" outside the bleached stucco façade of the cathedral, and tourists stood under the palm trees and waited in line for the horse-drawn carriages to fill and depart. A black man in matching yellow sweatpants and T-shirt played achingly slow hymns on a trumpet under a green café awning. As he ended each rendition, he pointed to the sky and mouthed the words "thank you" as he beamed beatifically upward. I placed my five dollars in his baseball cap. He nodded his head and informed me that I had displayed impeccable taste. I thanked him for the compliment.

"I know where you got them shoes." A voice called out to me two blocks southwest.

I didn't bother to turn around as I answered. "Decatur and St. Louis."

This was getting to be much too easy.

⁂

THE FERRY TO Algiers Point in the later part of the afternoon was almost empty. I paid the exact amount and sat down outside. The loading and unloading took longer than the voyage itself, even allowing for the gentle progress the boat made across the width of the Mississippi River.

This was only my second time in Algiers. The ferry terminal was much more elaborate than I remembered. There was a huge billboard with a map for tourists and a helpful numbering system to get them and their money from ferry to shops to bars to shops and back onto the ferry and back across to the city.

I followed the road to the left of the terminal, then climbed up the grass on the side of the levee to the footpath running along the highest point, where I could gaze out across the water.

I remembered that Algiers had sustained wind damage to roofs and broken trees but little actual flooding during Katrina. It had however suffered a blow or two to its reputation. After the storm, a number of its minority white population had armed themselves and cordoned off small sections of the neighborhood, threatening the majority black residents at gunpoint, firing their weapons into the night. There were witnesses who spoke of black bullet-ridden bodies in the terrifying aftermath of no electrical power and little police presence. The charred remains of a black man were discovered in the trunk of a car abandoned on the west bank of the levee.

Algiers was neither alone nor remarkable in the days that followed. Two black men were shot to death by police on a bridge in eastern New Orleans six days after the flood. One of the men was mentally disabled, and he was stomped and kicked as he lay on the ground dying.

It was and still is almost impossible to separate fact from myth during the immediate aftershock of the storm, and tales of destruction and death have gradually given way to stories of resilience and rebuilding. The desire for healing can clearly overcome a great deal, but the long line of criminal indictments stands as a grim and well-documented record of hatred and brutality.

Inside a roadside bar, a few late-afternoon customers nursed happy-hour drinks and squinted some, as the unforgiving sunlight filtered through the dirty windows and a seven-piece band went through the last part of a sound check.

The upright bass player was black and tall and dreadlocked and friendly and we talked at the bar when they were finally satisfied with the mix. I bought him a porter from Michigan. It turned out he made his own. We talked of many things but mostly we talked of beer. He'd drunk some of ours in Chicago and he approved. We talked more beer and we talked Chicago and then we talked Colorado. He named a few places in the state where they had played. They'd been to New England and Northern Michigan recently. We talked beer and we talked music.

All seven members of the band lived in New Orleans, which he claimed they loved, but where they seldom performed.

"It's a wild place to hear music but it sucks to try to make a living playing clubs and bars. No place charges a cover. Tourists know they can get it for free. Even a five-dollar charge makes folks go someplace else. Club owners know how much good music is around so they can be cheap and they can be choosy. We get gigs during the festivals and Mardi Gras for the exposure, but that's all."

"Why do you stay here?"

He looked at me as if I were thick.

"It's my home, and it fucking lives and breathes music. When we tour out in Colorado we make money. We're on the road for most of the summer. If we charged a five-dollar cover on tour people would figure we were shitty and not show up. So we charge them forty and sell them a CD for fifteen and everyone is happy. I teach keyboarding to second through fifth graders at two charters four mornings a week during term time. My girlfriend teaches pre-K all day at one of the schools. I blow trombone at every second line I can get myself to in the afternoons and weekends. Drunk tourists always want their second line weddings. It's an hour of my time and a hundred bucks a pop. A good weekend's second lining will cover our rent. We play the same songs and get some exercise. My girlfriend teaches dance to at-risk kids during the week in the evenings and I stay home and practice and watch our three-year-old. We have to pay a sitter during the day but she's great and lives close. She's teaching my daughter Vietnamese so she can be an interpreter if we ever have to go fight there again." He smiled and shook his head. "It's all a mess of work."

"Maybe you'll get a break."

"Maybe I will."

"Are there breaks?"

"Sure. All the Marsalis family are doing just fine for themselves. Shorty, too. The Nevilles pretty much own this town. Rebirth are a fine band doing real well. None of them are working as hard as I am. All that New Orleans bounce has probably already been and gone and I missed me that chance, but I'll survive that nasty shit till the next big thing comes down. You need to check yourself out some Big Easy street music."

"What should I listen to?"

"Get some compilation discs. Can't go too far wrong with the local labels. There's good music stores on Frenchmen and Chartres for you to go and check out."

"Do they carry your stuff?"

He smiled me a big smile. "They sure do. But I got some in the case right here. Ten bucks even. Giving you the preshow discount. Cash only. No tax on that."

"Will you sign it for me?"

"Be my honor. Sign you up for the mailing list too. Next time we're in Boulder you can stop on by and see us. You still making that Art Nitro?"

"We are indeed."

"Got yourselves a choice brew there."

"Thank you." I changed the subject. "When do you guys play?"

"Not till late." As he spoke he ripped the thin plastic off the CD and signed the front of the cover with a blue sharpie and a flourish. I handed him my money and we shook hands on the deal.

I walked back to the terminal. The ferry was just arriving. It would be a while before it turned around, but I was in no hurry.

A block down the road, a British police box blocked the entrance to a bar. Even though Daleks had scared the living shit out of me when I was little, it was a temptation.

⚜

MEL WAS GONE when I got back to the Square. Her bike was chained against the fence. This time her crate was pushed under the front tire. Inside lay a few strands of beads on top of what I would now refer to as her Blanche outfit. Wherever she had gone, she had gone there in her Marilyn persona.

For some reason this made me more nervous.

I asked one of the robots where she was. He chose not to break character. Our conversation was short and one-sided. The square was growing quieter. The trumpet player had moved on as the line for tables outside the coffee stand had shrunk. Jugglers were assembling outside the church, but they were still in the talking up part of their act, working the crowd, and they showed no sign of getting started anytime soon.

The assembled crowd was sparse and listless at the tail end of a hot day.

I headed northwest on Decatur. There were several bars in the first block. One was a loud franchise for distracted families, named for a singer of modest skills and formidable business acumen. It struck me as altogether too bright and slickly wholesome for Mel. There was a grocery store and a T-shirt shop and a voodoo emporium, but in truth every type of store would happily sell you a T-shirt. I looked in each window, but she wasn't visible.

Where had she gone? My guess was not too far. She'd left her bike and her costume behind. Her bike lock was cheap and flimsy and her stuff in the crate was unprotected and accessible to anyone.

I decided to keep on walking for another block.

She was inside the last bar on the left-hand side of the street. Their table was near the back of the room, half-hidden behind a pair of wood-framed glass doors. They opened to a courtyard where the waitstaff and the cooks smoked together and gave the busboys all manner of shit. The barroom was exposed beams of dark dried-out wood and powdering plaster walls water damaged decades before Katrina had taken the Quarter and shaken it some, before it moved on, splattering the lower-lying sections of town all the harder.

I will never understand the topography of this city, where it was possible to be a few feet from the banks of the Mississippi and still stay dry when the storm hit.

Mel's face was silly and florid behind a sea of empty glasses. Her eyes were half closed. The three boys at the table looked barely past their teen years. Two were clearly drunk but could still move, yet kept drinking hard. Their arm movements were synchronized, each word or two requiring the clinking of glasses. The third was almost passed out beside Mel. His mouth was open in a vacant half-smile, and his head was partially thrown back. One of his arms lay loose across her shoulder.

I walked closer to their table. When I was near enough to see that his other hand was up inside her skirt, and that one of her hands was inside his trousers and furiously moving, I stopped.

I had several thoughts:

It was none of my business and I should leave.

I could hit one of them before I left.

They were all consenting adults, although three of them were close to children.

It was none of my business and I should definitely leave.

Maybe he was her boyfriend.

Discount that last thought. Don't be so fucking stupid.

It really doesn't concern you, so why don't you just walk the fuck away?

And why do you care so much anyway?

As I reached the door of the bar, a waiter smirked at me and asked if I wanted a table in the back. I told him to fuck off and I felt very slightly better for a split second.

⁜

IN THE RECORD store on Frenchmen, the gentle goateed soul behind the glass counter looked anxious to answer any possible question I might have on the indigenous music of the region, but I didn't have the energy to let him loose. I stood in the Local Tunes section in the front of the store and stared vacantly at a handful of record covers. It was hopeless. I picked up *OffBeat* at the door and told the gentleman I would return another time.

Across the road stood the restaurant Nye had told me about. It would have to wait. I still wasn't hungry enough.

Two thoughts occurred:

Leaving this shitty town suddenly didn't seem like such a bad idea.

Beyond any rational sense of proportion, seeing Mel in that bar had bothered me.

⁜

FOR WANT OF anything better to do, I started walking, back to the corner of Burgundy and Dumaine, where Logan Kind and I had both done our streetside serenading. The market was closing up for the day. Inside the store no one recognized this one-time local troubadour. I bought my shrimp po' boy and Zapp's and stood outside under the canvas to eat. The bread was still warm. The chips were unbelievable. Then I thought about Mel and her boys again and lost most of my appetite.

I threw half the sandwich in the garbage and walked back through the Quarter eating the rest of my chips and wondering where the nearest bike shop was located.

There was a hardware store on Rampart only a few blocks away. I bought the cheapest cutters they had. It was all I would need.

Mel's bike took a half second to cut loose. Once again the robot said nothing, but I could sense he was trying not to get caught watching.

"You can relax. I'm giving it back to her." I got up in his face and spoke the words slowly and clearly. He might have thought about a smile. Her crate of crap was still there and attached to the front of the bike with two pink bungees.

Her bike rode pretty much as expected. I'm used to riding a police special Cannondale back in Boulder.

At the bike store on Frenchmen they sold good locks. The guy in the store wore a red and black bike shirt with a winged demon drinking a beer. He was far from impressed with my ride as he walked me to the door.

"The lock's worth more," he observed.

"It's a loaner," I told him defensively.

"It's a piece of shit," he calmly stated.

⚜

THE KNOCK ON my front door came close to the morning.

She looked pretty much how I imagined she would. She also smelled less than fresh.

"You took my bike away Mister Tourist."

"I was worried someone would steal it and take all your stuff. How did you know it was me?"

"This is my way home remember?"

"How do you feel now?"

There was silence. She was thinking her way through it. That I knew how she felt probably meant that I knew more than she probably wanted to talk about.

"Thank you for bringing it here. You cut my lock."

"It wasn't very hard."

"No. I suppose not." She wasn't that interested.

"The new lock is a much better one. It uses a four-number combination. I'll change it for you. It's still set on the default." I was starting to sound like an idiot.

Her bike was chained to the rails at the front of the house. I pulled the lock free and held it up.

"What's your lucky number?" I asked her.

She looked at me for a long time. "Do I fucking look like I have a lucky number?"

I said nothing and went inside to get her crate. I handed it to her. She took it and still said nothing.

"Do you want to get changed?"

"It doesn't matter."

"The other dress might be cleaner. I can lend you some other things."

She shook her head. "I really need to go now."

We said goodbye. On the sidewalk she got slowly onto her bike.

"Which one are you?" I asked.

"Excuse me?"

"Which one? Marilyn or Blanche? Which one are you?"

Her laugh was hollow. "Maybe I'm both of them. They were both fucked up."

I told her, "I like Blanche better."

"Is that so?"

I nodded.

"And why is that Mister Tourist?"

"I just do."

And then she managed a tiny smile. "So maybe you can tell me something they both had in common?"

I was ready for that. "Laurence Olivier."

"Very good Mister Tourist."

"It's Tom."

"I know it is. Good night, Tom."

"It's morning."

"No it isn't."

And she left.

I watched her as she rode her bike along the length of Elysian Fields as the sun rose in the sky.

ELEVEN

THERE WASN'T MUCH POINT IN going back to bed.

The café where I could replenish the dangerously low levels of boudin in my body was still closed, but the outside tables and chairs were spread across the narrow sidewalk and were available for sitting and waiting.

I sat down with my copy of *OffBeat* and tried to read as I waited. There was an ad near the front, for the record store I'd been to on Frenchmen. There was also one for another shop on Chartres. I assumed these were the ones the bass player in Algiers had been talking about. It was time to find myself some New Orleans street music. Help would be welcome, although *OffBeat* might as well have been written in Braille for all the comprehension it offered to the old, the vacationing, and the non-hipsterish.

Speaking of hipsters, the magazine cover showed one aging white specimen in an impossibly loud suit and a bowler hat. The story said he was traveling through South Louisiana and Southeast Texas on a mission to soak up the culture and trace the origins of classic swamp rock from the fifties onward. His pilgrimage would begin with the seminal recordings: the early cuts from Cookie and the Cupcakes and Bobby Charles. He was an Englishman, naturally, in his early sixties and hailing from the town of Crawley, which was just south of London. Back home he owned a mail-order record company and two small independent labels: Bayou Teche Tunes featured the finest in vintage swamp rock, and Los Hoyos Records put out modern day carnival music from east Cuba, principally from the town of Santiago. Both of these niche genres were apparently alive and flourishing in the United Kingdom and Germany.

All of this naturally came as news to me.

There was a gang of lesbian street rapper-poetesses who performed together and formed a militant ad hoc arts collective. There were six of them: three were white; two were black; and one I found was quite frankly impossible to categorize accurately. They were posed in a centerfold group shot that showed dark lipstick grins and an abundance of less than finely toned flesh, which they clearly couldn't give two shits about. The ladies were scheduled to stage a guerilla reading event tonight, part poetry slam, part agitprop declaration. The tenor of the article strongly suggested that those of us who possessed penises, and who used them in a heterosexual manner, were permitted to attend, but only if we promised to behave ourselves and "shut our prissy little asshole breeder mouths and let women talk for a fucking change."

It was the work of a spilt second to not schedule that event on my busy dance card for this evening.

I put the magazine down in defeat and looked at my phone.

I'd now been all the way through the archived obsessions of Croftertales and I'd read every theory and fan note contained therein. I still had more questions than answers about Logan and his last days and death. The mystery of the Deltatones was solved. Logan tuned a guitar and one of their songs got played that way the one and only time. The people who had spotted the similarity were to be commended for possessing a sharper ear than I could claim.

There was still the whole wide expanse of the Internet to trawl for more Logan lore, but my suspicion was that I had already covered the cream of the conspiracies, and that the balance would be a rapid descent into avenues of even more labyrinthine fancy and fixation.

I was still curious about "Circumstance." How come nothing existed on this other example of music theft? Was Stephen Park mistaken?

Where to look next?

My ruminations were interrupted by the sound of the café door opening. This was a welcome development. The boudin bank was now open for withdrawal. When I got to the front of the line I willed my arteries to relax and open wide, as I scanned the menu in a desultory fashion. Every breakfast entrée came with a cupcake for fifty cents extra. I considered the offer carefully. There was little possibility I'd eat it after the boudin. I was certain I would keel over and expire if I tried.

"Would you like a cupcake with that, Tom?" The same young lady had now served me twice. It was one of those places where they attached your first name to the order, and she had remembered mine for some reason. She smiled at me encouragingly.

"Why not?"

‡

IT'S STILL NOT clear to me where the divide between the Marigny and Bywater districts occurs. It may not matter that much, as my intended stroll along Chartres would surely manage to bisect both.

It was a ridiculously fine day.

My chosen route passed new urban planning: an art gallery; an environmentally friendly play-park, which naturally looked boring; a steep rusted footbridge over the train tracks; the first stages of a waterside common area with massed flowers and a spongy manmade path, the surface forgiving on legs intent on hitting the ground hard and often.

Marigny and Bywater were in classic rebirth mode. Next would come far higher rents, mass bohemian exodus, teardowns, and gentrification projects. The locals would certainly whine.

There was still isolated blight. I noticed the gaudy wrecks of an abandoned diner and a vegetable-canning factory. And, in the in-between stages: a clearly extant junkyard; artistically over-graffitied garage doors; a record shop; a bare-brick neighborhood restaurant boasting praline bacon. I just knew that tempting treat would react adversely with my not insubstantial boudin and cupcake base. It was wiser to keep moving, rather than lick my figurative chops and foolishly linger.

The record store seemed the healthier option.

The outside offered up a scruffy mural to the ghosts of New Orleans music. I recognized Fats Domino and Louis, Prima and Armstrong. There was a host of others I was unwilling to confess I wasn't familiar with.

A woman paid for a Two Gallants record with a twenty-dollar bill and received distressingly little change. I realized I didn't have much cash left on me, but one preoccupied, moustache-muffled grunt from the Fu Manchu lookalike behind the counter assured me that my credit card would do just fine.

Most of the main floor was devoted to vinyl and, as such, was of little use to me. Many years ago Nye and I donated our turntables and all the albums we owned to a soup kitchen where we volunteered.

An imperial stout–fueled pact preceded our altruistic act. We agreed that one year would have to elapse without a second spent cringing to the cracks and hisses of our long-cherished galleries of plastic. The allotted time had passed and we made our donations gladly.

We had both come to regret our spirit of largesse.

I could always start over. But my house in Boulder is a little one and space is restricted. And what would I do with all my compact discs? Find another needy church sale perhaps? I could give them to the homeless shelter in Boulder where I volunteer.

A veritably vicious circle of compulsive collecting and altruistic discarding insidiously beckons.

Fu was pulling records from a cardboard box and placing them on the glass countertop; it was primo punk plastic from the end of the seventies: Buzzcocks, Undertones, The Damned, Sham 69 et al, mostly in twelve-inch colored vinyl and picture sleeves. His face remained impassive. This had to be his buyer's countenance, his game face, the one he used to accompany shameless acts of barefaced lowballing.

He was appropriately turned out in a pit-sullied Stiff Little Fingers T-shirt, paper-thin and stretched across a substantial gut.

"Be with you," Fu mumbled without looking up.

The seller was an older gentleman in a short-sleeved Chicago Cubs shirt and pleated denim shorts. He was summoned over. The verdict was grimly rendered. A piece of paper was slid perfunctorily across the glass.

"I can maybe go more for trade," Fu said.

"You're kidding me, right?"

"Don't do that much punk."

"Could you go higher?" the Cubs fan pleaded.

There was a shake of the head before the delivery of a well-practiced pause. "Cash or trade?"

The seller's voice was good and beaten when it finally emerged.

"Gimme the damn cash."

A paltry sum of money changed hands, and the box was refilled and placed carefully behind the counter. Another in a long history of losses for the Cubbies.

The champ was ready for me now. At least he had the good grace not to be smiling.

I've noticed before that the relationship between locals and tourists in New Orleans is a bewildering one. The city needs out-of-town dollars badly and thus casts a forgiving eye on the more crassly loutish behaviors by the more exuberant vacationers.

You don't need a carnival to carnival in New Orleans.

But the city also insists on snapping at the feeding hand on occasion. As a marketing strategy this works up to a point. The hardier sightseers will often request that their slice of local life be served up roughly by the street performer who simultaneously insults and cajoles as he smiles and picks your pockets. There's a collective willingness to acknowledge the ever-present grift by both sides in the tourism game. Clearly no one wants the place mistaken for a Disney attraction, but the Big Easy denizens may push the envelope in their desire to offer a hardcore holiday. A sense of danger and real danger are two different things.

The guide books continue to delineate the safe zone of the Quarter, and hint at the danger lurking only feet beyond Rampart in the Treme section, but their warning tone seems intended as much to titillate as to caution, while unlucky vacationers do on occasion fall victim to a lot more than a good fleecing.

The huckster methodology can go too far. You can bullshit us with your historical quadroons and your antediluvian voodoo tales, cajole us with offers of bouncy tits and shiny beads, and mock us for our wrinkle-resistant Dockers. Yet New Orleans does want and need our cash, and we know y'all do want us to come back real soon.

All this talk serves as preamble to the fact that I was more than ready for the guy in the record store, a certified colorful character, with an attitude certain to be pungent with mockery.

Best to play along. I went with an innocuous opening. "I'd like to buy some local music."

"You want it on plastic?" A begrudged chance to not look like a total douche.

"No, on compact disc," I said, earning zero hipster points.

"What do you like?"

"All sorts."

"That doesn't help. Tell me the last five shows you saw."

I thought for a moment. "Carly Williamson in Oxford. Wilco in Chicago. War on Drugs in Boulder. Joe Henry. Andrew Bird. Punch Brothers." I realized that was six.

Was he maybe the tiniest bit impressed? Had he expected James Taylor or Billy Joel for fuck's sake?

"You're kinda old for most of that shit."

"You're kinda fat for that T-shirt."

"Fuck you, too." But he was smiling.

"Henry's about my age," I told him. "The guy who plays guitar for Wilco is older."

"Really?" Brutally sarcastic.

"Yeah. Really." Ditto.

"Cline's pretty cool though."

"Your sales technique sucks." I said.

"Like I give a fuck," Fu retorted.

We had reached a standoff.

"Get the fuck over here Mister Hipster."

He started handing me discs. We were shopping.

"Got a lot of compilations. Mostly jazz and funk and rap 'round here. The people you listen to aren't exactly known for their funk. Bird sung on a Preservation Hall collection. Henry was part of a Toussaint tribute. He produced some tracks on a compilation that raised a million bucks for musicians' houses in the Upper Ninth. He produced Aaron Neville and Toussaint, too, when he played with Elvis Costello. He even helped that actor from "House" make some New Orleans music. He's from the same place as you."

"He's English," I reminded him.

"The 'House' guy did his best. Music was decent. He had Dr. John sing a song. Irma Thomas helped out. Takes some monster-ass showbiz balls to go up against those two."

He handed me two more discs.

"These are okay," He allowed.

I read the titles. *From Piety to Desire: Music from the Crescent City Streets.* The sleeves were both identical, except for two different volume numbers in red ink. Both showed a black-and-white photo of rail lines and a saloon on Basin Street at the beginning of the nineteenth century on the front side. On the back were the track lists and musician credits, running times; not too much else. The label was Raleigh Rye Records. The company address was a post office box in the Garden District. No phone number. No website or email address or social media outlets were mentioned.

"Been seeing these since the late eighties. Strictly a local label with limited releases. There's been over forty," Fu explained. "Owned by a strange old dude. He put a whole bunch out after Katrina, and his numbering system kinda went all to shit. Not much rap. Gotta admit they're all really well produced."

He handed me volumes seven and ten.

"Why did you give me these two?"

He shrugged. "Only shit we have in stock."

"I want to see some live music."

"Lucky you. Meters are playing on Napoleon tonight."

"Where do I get a ticket?" I asked.

He smiled nastily at me. "Take care of you right here."

"I want to see a second line."

"The radio station website lists them. You got lucky again. Season just got started."

My haul now amounted to eight CDs at over a hundred bucks and a concert ticket for about half that. I summoned up my nerves and asked for a bag. It was grudgingly produced. I decided to make one last pitch for credibility and pointed at his shirt.

"I once owned Alternative Ulster."

He wasn't impressed. "Good for you. Wanna buy it again? Got a seven-inch first issue. Misprint on the label says Ulster was the B side. Let you have it for a hundred twenty."

"I thought you didn't sell much punk?"

"You want it?"

"No," I told him.

"Enjoy the show."

We were clearly done.

Outside the store I pulled up eBay and found a guy in London selling the same record for sixty dollars American, plus twelve to ship.

Same misprint on the record label.

Same two songs.

Better attitude.

⁑

THE METERS PLAYED slick mechanized funk in a famous city club, and the downstairs dance floor was organic and seething. There were none of their original members on the stage. The club used to be in a juke joint where a handful of people got together to watch Professor Longhair perform in the seventies. The Meters were once the backing band for Lee Dorsey. I'd seen them play before, at a Chicago summer festival held on a city sanitation department parking lot on a blistering day.

Outside, the night air was cooling and the funk sweat evaporated on the skin as I stood on Napoleon and took a few deep breaths. A rusted-out Chevy Impala pulled up at the intersection and a window rolled down.

A voice shouted. "Y'all are fucking yuppies." Three empty liquor bottles were thrown from the car. I ducked for no good reason. All three detonated harmlessly in bright splinters behind me as the V8 engine grew impatient.

"Fuck y'all." There was a stabbing of laughter as the big car pulled away. The plates were Louisiana. That was as much as I got. The color was maybe a sky blue and navy two-tone paint job. The eighteens were chrome custom and shinier than anything else on the vehicle.

⚗

THE METERS SHOW had ended early and the four-mile walk would get me to the Quarter and the last show of the night on St. Peter at around ten. Regular tickets were dirt cheap but required standing on the street outside. The inflated price of a sugar-sweet cocktail in a plastic cup afforded me all access to view the shifting urban procession.

The concert was an hour long, and the audience mostly perched on benches or stood reverently in the mildewed darkness as the band sat on wooden chairs in the front of the peeling wreck of a room and played. Their uniforms were white short-sleeved shirts crisply starched, dark thin ties, sharp hats. All ages and hues represented on the tiny stage. I had reserved a seat for a twenty-dollar upcharge, which got me a fast pass straight inside, and squatting rights to the thin edge of a hard wooden bench.

⚗

THE OLDEST BAR in town was lit solely by single candles on each table and looked to be closed when I got there at eleven thirty.

It wasn't. The back of the room was empty. The tables outside were half full and the front of the room was packed with seriously hammered women aged around thirty-five singing to vintage Bob Seeger cranked high on the digital jukebox and devouring pitchers of Voodoo daiquiris. They all wore tight bejeweled jeans with a lot of white stitching and T-shirts that were stretched taut and bore the wordy and identical legend JANET'S GETTIN' HER BIG OL' ASS HITCHED AGAIN IN THE BIG EASY SO US BITCHES ARE GONNA PARTY HARD ON BOURBON STREET!!!

I was surprised to see that the carriage tours of the Quarter ran this late into the night. Each carriage carried a half dozen people and was pulled by a single horse. Each carriage slowed down outside the bar. Each guide barked out the advanced age of the place, recounted the inevitable tale of long-ago haunting, and remarked on the lack of damage the place sustained both during and after Katrina.

And each time, a number of Janet's bitches would rush to the door of the premises and out onto the sidewalk where, with some effort, they would pull up their T-shirts, yank down their lace demis, and flash their tits while collectively cackling like fiends. Carriages full of young inebriates cheered loudly and threw their beads and empty to-go cups. Older passengers rolled their eyes, smiled stoically, and shook their heads in a weary show of indignation.

I sat at an outside table, drank a Turbodog, used my phone to check the second line listings for the next few days on the radio station website, and took frequent breaks to check out the impromptu burlesque each time a tour carriage arrived.

Janet's bitches showed no sign they would be putting the girls away for the night anytime soon.

‡

THE NEXT DAY at noon, I got my shoes on the corner of Second and Dryades in the Central City district. The Mighty Messengers of Concord were scheduled to march till four in the afternoon with four brass bands helping them out along the way.

The cinderblock bar at the intersection was to be the start and finish for the event. The place looked nothing remarkable from the outside; it was one of a half-dozen parade stop bars along the designated route. But it had some history. It had been one of the first places to reopen after the storm, and it had also been the scene of some alleged NOPD brutality. In 2006, the owner of the bar was tasered and beat down in full view of a dozen witnesses. No official investigation into the matter had taken place. The owner was black and in his mid-twenties; his customers were all older African Americans. The cops were white. The execution of five young men had taken place a week previous, just a few blocks distant.

Outside the front door, an older gentleman wearing a huge pink sash draped over a black shirt and matching black trousers was taking shelter under a gigantic pink parasol, with a cooler loaded with cold Dixies. He was doing brisk business at three bucks a can.

I popped open my beer and guzzled it while it was still icy. The amount of pompous shit I would take from Nye for drinking mass-produced gnat's piss from Milwaukee was considerable, but that was unimportant. Today was just the sunniest of marching days. The air was unmoving and marinated. This was a setting where even the terminally repressed can slip loose for a moment.

But more important, there was no way I was going to tell him.

The Mighty Messengers were an all-black ensemble, but there were plenty of self-conscious white tourists and lighter-hued locals in attendance further back, drinking from plastic cups, dancing mostly alone, taking pictures with cell phones or with complicated SLR cameras, and comprising a sizable minority in the egalitarian ranks of the second line. The Unity Soul Ten got things going with "Shrimp and Gumbo," which was on a Rebirth recording I'd been listening to that very morning. We marched behind the Soul Ten as they in turn marched behind the Mighty Messengers, who stepped proud and high, sang out loud, the men turned out in white tuxedos and white hats and white patent leather shoes, the ladies spinning their dainty white parasols and trailing a haze of long white feathers behind them.

Progress was unhurried.

The band and the first line looked riotously sharp.

And with considerably less sartorial splendor, we brought up the rear.

On either side of the road, yellow tape was stretched along the length of the route, and more people walked on the sidewalk behind the flimsy barrier. A black cop paced us on one side, but mostly he laughed and he danced, in as much as a man of his considerable size could be said to dance. There were maybe thirty Messengers and they all strutted and sashayed. Every once in a while someone broke rank and moved to the tape to hug an acquaintance.

I was reminded that New Orleans is a small town that grew even smaller after the flood, which made it easy for some folks to leave, and then made it hard for them to come on back.

The Soul Ten broke down their first song enough to make it last almost half an hour. Most of us in the second line were loosely dressed for comfort, but the band members were decked out in several layers of the loudest lilac polyester. As they hauled along heavy brass instruments, the Ten were freely sweating. Entrepreneurial kids kept an endless flow of bottled water coming to them. I did notice that the Ten never had more than one band member taking a break at any one time.

At the hour mark, another dozen musicians suddenly augmented the Soul Ten. This was Royal Orleans and they would be our tour guides for the next quarter of the march. The changeover was seamless as both bands belted out "Tootie Ma is a Big Fine Thing" together for a while. There were a few weak groans from the assembled hardcore. This was clearly solid tourist fare, and we solid tourists lapped it up.

"This ain't no Mardi Gras y'all," someone shouted.

There was mostly good-natured laughter to accompany this.

At this point, a tall black kid with a banjo joined us. He walked right alongside me, a skinny beanpole in loose black sweatpants with pleather strips down both sides and green and yellow Nike shoes on his feet. The polo horseman on his shirt took up a quarter of his chest. The shirt was black. The horsey and his jockey were a close match for the shoes. The kid was maybe fifteen.

I watched him as we marched and he tried to play along. His head was scrunched over the neck of the instrument as he gently fingered the few chords he knew. He wasn't strumming loud enough to be heard by anyone.

"How long have you been playing?" I inquired.

He grinned down at me.

"Just be tryin' this shit out right now."

"It's not easy."

"You play?" he asked me.

"A little guitar," I said.

"I wanna learn to play more."

"You should. Why the banjo?"

He looked down at the instrument. "Belonged to my Daddy. He died in Katrina."

"I'm sorry for your loss."

He shrugged once. "I was little."

"Could he play?"

He started to smile. "Everyone say 'bout as well as I do. When I get better I'm gonna walk up front with the band." He gestured towards Royal Orleans up ahead. "Make some pro money. Get me some new KDs."

I must have looked blank.

He pointed down at his feet. "These last years.'"

I nodded as if I understood.

Royal Orleans now had the gig to themselves, as the Soul Ten melted back into the crowd at the next intersection. There were a dozen musicians in the new band, mostly on brass, two on drums, in classic Blues Brothers attire: black jackets and black trousers, white shirts and black ties, black hats with sharp brims and the band name in loud glitter stenciled across the hatband in the front. They looked like bus conductors. One of the two drummers was a woman. The trombone player looked very familiar. I smiled and he nodded back. It was the bass player from the bar in Algiers.

We got close during the next break.

He had recognized me. "You're sure getting yourself out and about," he said jokingly.

"You too. This is a lot of fun." And I meant it.

"Glad to hear it. So where else have you been?"

We were both almost shouting.

"I saw the Meters last night."

He smiled. "You don't say. I was there."

"It was busy."

He nodded. "They're a big draw these parts. And now you're out here."

"I went to St. Peter, too."

He nodded approvingly. "Well you certainly shouldn't miss that. Did you find some street music to listen to?"

"I bought a few compilations."

He nodded approvingly. "That's good. Which ones?"

I could suddenly only remember the one name.

"*From Piety to Desire*."

"Which volumes?"

I was forced to confess: "I don't remember."

"They can be uneven. Gotta admire that weird old guy though. He puts them out at least once every year."

"That weird old guy?"

"That's not fair. Templeton Rowley is the name," he said. "He's a colorful resident, used to be from a fancy family up north; owned a couple of chemical plants up at Baton Rouge and they made a heap of money during the Second World War. Templeton was the family oddball. Didn't want to have much to do with all their money, though they did cut him loose with more than enough of it so that he could show up in New Orleans one day all hell-bent on being another unauthorized local music historian in a town already bursting with them. He soon starts in, recording all sorts of local music. Anything he can find that fits his credo of religiously putting out only the most obscure artists, whose material is only original work. Rowley himself produces, all the recordings are made in a small studio he has somewhere, and it should be mentioned that for being a total amateur he gets a very respectable sound."

"Have you recorded with him?"

"Never have had that particular honor. Shit. I need to stop talking. We're only playing for the next hour. What are you doing after this?"

"Marching some more with the next band?" I said half-heartedly.

He pretended to frown. "You wanna do something else?"

"Such as?"

"Play a jazz funeral?"

"I'd like that," I told him.

"Starts off at Washington Square. You know where that is?"

"I'm staying very close."

"We finish up down beside the water at Crescent Park."

"I've been there."

"It's a fifteen-block walk from the park to the river. The widower is bringing the ashes. We'll be real close to Piety and Desire at the end. You'd sure as fuck better like 'Amazing Grace' and 'We Shall Overcome' because we'll be playing them for most of the way there. You could bring your guitar and play. They're both easy."

On our first meeting in the Algiers bar I had mentioned that I played badly.

Maybe he'd forgotten the badly part.

"I should warn you that when he lets her ashes go, we're gonna be doing an Eagles song."

"Which one?"

"Believe it's called 'Desperado.' It was playing when they first met. Gotta confess I've never played it before. It'll probably sound fine." He sounded momentarily less than certain.

"A brass band playing the Eagles?"

"Sure. Why not? Everything in music is borrowed and everything is then remade into something else, into something that sounds like it's new, even when it usually isn't. How do you like our name?"

"I do. It sounds very fancy."

"Well it's a Led Zeppelin song. I really have to start playing now. Funeral starts at 3:30. Come and play, or at least come. Washington Park on the Elysian Fields side."

He left me then as the Royal Orleans began playing "St. James Infirmary." The tourists began to cheer as a number of the Mighty Messengers succumbed to what looked like a legitimate outbreak of swooning.

⚑

THE MOURNERS WERE already congregated on the sidewalk beside the park. There were maybe forty assembled. Most had to-go cups to sip from and the atmosphere was sunny on the surface with undercurrents of sadness. The event promised to be well organized. Flyers were being distributed and any inequities in bead and alcohol distribution were being hastily rectified.

I had brought my guitar, and I stood holding it self-consciously as the bass player introduced me to the rest of Royal Orleans. I was pleased. I could now stop referring to him as the bass player. His name, finally revealed, was Spencer.

The flyer enabled me to acquaint myself with the history of the recently deceased. Her name was Cheryl McAllister. She had been a chemistry professor at Loyola in the College of Humanities and Natural Sciences. She had two large dogs and no children. Her husband, Lewis, was also a professor at Loyola. He taught in the Art and Design Undergraduate Program. They were both nearing seventy and had planned to retire soon. They loved New Orleans. They danced together on Saturday mornings in the Evangeline Parish. They lived in the Garden District. He was born and raised in New Orleans. She was originally from Newport in Rhode Island. They owned a summer house in Jamestown.

The cancer had begun in her liver and shunted rapidly through her system. She had rejected almost all treatments, except the first few doses of chemo and a solitary blood transfusion. As she neared the end, she made her wishes very clear. She would die as gently as possible, with only orange juice to sip and as much morphine as the hospice could provide. As she put it: "I've been high a good many times in this life and I have no problem being high when I take my leave."

It was five days since Cheryl's body had been cremated. Lewis McAllister gripped his wife's ashes in a tarnished metal flask. The mourners were mostly white and ran from late middle age to very late middle age. They wore comfortable sandals, baggy cargo shorts and faded jazz heritage T-shirts. The McAllisters had cultivated magnolias in their garden, and many participants clutched branches of the white and purple and pink flowers in their hands. Most of the petals had browning edges as the blooms in question were now well past their prime.

Spencer introduced me to Lewis McAllister. Photographs showed his wife had been tiny and fit. Lewis was a bear of a man exploding out of an ill-fitting dark suit, with only a handful of long ginger hairs leaping upwards unrestrained from his ruddy scalp.

He shook my hand with unforced vigor. I mumbled the customary words and he noticed my accent immediately. Did I know his roots were primarily Scots? His family was from Fife. He and Cheryl had been there many times. She loved to visit Perth. Had I been there? Could I play "Amazing Grace"? They both liked the tune even though they were by no means religious. Cheryl had little time for churches and dogma, he said, but now that she was gone he . . . but that last thought drifted away. He had wanted to have a piper play knowing she would have loved it, but he had been unable to find one at such short notice.

When Lewis spoke, he kept slipping between tenses. In some his Cheryl was still present, while in others she was past.

Lewis McAllister was talking in lieu of falling apart.

When it was finally my turn to speak, it was difficult to locate the best words. I had been to Perth many times. Would it be okay to play "Amazing Grace" in C? It was a shame about the pipes and the piper. I was very sorry for his loss.

And by and large my answers seemed to be suitable.

He was happy with the C key so I was able to assure him that "Amazing Grace" was well within my limited abilities. He smiled then.

It was clear that my heritage was of more importance than my prowess on the guitar. That was equally fine with me.

We did play "Amazing Grace" in C. We played it in C many times. While it was simple enough, the experience of walking and playing at the same time was a novel one for me. The mourners sang with us. The words to the hymn had been printed on the back of the flyer, superimposed over pictures of Cheryl—artistically rendered in sepia—pulling hard against the twin bulk of her dogs, on her knees in a garden with a stretch of beach and the ocean and a high suspension bridge in the far background, and two-stepping hard on a cracked linoleum dance floor with a game and sweaty Lewis in tow.

There was some confusion as we neared the river and the park. There was either a high bridge to climb over, or the train tracks to navigate a little further along. Lewis was consulted and the gentler gradient of the tracks was selected. The band kept on walking. Each time we got to the end of the song, the mourners began anew. They were loud, especially at the first verse. We played it as slowly as they sang it. Spencer took an appropriately doleful solo on one pass through. On another there were several nods in my direction, an unspoken indication that I could take a turn and solo if I so desired. But I shook my head. I knew I wasn't good enough or confident enough or belonged enough to do much of anything except strum along quietly in the background and try not to smirk at the absurd amount of pleasure this event was providing me.

We passed people on the street. Tourists took cell phone pictures; all species of hats were solemnly doffed in our wake.

As we crossed the tracks, a woman jogged across our path in a bright red sports bra and shorts with matching red iPod and earbuds. I'm not truly certain she even noticed us.

Beyond the tracks, the footpath followed the curve of the river. A half-dozen wooden steps dropped down to the edge of the water. Royal Orleans arrived first and we stood there awkward and uncertain for a moment before Spencer called out for "We Shall Overcome."

We played it in G; I was able to keep up.

When the rest of the procession had caught up with us, Lewis walked to the front of the crowd. He gripped the container tightly in his hand as he pulled several sheets of paper from the inside pocket of his jacket. He had clearly prepared a speech that he began to unfold with a shaking hand. This process threatened to take forever with the container in the one hand slowing him down. He made to place it on the ground. Then he changed his mind. Someone offered to take it from him. Lewis began to hand it over. Then he stopped again. So it was that he stood there, hopeless and confused, utterly defeated.

It was a time-trapped heartbreak of a performance we were observing.

Two women stepped to save him. Papers were held and collated, and the urn was placed gently on the ground, close to Lewis, so that he could begin his speech.

Royal Orleans stood silently holding their instruments. The mourners awkwardly gripped their sprigs of magnolia and their drinks and their sheets of paper. The two ladies stood on either side of Lewis like end tables. Both were petite compared to him. One was even smaller than Cheryl McAllister. A closer observation revealed that, by default, she could only be the deceased's younger sister.

We all looked toward Lewis. His beginning was far from encouraging. He stared at the sheets of paper as if he had never seen them before in his life. Was he uttering some of the words silently to himself? Then he opened his mouth wide and his big, round red face collapsed in grief.

Royal Orleans began to play "Desperado" with stilted deliberation as Lewis' shaking bulk was delicately supported by the two doll-sized ladies. Several extended minutes passed before he composed himself, opened the flask, and began to walk towards the water.

It was reasonable to suppose that he would pause at the edge, but he kept right on going into the water. It was as high as his knees when he stopped and turned to face us. We watched him as he mouthed four words and emptied the ashes onto the water reluctantly.

"Goodbye my little one."

Cheryl McAllister's ashes lay on the surface. With a single beckoning gesture, Lewis invited others to join him. Several mourners walked out into the water, and soon the fading magnolia blooms were falling amid the ashes.

When it was over, the mourners waddled wet-footed back to the parking lot beside the bridge. As I heard the flapping of old Birkenstocks, I did wonder if the aquatic portion of the afternoon had been planned.

A number of cars had clearly been positioned there for the aftermath. We lost a few of the faithful at that point, but Lewis and many of his friends had gotten their second wind. Could we walk with him back to the park? Could we play some more? Royal Orleans never hesitated for a second. They surely could, because in truth this was what had pretty much been expected all along.

So "We Shall Overcome" was reprised. Things got a lot more jovial after that. If we had walked all the way to the river in a spirit of studied sadness, we returned to the park in jubilation. Lewis and his friends opted to dance all the way back to the park. Could we play "Tootie Ma"? Hell yes we could! Or rather, they could. And for the second time that day Royal Orleans played the song and, not having the faintest clue what chords to play, I beat out the rhythm on my guitar and did my best to sing along

It was interesting to watch the recently bereaved Professor Lewis McAllister as he strutted his way down the street with a variety of dance partners. He seemed cheerful enough. He was certainly laughing loud and hard. But if you watched closely, he hesitated between each song, as if he was looking for someone else to dance with, someone much smaller.

He missed her.

He had loved her.

Is it possible to feel both sorry for and jealous of someone at the same time?

In a number of staider locales, the visible display of frivolity would have felt a shade premature and been viewed as more than a touch unseemly, but in New Orleans you can only lament for so long.

TWELVE

THE SUDDEN INEXPLICABLE ONSET OF guilt will make you do
things.

I had called Faith Community in Boulder when I first arrived in
New Orleans. This was the church where once a month I worked in
the basement where the homeless were housed on the coldest nights.
I helped set up beds, take down beds, handed out donated socks,
and drank shockingly bad coffee for the last quiet hour of my Sunday
night shift.

I had started working there two years ago because I wanted to find
a man who also worked there, serving the lost, listening to their fears,
making them feel better about themselves, and then killing them.

I kept on working there after I helped find that man because
the place still needed volunteers, and also because the shitstorm of
publicity Faith was buried in after the killer was discovered made me
feel uneasy.

I had called because I would miss my night to volunteer. My
intention was to reschedule. But the lady who answered the phone
had offered another option.

"Would you like to do some volunteer work while you're in New
Orleans, Tom?"

The lady who answered the phone at the church was always
polite. I seldom called her. I knew my day to be there, and I almost
always showed up. Occasionally she would call to ask me to switch
with another volunteer. I usually said yes.

She was notoriously difficult to refuse, so when she posed her
question, I mumbled in the affirmative and tried not to sigh as I did so.

She had called me back in a half hour with a day, an address in the Lower Ninth on Tennessee Avenue, and a time early in the morning for me to be there. It was now that day and that time. And I was there.

We were required to cut the grass on long-abandoned properties. We were issued the first of many generic bottled waters, a scythe, work gloves, insect repellent and industrial-strength sunscreen that was so thick it barely squeezed out of the tube. The older kids were given lawn mowers and told to wait. The younger ones were sent ahead to scout for rocks. The handful of adults who showed up were told to spread far out, watch out for rocks and children, and commence swinging.

It was backbreaking, brain-numbing, and easy.

Tobias Watson who worked alongside me was was a strikingly black man maybe close to my age. He told me he lived a few blocks away on Flood Street. A sharp glance dared me to offer any conceivable response to the name.

We swung together in unison as he began to talk.

"Twenty feet of dirty canal water heading down my street. One church left with nothing but the steeple still standing right up after. When the waters fall there was these two rowboats still tied up. Church top was the safest place to wait out the highest of the water."

"Twenty feet?"

He nodded solemnly. "Like a flood. One house got swept into another church and beat it down flat."

I looked up and down Tennessee. The levee was nearby, visible through the gaps on either side of the road where other houses had once stood. Maybe one in six structures had been rebuilt. There were a few traditional structures next to a series of bright new homes constructed at the urging of a movie star. He owned a house in the city where he lived with his movie-star wife and their bunch of kids.

Tobias supported his efforts.

"Man did what was right. The houses look nothing like what they replaced, but all that sorry shit fell down. They painted them some pretty wild colors. I heard one of these new houses is built so as to float if we ever get washed away again. The man came here. He talked some to us. Real polite. He listened. Called me sir."

Tobias swung and toiled beneath an elaborate hat and netting ensemble that looked about right for chopping his way through the Amazon. He pointed towards the levee.

"Water came from over there like it was a wall and washed the street away. Army Corps knew the canal levee was weak."

Tobias pointed further down Tennessee. "Man over there, he rebuilt. Stone outside the front door in the grass all that was left of his place. Carved the name of his baby daughter and his mother on it. Both of them upstairs when his house done wash away.

Church over on Flood never got to be rebuilt. Pastor has his church in his new house down this road. Used to be a bigger church. Lost his flock to places like Houston. His new house had to be built twice; bad drywall rotted out the copper piping the first time. Volunteers did their best but used them some cheap drywall from a foreign place."

"Why are we cutting this grass?"

"Keep the city from taking away the property."

"Will these people come back?"

"Don't matter to me if they do or don't. This their places. Some can't prove it. Some don't much want it. Don't matter. It's theirs to do with what they see fit. Ain't the city's business."

He looked closely at me. "You got you enough sunscreen?"

I assured him that I had.

Tobias revealed his plan for the rest of our day.

"We cuttin' till lunch. We can stay and keep on cuttin'. Get a ham and cheese sandwich and a bag of chips for our trouble. Cut more grass all the afternoon. Or we go to Gentilly."

"What's in Gentilly?"

"Afternoon work. Paint a little house. Two sisters live there. Older ladies. Real nice. They both live on the same street. Both flooded. Both got the inside of their house fixed pretty with insurance money. But the money didn't cover all the outside work.

We paint the one last week. Look fine when we get done. She real happy with the work. Made some crawfish etouffee and cornbread for all us painters. Her sister's house got to be painted this afternoon."

"How was the etouffee?"

Tobias smiled. "Lady an outstanding cook."

I swung that machete harder.

We had a plan for the afternoon.

I offered Tobias a ride to Gentilly. The volunteer coordinator was a full-grown woman trapped inside the body of a ten-year-old boy. She thanked us for our morning labors and handed us two sandwiches, two bottles of water, two huge apples, and two individual bags of Nacho Cheese Doritos. We thanked her and placed our lunches on the back seat of my car hoping we wouldn't need them.

Tobias Watson gave me his Katrina story as I drove west on Claiborne Avenue.

He had fled Katrina at the mayor's first urging, heading north to his sister's place in Jackson, where he waited it out for a few weeks. Tobias' sister was married to a white man, a cop in Jackson. When Tobias was set to come back home, his brother-in-law made a series of phone calls. Tobias got his FEMA trailer quickly. He had his building permits in place faster than most, and his single shotgun on the unfortunately named Flood was habitable within six months and pretty as a picture within the year, which surely stood as some kind of city record. The interior of his single-story home was a sorry mess when he first returned, but the brick façade had stood firm. Tobias was handy and did a lot of the work himself, plastering and painting every day, and sleeping in his trailer at night.

"Did you ever consider not coming back?" I asked him, as I turned to head north on Franklin.

"I surely did," he replied. "But this my home."

We arrived at a two-story house on Cameron. There were ladders leaning against walls and teenagers everywhere, all wearing bright orange T-shirts that proclaimed their allegiance to Jesus and to a Presbyterian church youth group in southern Illinois.

On our arrival, a volunteer coordinator interrogated us on our level of handiness. Tobias passed, and was assigned to the repair of several rotted-out window frames. I joined most of the youth in the unskilled painting crew.

Tobias and I looked around hopefully. Lunch was either long over or else not happening. We picked at our sandwiches in somber silence.

We were offered top-ups of repellent and sun-blocking cement before we got down to work. I held the ladder while a girl in very tight jean shorts rained paint down on me from above. We labored in this fashion for about ten minutes. Then we switched roles for the rest of the afternoon. Her name was Tracy. I was a much better painter than she was because I was older and able to concentrate better; in other words, I wasn't distracted by having to flirt with the good-looking young man on the adjacent ladder. I was also much happier to be above Tracy than under her. Trying hard not to stare up at the rear end of a girl surely no more than sixteen was wearying.

The new arrangement worked for Tracy, too, as the boy on the next ladder also switched places, securing his place in the lower-level stabilizing gig. The smitten twosome was now free to chat while offering cursory support to their airborne work partners.

I painted carefully. My Buffs cap was soon sweat-sodden. My neck ached. I broke for water and more paint. The house would soon be a creamy yellow color. The orange-clad crusaders were singing some hideous power ballad about being in love with Jesus, which I just knew would be wedged in my brain for the rest of the night.

But I didn't care. The work was thoughtless and distracting and the time went surprisingly fast.

We worked until around seven. It was still warm and light and the house was finished. Tobias had worked on retrofitting busted-out window frames and then switched to rebuilding the back deck that now looked brand new.

We were working on Chantelle's house. Her sister Chevelle lived two doors down on the same street. They were both loud and large and mysteriously happy. At seven, ten folding tables appeared on the front porch as we washed brushes in the yard and cleaned up. Iced tea was served in huge pitchers. Dinner was brought out from the kitchen. Both sisters served us crawfish etouffee over white rice and warm cornbread.

I sat beside Tobias and tried not to match the shit-eating grin plastered across his dark sweaty face. I failed. We clinked our mismatched McDonald's glasses together and got stuck in.

It was getting dark as I drove Tobias back home. We were both exhausted and we said nothing for most of the way. At his house he offered me a beer and I took him up on it. We sat on his front porch and we drank. The spaces between the new and the surviving buildings were large so that, even though it was relentlessly level, you could see a long distance across several blocks to the deceitful levee, appearing as a long dark line drawn up against the night sky. A stray dog walked past Tobias' place looking furtive, clearly up to no good. Cars drove by slowly to circumvent the canyon-like potholes that booby-trapped his street. A ship's horn sounded far away. We sipped at our cold Heinekens.

"This place used to be full," Tobias told me. "Now it's just nothing but empty."

‡

I GOT SAFELY back to Elysian Fields without falling asleep at the wheel. I popped open a tall NOLA to cleanse the skunky beer taste and sat down in the courtyard.

I woke up a good while later. The night was still warm, as was my mostly untouched beverage. The fountain was turned off. I remembered it had been gurgling when I first sat down. My painting arm hurt, but my stomach was full of rich food, and despite the layers of SPF 5000 spackle, my neck felt charred, yet I crawled off to bed smiling.

‡

My painting arm still ached the next morning, as did every other muscle. I made some coffee in the house and sat outside in the last clean T-shirt I had. The washer and dryer, small modern and double stacked machines, were behind a hidden door in the back of the bathroom. I hadn't bought detergent but there was enough left behind by a previous tenant.

From Piety to Desire, Volume 7 was playing on the boom box I had found and connected to an electrical outlet on the side of the house. I wasn't close to being hungry. I sipped my coffee and tried to think of something I should know about Logan Kind that the Internet hadn't already told me.

There wasn't terribly much. Tracking down his old digs was maybe a place to start. He had rented an apartment on Esplanade before the storm. The building had closed and reopened as condos within the year, but Logan was long gone by then. The previous property company no longer answered their old phone number, and boasted no online presence. Logan Kind appeared to have never possessed a listed phone number in New Orleans, and his place of residence after Katrina was still something I hadn't uncovered.

So how had Logan lived? There had been music sales that had grown slowly and exponentially before and after his death. His sister Margot administered his estate after his death. There was a publishing company named Kindsongs, which held publishing rights to all the songs recorded on *Crofter*. Margot Kind was the only named employee on the website. No other performers, and no other songs, were legally represented by the company. It wasn't clear when Kindsongs was founded. Was it before Logan had died or after? My best guess would be post-demise.

Had Logan worked? Not in Oxford, according to Carly Williamson, although unpaid dog-walking had certainly taken up a good portion of his free time. In New Orleans he had played out on the street on occasion. It was hard to know how often he performed. The registered sightings by Croftertales subscribers were sporadic, but that was hardly a definitive record of employment.

Could you make a living performing on the streets? I had no idea, but if Mel's theatrical one performer-two-character revue required giving hand jobs to young drunks to stay afloat, then the profitability of Logan's intermittent busking seemed doubtful.

At that moment, an impossibly pure voice caught my attention. According to the brief liner notes, tracks seven and eight on the *Piety* compilation were recorded by Iris Cummings. She played a hammered dulcimer and she sang wistfully in both English and Gaelic. The first track was "Meddlesome Malcolm" and was lightly comic in tone. The name of the second song was unpronounceable and was a more ethereal composition. Her voice was quite wonderful on both. The production was simple and perfect. I could have listened to her forever. Alas, the two tracks were all Ms. Cummings delivered before a zydeco-speed-metal hybrid power trio laid waste to my eardrums.

This was, I judged, the perfect moment to move my laundry along. Once my clothes were safely drying, it was back to work.

It was possible to leave a message on Margot Kind's website. I contemplated asking her a few questions about her brother, but I couldn't quite work out what to say. I did want to get in contact with her eventually. But I wanted to be able to tell her something and that clearly wasn't possible yet.

Logan Kind had rented two places to live. He had existed. He hadn't had any kind of gainful employment as far as I could tell. But he hadn't actually starved. I wanted to know if he had made money. He went to clubs on rare occasions. *Crofter* had never been a million seller, but it had at least sold copies. Had he received royalties? Had anyone famous recorded his songs? Had he written a screenplay? Won the lottery? Sued some rich rapper for sampling his songs and settled out of court for a colossal lump sum?

The Internet could go some way towards answering these questions.

I loaded *From Piety to Desire, Volume 10*.

By the time my clothes were toasty dry I had plenty of answers. Three bands I had never heard of had recorded three of Logan's songs. His Amazon rating was a number several decimal points west of Beyoncé's. I did note that the Amazon ratings of the three aforementioned bands were very close to Logan's. He hadn't won the lottery. I had already discovered that Margot Kind had a book in the works, and that an indie film about Logan was in preproduction, but neither of these endeavors would have provided financial assistance to Kind during his lifetime.

The last site I visited was simply one person's list of sad music deaths, in reverse order, from ten to one. Logan's was number eight.

Two members of the band Badfinger had hung themselves, years apart, supposedly as a result of widespread public indifference to their well-crafted pop songs. Badfinger had once drawn favorable comparisons to the Beatles, who had signed them to their own record label. One of their songs did become a huge hit twice over, but it was too late by then. Even very recently an acclaimed television show had featured their finest song in the last scene of the series finale. But it was still too late. The website listed Badfinger's members as rock's saddest deaths. It was hard to argue.

Guess I got what I deserve
Kept you waiting there too long, my love

The courtyard was now quiet. The music on the compilation discs had proved to be mostly distracting; not because it was especially good or bad, but because there was so little attempt at continuity. It was rap to jazz to rock. At one point what sounded like a couple of ADHD kids beating a handful of large plastic receptacles to death gave way to plainsong: barely whispered spoken word, as an earnest woman emoted on the subject of childbirth, over what sounded like a duet for pregnant whale and theremin.

I had managed to enjoy Iris Cummings, despite the unruly juxtapositions. I was certain that I would have appreciated some of the other artists in a more supportive setting.

THIRTEEN

THE INTERNET RECOMMENDED Nashville tuning for "Wild Horses," but that wasn't about to happen.

It was two hours later. My body hurt despite four Ibuprofen, and I was back on the streets in the early afternoon, guitar in my lap, another sorry-looking chair from the courtyard securely wedged under my rear end. Once again I had been able to procure shade under the store awning, with my guitar case lying open in an act of incurable optimism. I was fully watered, with all manner of ablutions successfully completed.

I still wasn't sure why I was doing this.

It was remarkable, given the limitations of my talent, how willing I was to be this exposed. Perhaps it was the spirit of the city. What else could it be? I reviewed my previous history of public performance: third wise man in a Sunday school Christmas nativity program with a solitary line of dialogue ("We seek the Christ child"), and that was all she wrote.

What made more sense was the degree to which I felt drawn to Logan Kind and to his music.

I had looked again at the attempted tablatures of his recordings. The more rudimentary versions were within my abilities. I'd persevered, hoping to be able to play at least one song from *Crofter* and do it justice. The problem was that the simple notations still sounded nowhere close, while the more advanced versions were light years above my skill to duplicate.

So I stuck to playing covers and, for reasons I couldn't explain, was tending to play older songs. Personal taste was not the determining factor; I'm no chronic nostalgic, and plenty of new songs that I loved were transposed and posted and eminently playable.

It wasn't that.

On my commandeered corner in the Quarter, I was playing nothing but vintage songs, or newer songs by people who were themselves vintage. I played Richard Thompson and Lucinda Williams, the more strummy acoustic Beatles and Stones stuff, even early Sir Elton for God's sake.

And the question had to be why?

My simple answer was Logan. It was true I couldn't play him or play like him. But I could play his era. The songs he might have listened to and liked. The Croftertales postings had listed the covers he had played, and I had shamelessly co-opted as many as I could, all the while assuming he must have had his own good reasons for picking them.

And I was aware that as I played I was trying to simultaneously sound like both Logan and the original singer, a vocal hybrid, of Logan and Mick, of Logan and Lou, of Logan and John or Paul or even George, when I was capoed up impossibly high for "Here Comes the Sun."

When I listened to Logan, I heard his guitar-playing first and foremost. His voice was a young and reedy tenor that had grown on me as I played the songs over and over. His college-sieved North of England diction was stark and unmistakable on every track.

"Here Comes the Sun" had been the first song of the afternoon. I thought it went splendidly. It produced my first genuine request, other than the usual ones to stop fucking sucking.

"Can you play any other Beatles songs?"

"I can play 'Let It Be'."

"Anything else?"

"In My Life."

"Can you play that for us?"

"It would be my pleasure."

And these memories lose their meaning,
When I think of love as something new.

Two ladies, perhaps a decade senior to me, danced with each other as I played. It was an old-fashioned affair, with elaborate twirls and hand-holding, with not-quite-ironic curtsying to each other at the end of the song, and a smattering of girlish giggling both before and after.

They'd dropped a crisp ten-dollar bill in the guitar case, and since I hadn't lost my seat yet, I was now ahead, at least so far.

Later in the afternoon I played "Let It Be" and two more ladies showed up. They offered to sing along with me. I had a printout of the words and the chords. I stood in the middle and painstakingly flatpicked. They stood on either side. One held the lyrics high while the other constantly took selfies. They barely looked at the words. They sang very well. When we were finished, I willingly surrendered my cell phone number and the pictures were texted. I looked happy. My neck was indeed seared red from the rigors of yesterday, and I thought it might be time to retire my CU hat, or at least wash it.

Another ten-spot came my way.

And still no furniture malfunctions.

⁂

"Perhaps you would honor me with a song of your own, young man."

His jacket was a light cream color and his ample trousers a thick brown nubby fabric that would surely endure forever. He wore brown polished walking brogans and carried a walking stick with an elaborate yellowed bone handle and a bright metal tip. He carried the stick under his arm. The outfit seemed too warm for the locale, the style more landed English gentry than something appropriate for the stagnant heat of below-sea-level Louisiana. He had simply appeared, materializing crisp and unfazed by the heat in front of me. I assumed the cane to be mostly an affectation, as his arrival had been soundless, unaccompanied by punctuated taps of steel.

He was smiling at me.

"I'm sorry. I don't have any."

His tone grew a shade darker. "Then do you not compose, yourself?"

"I can barely play, let alone compose."

"You're not a native of these parts."

"A foolish tourist."

"That's very curious. Are you a traveling musician?"

"I'm actually a semi-retired businessman here on holiday and clearly pushing my luck."

"I hear in your voice that you hail from a faraway land. I have sadly never once left this state. We do have the evanescent nature of occupation in common. I, too, am barely required to work. You have come a long way to be here in this wonderful city of ours."

"Not so very far. I live most of the time in Colorado."

"And how long have you played?"

"I played a little as a boy."

"And now you find yourself playing as a man."

"I'm trying to begin again. There was a long gap."

He nodded. "I have some understanding of what it means to begin again. I would imagine it's less than easy after such an extended break."

"I like to think I'm doing much better than I first hoped."

"Then allow me to compliment you on your progress."

"Thank you."

He took a few steps backwards and then stood. He was clearly waiting.

Feeling unaccountably nervous in his presence I began to play.

He spoke again when I had finished.

"Were you aware that Lead Belly, who was born on a plantation near Mooringsport, Louisiana, recorded that very song in 1944? He called it "In New Orleans." It was also recorded earlier in 1937 as "The Rising Sun Blues.""

"Who originally wrote it?" I queried.

He smiled warmly at me. "Who indeed? It would fall under the wide umbrella of an uncertain provenance."

He moved surprisingly fast, placing something inside the guitar case and turned towards me.

"I wish you all good luck on your new beginning young man."

When he walked away, his cane stayed tucked under his arm and never once touched the ground as he headed northwest on Dumaine.

Inside my case I discovered a new hundred-dollar bill slumming with the two tens.

I knew what to do with the money as soon as I saw it.

But first the guitar and the chair had to be safely escorted back to the house. The walk took me down Frenchmen and past Washington Square, where the funeral walk had started and ended yesterday.

A stooped man in sweat-soaked overalls was singing loudly and tunelessly as he swept a fine dusting of flower petals from the oak-sheltered path onto the grass. I wasn't altogether sure what purpose the repositioning of the dead flowers served. I could have asked. It would have stopped the singing. But I chose not to.

The chair was returned with some pride to the courtyard, and the guitar was placed on the bed, with the overhead fan cranked to the second highest setting.

When I got back to Jackson Square, the place was bursting with all the ingredients of Big Easy hustle.

Outside the market café a tense standoff was taking place between a tourist on foot and a tourist in a white Toyota Camry with Indiana plates. The pedestrian was a black woman. The driver was the same color as his car. She had been taking her time crossing the street when he had inched his vehicle too close. She was building to incensed, whereas he was mostly embarrassed. She wasn't about to step aside any time soon. He also wasn't going any place, as his car was sandwiched between her and more traffic. Horns were honking behind him. The woman was building a supportive audience. There was scattered cheering as her finger commenced to wag. She smiled at her new fans. This was all going her way.

The driver had a measure of my sympathy. Someone had once advised me that going crosstown in New Orleans was possible on foot and ill-advised in a car, unless you chose to take Claiborne Avenue.

I found Mel in predatory Marilyn mode. There were two young men standing close by, faking coy, as she blew them a series of very deliberate kisses. One was the primary target, slickly overripe and disagreeably handsome. The other was pockmarked and petulant. She was soft-whispering a song about Little Rock. It was mostly a breathing exercise.

I got closer. She saw me and smiled. I held out the hundo. Her face did something weird for a split second before she recovered and took the money.

I blew her a big kiss of my own and left.

Still twenty bucks clear profit. I was suddenly hungry. When was the last time I had dined at the corner of Chartres and St. Louis? I had enough for a half muffuletta, a side of jambalaya, and two Abitas. An internal debate lasted less than a second. Done and done.

This was the very first place I had gone to in New Orleans, on the occasion of my very first visit. On that occasion I had been in the process of falling in love.

⁑

THE TRAIN HAD headed south from Chicago. I was then thirty-seven and my marriage was breaking up. The journey had been taken on impulse, in a life not thus far noted for impulsiveness.

It had come at the conclusion of another journey, this one northwards, to Michigan, where a friend had become lost and where the mapping out of his last days had become an obsession built on a solemn conviction that his closing had gone neither well nor naturally.

I had been too late to book a sleeper car to New Orleans and instead sat through the night with a young woman ten years younger than I was. Her name was Kate. She was to meet up with a female friend in the city. We sat together. Then we fell asleep in the early hours and woke to find ourselves tangled up.

A handful of memories prove indelible. Mostly they comprise fearful moments, shameful acts of exclusion and intended cruelty. A few are more pleasant, like the wildly inappropriate notion to kiss a sleeping stranger's forehead as she smiles and begins to stir to an unexpected wakefulness in your arms.

Yes, it was an indefensible act of intrusion, and I hope I never forget doing it.

The train had offered breakfast service and we drowsily partook. The eggs were a grim rubbery affair. The coffee was altogether too welcome to justify criticism. She told me her post-grad work was in anthropology. She was looking for a research job in that field. I had just read an Oliver Sacks book about color blindness, and tried to bluff my way through a quasi-scientific conversation that I didn't want to end.

I was staying near the Audubon Zoo on Calhoun. Kate had been able to secure herself accommodation in the Tulane residences, on the strength of a student ID that was still valid, and which allowed students to stay cheaply on campuses across the country.

Later in the day I would take the St. Charles streetcar to my bed and breakfast and be surprised at how many blocks south I had to walk to get to my digs. I was a good deal younger then, but ironically not as healthy as I am today. I had bought a guidebook at the Amtrak station. There were a dozen walking tours laid out in detail and I boldly intended to take each one.

We took a taxi together to the quarter from the train station. The train had been late arriving after over an hour spent simmering on a rail siding a few miles south of McComb, Mississippi. Every time the announcer apologized for the delay we were reminded how close we were to the birthplace of new teen singing sensation Britney Spears.

Kate found a payphone and called her friend and they arranged to meet in an hour's time. We stood outside the restaurant. A sign hanging overhead claimed the place had been there since 1797. The crumbling plaster walls and peeling white paint outside made that claim seem entirely plausible.

We were comically unsure of what to do next. We wanted to walk and to explore. She had a backpack. I had my shoulder bag. We were both travelling light but not quite light enough.

We weren't especially hungry.

I looked in my guidebook. The restaurant was favorably mentioned. She asked me if I planned on making all my decisions after consulting the book. I pantomimed the taking of mild umbrage in grumpy response.

We each ate small bowls of gumbo and guzzled our late morning hurricanes like the shameless tourists we were. The waiter's white shirt was far from clean. The flaking stucco walls inside the restaurant's front room were in as dilapidated a condition as the place's exterior. There were palm trees in a courtyard. At the back of the building was a larger and much fancier dining room with freshly painted walls and wood trim and clean white tablecloths that didn't have a sheet of grubby clear plastic placed on top of them. We wordlessly opted for the determined squalor of the front room.

Kate would have to leave soon. In a hurry I had looked some more in my guidebook. There was a grandly columned hotel on St. Charles Avenue. It boasted a many-roomed bar and a huge deck with fans overhead and white wicker chairs. It offered live jazz at night. It was an old city tradition in a town overloaded with old traditions. The guidebook told me not to miss the mahogany stairwell that led to a stained glass skylight. It warned of the likelihood of having to endure clusters of yappy college kids hitting on each other loudly, but promised that the place was dark and sprawling and there were plenty of carpeted corners to submerge yourself in.

I asked if we could meet and have a drink there later that night, and Kate said she would like that.

We arranged a time.

Our hour was almost up.

She told me that she had to go.

She got up and kissed me on the cheek.

"Now we're even," she told me.

She was right. We had now kissed each other once.

And she left.

We never saw each other again.

⁂

AT 6:45 I was sitting at the hotel bar with my guidebook open. I looked up as instructed. The bar ceiling was mahogany wood imported from Honduras and was positioned fifteen feet above the dark wood floor. The chandeliers were bronze.

On a more practical note, happy-hour prices were good until seven.

I was asked if I cared to sample a Sazerac. I saw no reason to appear churlish.

At precisely seven o'clock the hotel intercom summoned me by name to the front desk where I was handed a note. I had two distinct thoughts as I opened the folded paper.

It felt like a melodramatic moment in an old film.

It would unquestionably be bad news.

Kate had swung by the hotel on the way to the airport to hand deliver it. Her mother had called her at the university residences. Her father had suffered a heart attack. There was a ticket home waiting for her at the airport. She had to leave right away. She was very sorry. Goodbye, Tom.

If I remember correctly Humphrey Bogart had read his note at the train station. He now has to leave town without his best girl. He reluctantly gets onto the train. His face is all broken. In an angry gesture he throws the letter away. The black piano player is with him, which is of some small comfort. As the train starts to foggily depart, a rush of sickly violins rises up and mocks him.

I read my note twice. Once at the desk and a second time at the bar where I returned to finish my discounted cocktail. When I had completed the second reading I folded the paper and put it inside the back cover of my guidebook for safekeeping. There were more architectural details to read about but I no longer gave much of a fuck one way or another. In truth I didn't much care about historic Louisiana décor. I had only wanted something to talk to Kate about when she arrived, so that she would think me urbane and sophisticated.

I knew her last name and where she had been planning on staying. I could have employed the university or the Amtrak people into helping me trace her. I didn't know where she or her parents lived, but I could certainly have endeavored to find out.

But I didn't. I was still married. I was older. I was mostly a miserable excuse for a living soul. And I also entertained the weird notion that what we had experienced, however fleeting, was oddly sweet and perfectly complete just as it was. The rest would undoubtedly have turned out to be so much bitter anticlimax. That was the illusionary concept I initially fashioned at the hotel bar as I nursed my second, now full-priced official cocktail of the city of New Orleans.

I've since googled Kate twice. Both times drunk, and both times not drunk enough to not feel like a complete dolt for doing it. The episodes were ten years apart. The first disclosed a spell of adjunct professorship in one of the thousands of small liberal colleges littering Ohio. The second revealed high school teaching in a suburb of Toronto, a husband, two very small children, and a head full of prematurely grey hair that looked extremely becoming on her.

She looked quite happy on both occasions. Her life had clearly survived the gut-wrenching trauma of losing me.

I still have the guidebook and her note in my house in Boulder.

I did follow every tour in the guidebook when I was there, and I silently dedicated my series of pedestrian pilgrimages to Kate, my newly lost love. On the first junket, my hurricane was served in a jumbo souvenir bucket and hastily downed outside a voodoo shop. Inside the shop we were encouraged to purchase a trinket to offer to a legendry dark enchantress whose slogan-scarred grave was the next stop we were to be frog-marched to on our frenzied itinerary.

When we arrived, I dedicated my cheap plastic amulet to the smirking gods of thwarted love and placed it carefully beside a discarded bottle of the voodoo queen's reputed libation of choice.

Such was the insidious charm of the Crescent City: my wallow in romantic loss soon morphed into utter delight.

‡

I WAS SITTING on my front step in the early evening when Mel showed up.

"Good Evening, Tom," she said.

She was back in her Blanche ensemble. Of the two it seemed the more practical—best for bike rides, more suitable for social calls before and after working hours.

She spoke again. "I was able to leave early tonight."

"Is that right? I'm very glad. Business must have been good."

"I was able to meet my quota." Her voice was coy.

"Are you going to say something about the kindness of strangers?"

She was smiling. "Wouldn't that be a little trite?"

I smiled back. "Perhaps a little."

There was a long pause.

"I wanted to thank you."

"Please don't. I was given the money under false pretenses."

"Didn't you give it to me for the same."

"I don't need it."

She didn't reply.

I had of course said the wrong thing. If there is a way to acknowledge the giving and receiving of charity without embarrassment, I've yet to encounter it. If it's possible for two people to comfortably converse about and confess to a wide discrepancy in their respective incomes, I've yet to see it successfully accomplished.

I tried to recover: "I like your act."

She answered curtly. "No you don't. When I was younger I was better at this. There was a nightclub on Bourbon where I performed.

It was almost a real show then. Now it's just a means of hollering, of calling attention to myself and begging and . . . "

I cut her off. "You don't have to say it."

"No?"

But she changed the subject.

"So the money . . . "

"I was playing out again in the very same place as before. An older man gave me the hundred dollars."

"You say you're not very good."

"That's putting it mildly."

"Maybe he thought you were cute."

"I'm not."

She looked hard at me. "You're not un-cute."

"Thank you. It isn't a matter of cuteness."

"So why did he give you so much?"

I had given the matter some thought.

"I have a feeling that he rewards effort rather than talent. He has money and he's on an errand to seek out new musical endeavors, even god-awful ones like mine. I think I got credit just for being there and trying."

"What does he look like?"

I described him as best I could. Mel looked blank.

"I'm sure I've never seen him." She turned petulant. "I wonder why he's never been to see my act."

"Do you sing or play an instrument?"

"Not especially." She pouted at me then.

I smiled. "Maybe you should try."

"I can't really sing."

"Do you know any songs?"

"We performed 'You Are My Sunshine' in my first-grade class. I was dressed as a sunflower. It was my first time in a costume. I remember it was all kinds of fun."

"Where did you grow up?"

"A small town in Indiana."

"Does it have a name?"

"I'm sure it does." She paused. "Do you know how to play that song?"

"It has only three chords and I know all the words to the chorus."

"It's a children's lullaby. It has a lot more words that we had to memorize and it gets weird."

"How weird?"

"It's a very sad song. An old governor of Louisiana wrote it."

"Is that true?"

She hesitated. "Yes. I think so. Maybe."

I found my laptop and my guitar and my last Hopitoulas and a small glass. Mel only wanted a sip. The rest was to be all mine.

I found the lyrics. Mel was right. It was weird.

Neither of us could claim to sing well. Mel's voice was deeper than I expected and she sang hesitantly at first. I was louder. Not any better, just louder. I played it in a handful of keys before we settled on A. We sang it once through. Then we sang it again. We took turns on the verses and we shared the choruses. I tried to sing harmony. It was grim. Mel laughed at me and we went back to unison.

We were both giggling by the end of the second run-through. She was leaning against me on the step in order to read the words on the screen. Her bare arm rested on my leg. I adjusted my guitar in my lap and slid very slightly away from her.

If she noticed me move away, she said nothing.

When we had finished singing we went to the Internet, and on YouTube found no shortage of recorded versions.

"You choose one," I told her.

"I don't care." She said. "You choose."

So I did. We listened to Johnny Cash when he was an old man, and we listened to Johnny when he was a younger man and singing on a television special with June, and afterwards we sat for a while and said nothing until it got dark.

Mel had a light attached to the back of her bike. I watched as it grew smaller and smaller.

FOURTEEN

THIS WOULD BE MY LAST day as a street performer.

The day began with thick fog washing across the Quarter, coughed up from the river. The air was the coldest it had been since I had arrived in town and kept the tourist count low. I played for about an hour. No one stopped. No one sang along. I wore my jacket the whole time and I performed without once sitting down.

At the end of the hour I put my guitar away and walked towards the market café.

In the Square the crowds were thin. Mel was sitting on a park bench. She had a wool shawl draped across her shoulders. She was in her Marilyn outfit. She looked cold. I offered to get her some coffee but she declined. I told her she should go home. She agreed but her response was a half-hearted one. She kept glancing up and down the path looking for her customers, for her young men, for her stock-in-trade.

I said goodbye and headed over to the café.

Green plastic walls enclosed the café, and inside, the place was mostly full. I got coffee and an order of beignets and sat down at one of the unoccupied tables outside. A daily paper had been abandoned at the next table and I quickly grabbed it. The forecast was for the fog to last well into the afternoon, when the sun would reappear, and the temperatures would rise to become more seasonable.

Most of the Square was visible from where I sat, but thick bushes obscured the bench where Mel had been sitting. It wasn't warm in the exposed seating, and I made sure to eat my powdered pastries quickly while they were still fresh and hot. I threw one chunk at a bold pigeon darting between tables as I read *The Times-Picayune* from cover to cover.

Then I thought some more about going home.

This had been lots of fun, but I was fooling no one. I now knew a lot about Logan Kind. I'd got to hang out in New Orleans and play guitar. But most of the questions I had wanted answers to remained unanswered. The things I knew about Logan could have been found by anyone anywhere with a little patience and a working Wi-Fi connection, although I suspected that I wouldn't have found them if I hadn't come here.

Because context is everything.

But I was playing guitar again, with Logan as my newfound muse and inspiration.

A moment of delusion had me heading back north, pulling rank, bullying Nye into letting me playing at Belvedere, or even at Cygnet, where surly barista and stoutmaster Jesse would surely cherish the opportunity to mock me mercilessly. There were open-mic nights everywhere, which were not restricted to the young or the prolifically talented. This was good, as I was clearly neither.

Then the moment ended. The street corner in the Quarter where Logan had played was going to be my only gig for a while. The near future would see me sitting on my porch in Boulder, noodling up a storm, staring up at the mountains. If I got good enough, I might play someplace else, but not until I was ready, until I was better.

There would be no playing on the streets anywhere, not on Pearl Street, and definitely not down by the creek.

My street performances in the Quarter were a form of devotional, not the beginning of any kind of busking career, because the streets were for the hardened and the needy, and not for the dilettante.

So much for stardom.

Stephen Park, the young man who died in the coffee shop, was still all kinds of an unresolved mystery. So were Logan's last days and a huge chunk of his earlier life. So were so many other things. I didn't have a clue what "Circumstance" was, beyond being a reference to a song that didn't seem to exist anywhere. I didn't know how Logan Kind sounded like no one else when he played the guitar.

About the only thing I did know was why the Deltatones song sounded like Logan's.

I thought about Boulder and Michigan and about Art and Keith. Back then all the answers to their deaths had depended on clues that had been visible to me. When I thought about this search there were several unfortunate possibilities.

There were no clues.

There were no clues I could see.

There were no clues I could see or understand.

I wanted to know why two people had died. There was no good reason that I could see.

There was no good reason why there should be a good reason.

I desired a certain resolution.

It wasn't about to happen.

I did suddenly have a thought.

The newspaper article about Stephen Park was a lot harder to read on the tiny phone screen. His interests were listed, the subjects he studied in college, the paper he wrote. Everything was as I remembered it.

"The Town Where She Loved Me."

The title had reminded me of something. I thought perhaps it was poetry. Whether I was clearly wrong or if I was right, I had no idea what poetry it was.

Stephen Park was also reminded of something. I had assumed it was a song, but I found I was wrong again. Stephen had written about Scottish poetry when he was a student.

Logan's song had reminded Park of a poem.

And he was correct.

"Circumstance" was a short poem written by a Scottish poet named Norman Allan Haig in 1996. It was readily available on the Internet.

The first verse read as follows:

Is it so surprising to you?
That a wonderful place would kill my love dead?
Both you and I came from there once,
From the town where I loved you,
From the place where you told me goodbye.

The first few lines of Logan's song were as follows:

It's a wonder to me that the place that we came from,
Is a wonderful place where you love me.

You and I came from there once long ago,
From the town where I once loved you.

From the town where she loved me,
From the place where I told her goodbye.

In Logan's version the last two lines were repeated, and formed the verse of the song.

I stared at the two pieces of text for a while.

⁜

MY BRIEF *Eureka!* moment was broken by the sound of someone screaming from the direction of the Square and I started to run.

I got to the young man just as he brought his foot down hard on Mel's skull. She lay still on the ground. There was a sharp crack. Her whole body quivered. He raised his foot again. I grabbed him and threw him onto the bench. He hit it hard face first and turned around, surprised. I jumped on top of him and punched his face several times. Then I grabbed him by his hair and smashed his head into the top of the metal bench as many times as I could until the cop pulled me away.

I ran to Mel and held her broken head in my hands. Her wig was gone and blood poured from her hair through my hands. There was more blood covering the bodice of her dress where the knife was shoved deep into her side. The skirt of her dress was far enough up so that her underwear was exposed and you could see the bulge of her cock and her balls. I pulled the skirt all the way down as quickly as I could and I smiled at her face and I held onto her.

"I'm all broken, Tom." She whispered these words before she died in my arms. The ambulance and many more cops showed up, and they made me let her go. By then I was crying, and my tears had fallen on her dead face and washed some of her blood away.

The cops talked to me for a while but I wasn't listening. Someone from the café brought my guitar and my cell phone, which I had left lying on the table. My coffee had been thoughtfully transferred into a plastic cup and I gratefully sipped from it as they asked their questions. The knuckles on my right hand were red and very sore. I was provided with an ice pack.

The cops asked me if I knew Melvin Taylor. I hesitated, then I told them that I did. They asked me how I knew him, and I told them everything, which wasn't very much. They asked me several harder questions but they were for the most part friendly. The New Orleans police enjoy an unenviable reputation, but these fine men were both professional and courteous. The cop who had pulled me off Mel's killer had heard the same scream and been two blocks away at the time. He was young and fit and he had arrived at the scene very quickly.

But we had both been too late.

They hastened to tell me more than once that I wasn't in any kind of trouble. There were eyewitnesses with cell phones, and no one had said or recorded anything that made me look anything other than overzealous. Mel's killer had regained consciousness and was on his way to the hospital. One of the cops was an older man. He knew all about Melvin Taylor.

"He's worked down here for a good long while. The Bourbon revue clubs at first. Doing his act on the city streets more lately.

As he's gotten older there's been more sex for cash stuff, head and hand jobs for the most part. He used to be a real cutie when he first showed up in town. Passed easy for a chick. Must be close to twenty years ago. Y'all knew he was a guy."

I told him I did. He looked at me strangely for a moment.

"As he's gotten older the trade he's taken up with has gotten rougher. Mostly he hooks up with handsome young drunks who would fuck a goat if it wore heels. But he's gotten himself injured before, spent time in the hospital emergency ward, hit by macho types who sober up and get seriously pissed when they find out they got it on with a guy in a dress. That's how they try to tell it. Lying fucks mostly. Truth of the matter is they knew what he was and liked it just fine. When we get a statement from the hospital bed that's what he's eventually gonna tell us. A real stone-cold ladies man who went and got his masculinity all fucked up and felt all threatened."

I asked how he was.

The cop smiled. "You were in the process of fucking him up nicely. The guy who pulled you off says you would have cracked his fucking head wide open. He says he's feelin' kinda sorry he had to stop you. Were you thinking of leaving town soon?"

I told him that I was.

"Then don't. Stay here for a few days. We'll have some more questions for you probably. You shouldn't need to be worrying any. It all looks pretty righteous. We can give you a ride back to your place in a while if you like."

I was tired and covered in blood. I told him I would appreciate a ride.

The cops were still tidying up as I left. Mel's bike was still chained to the fence. They were having some trouble getting the lock off. They had already taken away all the stuff in her basket, her Blanche dress and her beads and her Blanche wig and all the rest of the worthless shit that she had littered the road with when we first met.

I looked at the empty basket, her crappy bike, her drying blood on the path. I could hear a siren far away. The air was already warmer. The sun was beginning to burn away the morning fog, just like the forecast said it would. A trumpet blew an extended note outside the market café. It was the same gentleman from the other day, the same jogging suit, the same finger extended skyward at the end of every song, to give it all back to the big guy upstairs, the same big guy upstairs who had just let Mel get killed.

He began to play "Abide with Me."

I was soon crying.

I really had to leave.

They sat me in the back of the police car.

The ride was short.

I remembered last night.

Mel had moved close to me as we sang together.

Now I wished I had held her, but it was too late for that now.

FIFTEEN

FOR THE NEXT TWO DAYS I mostly stayed on Elysian Fields and
shamelessly sulked. I had more laundry to do now. I bought my
groceries at Whole Foods, some beer and some laundry detergent
and tissue paper. I played my guitar in the courtyard during the day.
I tried to play "You Are My Sunshine," but I wasn't able to finish. I
sat on my front step in the evening. I listened to my compilations a
little but mostly I listened to *Crofter* over and over again.

The cops showed up on the second day.

The hospital had released Mel's killer and the cops had him in
custody. It would be a simple case, with copious cell-phone video
and a lot of supporting testimony. The video clips included my act of
retribution, which was apparently a popular item at the station, but
I was assured it was not going to be seeing the light of day any time
soon.

I was officially free to leave town and unofficially encouraged to
hang around for a few more days.

※

ON THE MORNING of the third day, I walked back to the Square.
Mel's bike was still chained up; her crate had been replaced by
another one, which was overflowing with a fresh supply of beads
and flowers and notes and photographs of two famous film stars
and flyers that announced a funeral march planned for Sunday
morning of the next weekend. It would start late on the Square,
and end where Mel had lived, an apartment building on St. Claude
Avenue and Feliciana.

Near the bike, a young boy was selling flowers from a box. I bought a small bunch and placed them inside the crate. The act of death was no more or less a hustle in New Orleans than anything else.

‡‡

A REMARKABLY LARGE and detailed obituary ran that same day in the newspaper. Melvin Taylor had been thirty-eight when he died. His surviving relatives were a sister and a father, both from Indiana, and both now in town to make funeral arrangements. He had been murdered by an as-yet-unnamed male tourist, several days after the two of them had encountered each other during one of Mel's street performances, and then, shortly after that, in an unnamed Quarter bar. No motive for the murder was provided in the article.

Melvin Taylor had left Indiana when he was eighteen. He had finished high school there. He had known he was gay for as long as he could remember. He had loved old movies with Joan Crawford and Bette Davis. His favorite film was *Gone with the Wind*. There was a photograph of Mel from her early days in New Orleans and she looked uncannily like Marilyn Monroe. Melvin always insisted that he was an old-school gay drag queen, not a pre-op or post-op transsexual or transgender or anything else currently fashionable or tantalizingly ambiguous.

Funeral arrangements were pending. Donations could be made to the local gay-lesbian-transgender-straight alliance chapter. An address and a website were both provided. There would be a march on Sunday. Details of the march were also available at the GLTSA, and on the radio station website, where most of the street events were found.

I decided to stay at least until Sunday. I called Nye. It had been a very long time since our last conversation.

"The place where you are staying is available to you until the middle of next week," he told me.

I thanked him for taking care of the lodging arrangements.

"How was Colorado?" I asked him. It felt as if I had been away from home forever.

"Wonderful. You now have a tenant."

"Can I ask who?"

"You most assuredly can."

"Then who?"

"Neal."

"I thought he was my gardener."

"You might want to think of him now as a temporary live-in gardener."

"He's no longer with Gus." It wasn't a question.

"That would be accurate. He showed up at your place one night when I was there. He was upset and emotional. I made him tea, which he drank with an incredible amount of sugar."

"And thus we solve the sweet mystery."

"In moments of crisis many turn to sweetness for a temporary solace."

"Thank you for being there for him."

There was an extended silence. I had no idea why. Then he finally answered.

"It was entirely my pleasure."

I had bought my little Boulder place from Neal and his partner Gus. They had happily sold me the dwelling, but the green-thumbed Neal had been unwilling to let go of his wildflower-clogged garden, and I was happy to have him keep on making the place look lovely, while I hogged all the horticultural credit.

It was a winning arrangement. He showed up and worked. I served him wine. He told me wistfully how much he worshipped Gus. I served him more wine, and was careful to nod on cue at the end of each fiercely pro-Gus utterance.

But I never quite warmed to his younger partner. Gus seemed dramatic and flighty. I did like Neal. I liked his flowers. I liked his patience. I admired his pursuit of beauty, even if I thought it occasionally misplaced.

"You didn't ask me if Neal could stay."

"I didn't. How you would have responded?" Nye asked.

"I would have said yes."

"That was the presumption I made."

"Can I ask how long he intends to stay?" I asked curiously.

There was another long pause from his end.

"I would suggest you ask Neal."

I changed the subject.

"Tell me how much you've missed me at work."

Was that a derisive snort?

⁂

Two funerals in less than a week seemed gloomily excessive, even if the New Orleans concept of funereal did seem an altogether funkier version of the death rite.

Mel's certainly hit the ground running. From the outset, it was an exercise in hollerin' good-time raucousness, but it ultimately transposed itself into something far more wrenching in a keening emotional coda.

Strippers and drag queens, even the band, must have set some sort of record for streaming mascara. Everyone lamented loud and wet behind Big Tootie's Triple D Brass Showgirls funking it up big time to the sounds of "Zulu King." The brass was blasting and drums were drilling balls out, accompanied by showgirls who were a buxomly vision averaging three hundred pounds per head.

We all got to participate. The words to the chorus were easy to remember.

There were a few familiar faces in the crowd, including the older cop from the death scene who spotted me and nodded once in what looked a lot like approval, and the cardboard and spray-paint robot from the Square who had occupied the performance space close to Mel. If he recognized me, he chose not to show it. He was attending in full costume, and he wasn't alone. Many other street performers came decked out in full office attire.

A middle-aged woman who could only be Mel's sister was marching in front. She smiled as strands of beads were placed around her neck and her cheek was kissed. Beside her was an older man in a wintry gray suit who walked with some difficulty. His face showed little reaction as the same gifts were bestowed upon him.

Our route passed by the park and my rented place on Elysian Fields. We got to the corner where Mel had dropped under the front of my car. From there we turned right and walked another three quarters of a mile to arrive outside the apartment building on St. Claude.

We paused there. Bouquets of flowers, full to-go cups, parade-quality trinkets, Halloween-quality wigs in various shades of blonde, a paperback Tennessee Williams anthology, an expensive-looking coffee table collection of Marilyn Monroe photographs—all were placed on the cracked steps, once someone had procured a broom and swept away the dirt and garbage.

This would be the officially designated parade end, but there was an unplanned addendum.

If we chose to, we could proceed another block along St. Claude to arrive at a bar, the very same bar where I had once sat in a peeling leopard-skin booth and watched gay Mardi Gras hardcore porn shot on grainy VHS tape. The subject matter hadn't been my choice or, as far as I could tell, the choice of anyone else in the bar. The beer had been crypt cold and cheap, and mostly the place was filled with shitty art, shitty artists, a huge mural of a planet, and a smattering of tourists either terrified or thrilled or weirdly transfixed in a location somewhere in the middle.

The sidewalk outside the bar was offered as an ultimate destination. There were tables covered in bottles of generic vodka and cranberry mix and crushed ice and bowls of pureed cherries, which were to be combined in a secret ratio to manufacture the Flaming Mel, the event's signature potation. There was also a well-stuffed donation jar.

It was an agreement arrived at unspoken.

We were all more than game for a brace of Mels.

The sugar-sweet beverage thoughtfully came in a funeral souvenir plastic to-go cup. There were actually two versions. Both had a grainy picture of Mel on the side. One was as Marilyn. The other was as Blanche.

The fat man in a ginger mid-length wig and black leather pantsuit directly in front of me clearly had the right idea.

"I'm getting myself one of each because I loved Mel both ways and this way I get to drink much more booze much faster and y'all should be doing the same as me. You hear what I'm saying to you?" he sagely and breathlessly advised.

I followed suit eagerly and reached for two Mels.

When both our hands were filled we clinked our plastic Mels together.

I was singularly uninspired. "To Mel." I drank from one.

"To Mel," he responded. He drank also from one.

"To Mel." I drank from the other.

"To Mel." He did likewise.

We were done with the toasting. We both looked somber and grave.

There lurked a larger problem. I spoke up urgently. "Which one are you drinking first?" I asked.

He looked at both of his cups in some confusion.

A light dawned. "You drink one first," he told me, "and I'll drink the other at the same time and that way we cover both at the same time."

I smiled slowly at him. It seemed like the wisest of plans.

After careful consideration I chose Blanche.

He was left with Marilyn.

He was gallantly acquiescent.

In forty-five short minutes we had partaken of numerous Flaming Mels and the showgirls were softly playing hymns, standing still and tall under the bar awning and sweating a good deal less. Mel's sister had spoken and offered us her thanks. Mel's dad had attempted to do the same, but had been unable to summon much beyond a smile.

The music and the vodka worked its magic. We began to sway and sob as the atmosphere dive-bombed into one of abject loss.

When a clear a cappella voice broke into "I Wanna Be Loved by You" we managed a rally, but it was a brief respite from the pathos.

I ventured inside the bar for a light break from the maudlin.

It was cleaner than I remembered. The décor about the same but less shambolically disarranged. The back room was bigger, or else emptier, and the stage was in use. I had the feeling that the music was incidental to the events outside, an honored booking made before the annexation of the place in the aftermath of a sudden tragedy.

They were five pale young men from Mississippi and the Hamtramck section of Detroit playing leering rockabilly on upright bass, drums, two guitars, and a pedal steel.

The lead singer deployed his acoustic guitar like Elvis in movies while looking like Jerry Lee at his swaggering finest. He sung two short songs badly and indifferently before surrendering the microphone to the lead guitarist who wore horn rims on a babyishly round face. He played a vintage Telecaster through a Tweed Deluxe amp manufactured sometime in the reverb-rich fifties.

All the way from the Killer to Buddy Holly.

He sang the song shyly and expertly and gave the microphone back to the lead singer with a relieved smile when he was done.

The room was almost empty.

The next song implored us to come home to Louisiana.

For all the strut, he was a piss-poor excuse for a singer, and he was preaching to the choir.

I used the restroom and ventured back outside to the sidewalk lamentations for Mel.

Unsolicited remembrances were forthcoming. Most were tearfully sentimental. Many were warm. Some were close to incoherent. Many more specialty Mels were consumed.

At some point, I learned that Mel had adored small children.

It was very hard not to cry again.

Later in the evening we mourners ventured indoors after draining the sidewalk table dry. The event struggled to evolve into a cash-paying venture, and some ugliness ensued during the transition. Many of the gathered were revealed to be less than wealthy and the strapped mourners included Mel's two relatives. There were sundry grumblings. Management dug in their collective heels. A proposal was hastily arrived at and those of us with the wherewithal were asked to pony up and supply the funding for the rest of the night, which we dutifully did.

As a result of my largesse, I was kissed on or near the mouth several times.

At some point the rockabilly band ceased playing and a flood of desolate drunks then torch-sang from the stage.

I slurringly told anyone who would listen how I came to know Mel.

Mostly they smiled at the unlikeliness of the tale, which seemed a little less surreal each time I recounted it.

I must have walked home sometime in the early morning.

SIXTEEN

THE INTERNET PRESENCE of the plagiarizing poet Norman Allan Haig was restricted to four short entries. It took me about as long as drinking one large cup of coffee to peruse them all.

He had no published books or chapbooks to his name, and there was a notable absence of websites hosted by or dedicated to him. His work had appeared in only two anthologies. "Circumstance" was part of the collection *Crossing Cumbernauld,* and "Devotional" was included in a compendium titled *The Highland Moderne.* Haig was reported to have read his work in public twice: once at a library-hosted young adult readers' poetry night, and once at a poetry 'n prose slam in a Leith wine bar.

My extensive listening to *Crofter* allowed me to read "Devotional" in *Moderne* and quickly ascertain that it owed nothing remotely discernible to Logan Kind.

Norman Allan Haig was unknown and, if I was any judge of poetry, likely to remain that way. His lifting of Kind's lyrics had been noted by Stephen Park and apparently by no one else.

The effort to further expose his literary theft seemed of little practical worth.

It would be best to let it go.

Another small secret revealed.

My morning coffee was finished. My stomach was not quite ready to receive anything more substantial.

‡‡

A PATCH OF neutral ground runs as a grassy median right down the center of St. Charles Avenue. The streetcar stop is right outside a diner on the corner, where St. Charles and Carrollton Avenue intersect. Later in the day I parked my car, optimistically got myself a small burger and fries to go, and waited to board the more whimsical of public transportation.

My notion was to intermittently abandon the streetcar and wander the Garden District. There were a few places I had wanted to visit: some storied old hotels, a pretty park I remembered liking a lot, and the appropriately gothic home of a famous author I had once read. The rest would be largely a matter of impulse and impetuousness.

Most of the afternoon lay ahead of me as I sat on the grass and ate.

The large number of tourists waiting outside the diner forced me to reconsider my plans. I can't claim to know the exact seating capacity of a streetcar offhand, but my guess was that the line in front of me would easily fill the next half dozen cars.

So I elected to walk down the length of St. Charles instead. It was warm and sunny and the median already had an assortment of bikers and joggers and dogs and their attendant walkers. It would be easy to fit right in.

The famous author's house was closed to the public that day. Maybe it was for the best. The author herself had sold the property where she and her poet husband had once lived, and had moved north and west over a decade ago. The former convent-orphanage building where her doll collection had once been housed was in the process of becoming a block-long condominium development.

Best to keep right on walking.

Outside a university building I was cheerily invited to help fund the ongoing restoration of the city's many cemeteries. I handed my money over without protest.

The dead will always need the help of the living.

In a remarkably short time, I was standing in the shade of a huge oak tree on the 3800 block of St. Charles in the Upper Garden District. I gazed up at the large porch columns and the wicker chairs and low tables on the verandah. Crisp-shirted waiters milled about attentively serving the supping clientele who lapped me by several decades. There were several sipping their Sazeracs. I had been in this exact place once before, sipping a Sazerac as Kate had rushed out of town. I was abandoned, left to sullenly contemplate the hotel's lovingly restored antiques and the dark-stained paneling.

As I studied the people on the porch more closely, I noticed one older gentleman was staring back at me, leaning forward in his chair, wedging both his hands between his chin and the elaborate handle of the walking stick, the walking stick that I recalled was much more prop than necessity.

My mysterious benefactor was once again resplendent in the tweedy attire more befitting the lord of the manor on a ramble around the estate on a blustery day.

He was the source of my crisp hundred-dollar bill, my most glaringly generous of patrons.

My wave was one of hesitant acknowledgment.

His reciprocal motion was a beckoning gesture of welcome, so I approached.

There was an open seat beside him, which he pointed to, and which I silently accepted. Within seconds a waiter had materialized at my shoulder. There was a menu on the table but I boldly ordered without seeking its guidance.

"I'll take an IPA if you have one, and I'd like to buy this fine gentleman a drink if I may." I made this request as pleasantly as I could.

Yet the waiter clearly hesitated.

Then the fine gentleman spoke up for himself. "You may not, sir. I limit myself to two drinks before sundown." He pointed to his nearly empty glass. "And this, I must sadly confess, is already my second. But I do thank you for the kindness."

I turned to the waiter, who was still hovering, and who was clearly relishing the archness of our exchange thus far.

I decided to play along.

"Would it be possible for me to purchase a drink that could perhaps be served to this gentleman sometime in the near future?"

An eyebrow was lifted. My request was clearly unorthodox. The waiter again deferred to the older customer. Brief nods were rapidly traded.

Then I was addressed again. "I will gladly take a sidecar on some future occasion if I may sir." He then turned to the waiter. "Stanley, would you please arrange for said libation to be made available to me tomorrow at the usual time?"

There was a slight smile and an accompanying bow. "It would be my pleasure, Mr. Rowley." Then he turned to me with a gentle smile. "Let me see to that beer for you now, sir, if I may."

I elected to push my luck at that point. "Thank you, Stanley," I said in lordly fashion.

Even though I had already provided two people with a small measure of sport, I would clearly have to tip this man excessively.

After Stanley left, we both rose and formally shook hands. He was spry, and fully upright well before me. I told him my name.

"It's my distinct pleasure to see you once again young man," he informed me. "I'm Templeton Rowley."

Then I hesitated. "The pleasure is all mine Mr. Rowley. But I believe I know your name from somewhere."

His smile was a wicked concoction. "It's certainly quite possible that you do. Indeed it is. But you look puzzled. So let me help you. Tell me young man, are you a music fan in addition to being a player?"

It was my turn to smile. "You're being much too kind. I'm truthfully a lot more fan than player, and your gift was far too generous. But I'm sure I've heard of you before . . . " At that point I began to falter.

He waved the last of my words aside before he explained.

"I try to record all manner of the New Orleans street music when I am able. I own a very small label right here in town. Our name is Raleigh Rye. Perhaps you've come across some of our *From Piety to Desire* compilations?"

"I've been listening to them."

He was quite unable to hide his happiness. "Have you indeed? That's wonderful to hear. May I ask which ones?"

I was required to hesitate. "I don't actually remember the numbers. I'm sorry. I do remember that Iris Cummings was on one."

His grin was a sad and knowing one. "A most pure and pleasing voice."

I had to ask him. "Why do you smile?"

He shook his head. "I really shouldn't be telling tales," he said.

I waited for the inevitable tale to be told.

"You would doubtless be shocked to learn that the young lady in question was a veritable wreck of a soul barely able to remain sober long enough to make that single recording for me. Afterwards she managed to be quite ill all over one of the better rugs in my living room."

"She was at your house?"

"She surely was. I always record at my home. My basement is a large one and over the years I've filled it with the barest minimum of sound-dampening technology and far too much old analog recording equipment. I record with a selection of vintage Shure microphones onto my trusty reel-to-reel tape and the results are generally much to my liking. I was once lucky enough to visit Sun Studio in Memphis where Mr. Sam Phillips recorded Elvis and Jerry Lee and Johnny Cash at their wildest and finest. I was shocked to discover how small and primitive his studio setup was. But that pilgrimage would become my working model. I wanted to find a sound that had a little of that famous Memphis slapback to it, not too insulated, and not too sterile."

"How are the compact discs produced?" I asked him.

He laughed. "I'll be damned if I know. I send my master tapes away to a collection of tattooed young men in Slidell who convert my recordings to disc and see to the pressings. I'm sorry to say that we don't press very many. I have a young lady in Mid City to lay out the label and help me with the liner notes. She works with the Slidell boys and I receive not inconsiderable bills from them both. The recordings arrive in boxes. I send them to all the independent stores in the state that will agree to carry them for me."

Templeton Rowley had long thin fingers, and as he spoke he twisted an old black onyx ring on the third finger of his right hand back and forth. The ring was very large and hung loosely between his prominent finger bones.

"Can I ask if you make much money, Mr. Rowley?"

He laughed once again. "Oh dear God, no!"

As he recovered, Stanley arrived with my beer and I took a sip.

"Then can I ask you why you do it, sir?"

"I do it, sir, because it's wonderful fun, because it's an efficient way to use up my dear family's money in a way that they thoroughly despise, and because I'm not altogether certain that this fine city will survive in the bye and bye. Let me try and explain this to you." He paused and took a deep breath. Then he continued.

"I was already doing this for a long time before the storm came. I started out when I first arrived here in the early part of the eighties. I'm from Baton Rouge originally. I have some of my family money that I mostly didn't have to help in the earning of. I have a music history degree from an expensive college up north that my father thought was a hilarious waste of both my time and his money. My recordings were more of a pastime for me in the beginning, although my desire was always to preserve the sounds that I heard on the street, sounds that I was quite certain no one else was interested in preserving. My wonderful family was initially mildly amused. But let me say right now that I never was. I am very serious about what I do, especially now in the years since the shadow of the storm."

I interrupted him at this point. "Are you sure I can't buy you that drink now, Mr. Rowley?"

He shook his head and smiled. "You may have noticed that I talk plenty with or without a cocktail in my hand young man."

I nodded and smiled in agreement.

He continued. "From the beginning I have established a few stipulations, ground rules that I adhere to. They are as follows. There can only be two songs per artist on each of my recordings. I do this for the variation. I do this so that there are no star turns. I do this for a balanced representation. I don't try to program my collections. Sometimes the contrasting styles are complimentary. Sometimes they most assuredly are not. I don't choose or go out of my way to find artists I particularly like. If I did, my collections would be filled with Dr. John and the Neville Brothers, and they certainly don't need my help to get themselves recorded in this town. No. I'm looking for what I like to call the other New Orleans music. No artists I record will have a recording contract anywhere else or with anyone else at the time I record them. I only want their original work. That is important to me because I want to help creative talent and because it makes it easier for me legally and contractually, not having to deal with copyrights and song permissions and so forth."

"How many volumes are out there?"

He laughed once more.

"Ah. That's a fine question. I started out with two a year. That was my grand plan. I was quite dutiful with my numbering system in the early days."

"What happened?" I asked.

He replied. "Oh that's easily answered. The storm happened."

I waited for him to continue.

"In the months after Katrina, I rather lost my mind. I became convinced that the music would all be lost and that the town would never recover. So I made it my mission to save all the songs of the city. I recorded everyone I found. I think I waited less than a month after Katrina struck to put out a new volume, and then I'm afraid the metaphorical flood gates opened. I walked everywhere I could and I found all the people the storm had left behind. I found them still singing and dancing and playing and I brought them to my home. I recorded them all. I paid out far more than I had in the past. I must have released a dozen new discs in the first post-hurricane year alone.

These are now some of my favorite recordings. They are far from being my best; I was in a ridiculous hurry. But they are filled with all kinds of the most wonderful, indigenous, threatened music that I was so very grateful and honored to have helped give sanctuary to. I believe that this city has always been an innovative music frontier, dating back to the beginnings of jazz. Today we are still vibrantly relevant. Did you know that this city is the bounce capital of the world? I'm happy to say that I've recorded several gentlemen and ladies who have become stars in a genre that frankly I find utterly baffling and more than a little lewd. I'm proud to say that there has been bouncing in my basement. My esteemed father would no doubt have pretended to a deep horror."

"Are you still worried about the city?"

"Of course I am. Look at the slow rate of our rebuilding. The population is less than it was before the storm and the poorer and blacker folks are the ones we have lost. We've gotten whiter and we've gotten wealthier and I believe that the city leaders are more than happy to encourage this reckless economic redistribution and cultural bleaching. There are places in this city that were all but washed away. They still need so much of our help today. If we were in a wealthy northern city, we would not be relying on church groups with paintbrushes and well-intentioned actors. It would all simply be getting done through the impetus of a solid economy and a collective will. We would be fully rebuilt by this late stage. Of this fact, I'm very truly convinced."

"You must love this city."

He looked me squarely in the eye. "That I do, sir. That I truly do."

I had another question for him. "Why did you give me your money when you heard me play on the street?"

He smiled. "Another of my rules, I'm afraid. I always give my money to music. You were playing on our streets. I applaud your courage and your contribution to the sound of the city. You were playing songs recorded and written by other people. For that reason, I will not seek to record you. But I do commend you, and my money stands as my acknowledgment of that commendation."

"I was flattered and very surprised. I'm a hopeless beginner. But you must have known that as you heard me play."

Templeton Rowley said nothing but continued to smile at me.

"Can I admit something to you?" I asked him.

"Of course you may, young man."

"I gave your money away."

"I would assume to someone you thought more deserving?"

"I did think so, yes."

"An artist perhaps?"

"I would say so."

"Then for what it's worth you have my approval. You will notice my stipulation of course. When you give away your money you surrender the right to question its use the very second it leaves your hand. I am firm in that belief."

I thought he was right and I told him so.

I had given Rowley's money to Mel because I felt ridiculous taking it in the first place, and because I wanted to stop her from taking boys to a bar. It hadn't made a difference in the end, and I had been wrong to do it.

"By now it must be my turn to ask you a question."

"Please do," I told him.

"I did wonder why you had elected to play at that particular location?"

"Why do you ask that?"

"Please humor me."

"I'm sorry. It is your turn. The reason I was there was because someone I admire had once played there."

"And who was that?"

"His name was Logan Kind."

There was a long pause. "I must confess that I don't know that name." He sounded disappointed.

"I had hoped that you would." I must have sounded disappointed too.

Then he hesitated once more.

"Was he a singer?" he asked me.

"He was."

"And was he a guitar player?"

I answered quickly. "A very good one."

"And from the same part of the world as you?"

"Yes he was. Very close. Why?"

He continued. "Is it possible that he played under another name?"

Now I was curious. "I suppose so. It it possible. What was the name?"

Templeton Rowley looked at me carefully before he spoke again.

"In the first month after the storm I came across a gentleman named Willie Mac. He was playing and singing right where you were. Dumaine has always been a favorite street of mine and I walk there often."

"Are you sure of the name?"

"Of course. I have an excellent memory. Please forgive me. I'm in danger of being coy with you. I should tell you that Willie Mac was the name I wrote on the contract that we both signed after he had come to my house and played for me."

There was something about the name Willie Mac.

I frantically thought backwards, mentally skimming in reverse through the mountains of Kind trivia I had uploaded and pored over. There was something . . .

And then I remembered: In his youth, Logan had admired a long-dead Scottish poet. The poet was famous and famously awful. His name had been William McGonagall.

It wasn't too hard to get from William McGonagall to Willie Mac.

"You recorded him?" I was very close to shouting.

He nodded. "He came to my house with his guitar. Two of his songs did end up on one collection. Even I'm not exactly sure which volume it was. Would you care to hear all his songs?"

Was I hearing this right?

"What do you mean all his songs?"

"We recorded that day for a long time and ten songs were completed when he was finished; ten songs that I remember him being happy with. Two went on the disk. The other eight I've kept for him since then. He liked my basement studio. He liked the acoustics. I was careful to mike his guitar very carefully. He was an extraordinary player and I think the levels sounded just right to him. I must tell you that I wasn't much taken with his voice. The overbearing idiosyncrasies of folksingers I can well do without. I told him I would keep his other recordings safe and sound. I would never release them or do anything with them without his consent. He seemed quite happy with this arrangement. I told him I would wait to hear from him. I paid him for the two songs. We talked about his recording with me again. When he was leaving he told me there was another song that was close to being finished that he wasn't yet satisfied with.

"Would it be possible for me to hear the songs?"

He smiled and nodded.

"Of course. My house is on Robert and is not far from here. Do you like to walk?"

I told him that I did. He seemed very pleased.

⁜

HIS HOUSE WAS at the intersection of Robert and Baronne Streets, some fifteen blocks from the hotel; a short enough journey at Rowley's brisk pace.

It was a large two-story house with palm trees outside and ten whitewashed columns of its own, which framed a ground-level porch and supported the exposed balcony on the second floor.

Templeton Rowley liked to walk fast and he liked to talk as he walked fast.

He told me that his family business was chemical manufacturing. Actually they still were in the business. But he wasn't. He had chosen to cash out early. He had headed south and there had been little opposition from the rest of his relatives.

He spoke about his city immediately after the flood.

"This was one part of town that somehow stayed dry. Oh I've heard all the theories about the rich people, about the mysterious explosions blowing the levees up to sacrifice the poor folks in places like the Lower Ninth. I'm not quite that cynical. The French Quarter was also spared but the place was deserted for a spell. The Quarter was dry but the people were all gone. Restaurants had no staff and no food to cook with. People were displaced and if they still had a dry place to work, they didn't have a dry place in which to live. I walked wherever I could during those days. The streets were blocked off. There were few police around, and by then the stories surrounding them just made you nervous when you saw them. Power was sporadic and garbage pickup equally so. Those were bad times for this city."

"And Willie Mac was just out there playing on the street?"

"Indeed he was. I saw him on two occasions. He was alone both times. Playing at the corner of two deserted streets."

I told Rowley that Logan Kind had drowned several months after they had met. I told him that his one previous recording had been much admired, that he had loyal fans, a daughter somewhere, and a sister, who had assumed control of his interests. I told him that Logan had evolved into a lesser cult figure. I didn't tell him that the songs Logan had recorded might be of some value now.

"Do you suppose he killed himself?" Rowley asked me.

"No one seems to know."

"But what do you think?" He was insistent.

"I think he wanted to live. He was playing songs again. He was a very good swimmer. And now you tell me he had recorded new songs with you. Let me ask you this. Did he seem happy to you when you were with him?"

"That's hard to answer. I can't in all honesty say that he was unhappy when we met." He allowed this.

I sensed that he wanted to say more, so I encouraged him. "Please tell me what you think."

"I just wanted to say that it does seem to me that trying to make a distinction between an accidental act of dying and an intentional one in the strange times following Katrina is a highly superfluous undertaking." He made this observation carefully.

And we arrived.

If I had expected a house full of eccentrically compulsive clutter, I was to be disappointed. The living room was large and sparse and dust-free and luminous, with pale wood floors and red Persian rugs of obvious quality and a soundly sleeping dog and a housekeeper named Anita, who silently delivered a pitcher of iced tea and two tall glasses that no one had asked for. I was assigned a seat next to the large screen door that opened onto the porch and through which a humid breeze tenderly blew.

In no time at all, Templeton Rowley left and reappeared with two discs. One was enigmatically blank. The other was a factory sealed copy of a *Piety to Desire* compilation. It was labeled volume 42. He handed it to me.

"This is for you to keep. Please don't insult me by offering to pay for it and please don't ask me to explain why it is numbered 42, because it simply is. I'm going to let you listen to the other songs Mr. Mac recorded when he was here, but I'm not going to give you a copy of the recordings. I truly don't know what he would want me to do with his songs. I'm naturally assuming that these were in fact recorded by your Mr. Logan Kind, and that he is as dead and as gone as you have informed me he is. I also assume that you will confirm the identity of the artist when you hear these. I do realize that assumptions are seldom made wisely."

And then Templeton Rowley placed the blank disc in an expensive-looking single CD player. The first track opened with acoustic guitar—two mysterious chords alternating, and an ascending pattern plucked between them. I waited until the vocals began purely as a formality. Templeton Rowley was watching my face intently. I nodded slowly and he looked away satisfied. In truth I could have informed Rowley that we were listening to

Logan Kind with the first few notes. I could have told him this with utter certainty.

The first track ended.

Together we listened to all eight songs. Anita returned with an empty tray. She looked at the untouched drinks and shot Rowley a brief reproachful look. Then she wordlessly removed both glasses. Rowley took the first disc from the player. I handed him my copy of volume 42 and, after tearing the plastic away, he cued up the two Willie Mac songs.

We listened again in silence.

Afterwards I had a question. "What made you pick these two songs for the collection?"

He was quick to answer. "These were the first two we recorded. I told Mr. Mac I would use only two and these were the first ones he played for me. Later he mentioned there were others he wanted to play, and he asked me if I would be willing to record them for him. I told him I would be more than happy to."

"Can I ask you about the payment?"

"I pay one thousand dollars per song. I have always paid one thousand dollars. If someone were to ask me for more I would probably refuse. But they never have. When they ask me for less I always shrewdly counter with my offer of one thousand dollars, which they have always managed to find a way to accept. Once again let me be clear, sir. This is not, nor has it ever been, a money-making proposition."

"You paid Willie Mac the two thousand?"

"I did. I offered him my personal check, which is how I prefer to make payment. He asked me instead for cash, which I did not have on me at the time."

"So what did you do?"

"I went to the bank the next day and withdrew the cash. I placed it in an envelope and bribed a cabdriver to take me to a house in the Ninth Ward, a flooded property on a block of Lizardi close to the levee. It was on the 700 block. I forget the exact address. I knocked on the door and I waited for an answer. I should mention that Mac had given me the address and I had written it down. It was in the late part of the morning. As I say, there was no answer, which was not terribly surprising. The place was in decay and it was hard to imagine anyone choosing to live there. I placed the envelope in a mailbox outside the premises and I left before my very nervous cabdriver took the full fare I had foolishly paid in advance and drove away. I can't say I would have blamed him. The drive there was truly alarming. Only one road and one bridge over the canal at St. Claude was open to get to the Ninth. The street had been battered into submission less than two months previous, with overturned cars, trees picked up and thrown onto the side of buildings, a waterlogged mess of soggy dereliction. The house in question looked to be at least intact. I do remember that as I stood outside I distinctly heard the sound of gunfire."

"Why did you go?"

"Because I said I would. As I told you, this was the address that Mac had given to me the day before."

He paused.

"Would you care to listen to the other songs again?" he asked me.

"I would be honored," I replied.

"Anita will be bringing more drinks when the sun goes down."

"More iced tea?"

He might have shivered there and then. "Certainly not. Perish the thought, sir."

Before Templeton Rowley and I parted, I told him most of what I knew, which wasn't much, and most of what I thought, which was only slightly more substantial.

I told Rowley I would contact Margot Kind through her website and tell her about her brother's last songs. He told me that he would write to her because he did not care much for the Internet. I pulled up her home page on my phone. There was an address listed in the North of England, which I carefully wrote down for him.

Mr. Rowley had bought and paid for the two songs on his compilation. He offered to show me the contract. I told him it wasn't necessary. He had undeniably acted in good faith, as I suspected he usually did. His family may have disowned him but he struck me as an honorable man who passionately loved his adopted city, was fiercely protective towards its music and kept his word. Together, he and Margot Kind would have to work out what to do with the other eight tracks.

I had a vested interest. But it wasn't my place to mediate.

"I will write to Ms. Kind this evening." Rowley told me. "Her late brother's songs will see the light of day if I have anything to do with it. You have my word on that."

I found myself believing him.

"I might even make some money." He spoke these last words wonderingly.

"You very well might." I had no choice but to agree with him.

He smiled a sly smile all to himself. "My family will be ever so delighted."

Later I got up to leave. He walked me to the front door. I spoke first in parting.

"You didn't ask me what I thought of the songs."

Rowley shook his head ruefully. "It wasn't required. I took the liberty of watching your face as you listened. You were simply transported. I've often found that a love of music does that."

I could only agree with him. "Logan Kind only made one record when he was alive. It's very much loved. The sound on that first record was stunning, but your recording might be even better." I extended my hand. "Thank you so much, Mr. Rowley."

He beamed at me. His grip on my hand was a hard metal clamp.

"You are most welcome, young man," he said.

⁂

MY CAR WAS a sauna. I opened all the windows and the sunroof as I drove away from the diner.

First thing tomorrow morning I would go to the house on Lizardi where there would assuredly be nothing for me to see.

The years had unhurriedly bypassed that part of the town. The floodwaters had destroyed in an angry rush. I would either find ruin or reclamation. My money was on the former; but all trace of Logan Kind would surely be long gone.

But then, you never know.

I told myself that anything I did recover would go to the people I thought most deserving. I did understand that this notion was more than slightly subjective, and thus highly elastic.

The most I allowed myself to hope for would be an afterimage of an afterimage, a lingering remnant of a life's abrupt closing.

This journey south had been a fool's errand because all the intuition that had driven me on two previous occasions had been patently false in this instance. I now knew a few things that I hadn't known before. But the reasons why Stephen Park and Logan Kind died were still largely hidden, or at least they were hidden from me.

The drive took me back along St. Charles into town. There was a streetcar ahead of me and I slowed down to keep pace with it. When it teasingly stopped alongside the hotel's tall columns I did the same. The afternoon trade had been replaced by a horde of younger college-age kids and a smattering of sun-stunned tourists. They were drinking harder and louder. The waiters were working faster, doubtless making much better tips, but looking a whole lot more irritated in the process.

My route took me down two sides of the square. Mel's old bike was still chained to the fence. I braked. The flowers in the basket were mostly brown flakes and several had fallen on the ground.

I was finally hungry enough to go to the restaurant on Frenchmen that Nye had told me about. It was closed for a private event.

The house on Elysian Fields would be vacant in the morning. In the courtyard I found the caretaker still looking at used car ads. She had narrowed her choices down to two gently used Toyota Camrys. I handed her my credit card and we settled up. When

I asked if I could reimburse her for the stolen chair she had the nerve to giggle at me.

⁂

THE CAFÉ NEARBY was still open in the early evening.

There was still time for one last meal.

I ordered a plate of boudin and grits and a cup of coffee.

I gave my name.

The girl behind the counter was a different one. She consulted a long list.

"We already have a Tom ahead of you." She told me with a bright smile. "What's your last name?"

"It's Frost," I replied.

And I smiled right back.

PETER ROBERTSON is a native of Edinburgh, Scotland, and currently lives near Chicago.